MW01520107

The Mystery of the Smoldering Mattress

A Nancy Drouillard Mystery

©2023, Kathryn Crabtree

All rights reserved. This book or any portion thereof may not be reproduced or used in any manner whatsoever without the express written permission of the publisher except for the use of brief quotations in a book review.

ISBN: 979-8-35092-984-3

ISBN eBook: 979-8-35092-985-0

A NANCY DROUILLARD MYSTERY

THE MYSTERY
OF THE
SMOLDERING
MATTRESS

KATHRYN CRABTREE

CHAPTER 1

Nancy was in a foul mood; she felt resentful and humiliated. "Damn that twit, Todd. He gives lawyers a bad name! He is nothing but an arrogant ambulance chaser." She mumbled. "Treating me like a foolish, insignificant old woman, what an idiot. As if being a widow living in a 55+ Community makes me senile."

She drove past the Village gate attendant without her usual smiling wave to the staff member. Distracted, the welcoming sense of home she felt upon entering the 55+ Retirement Village was absent. The desert palms, cacti, and abundant flowering bougainvillea were lost in passing as she relived the past half hour.

She had such high hopes entering the law office of Todd Myers, the son of a friend from her earlier defense lawyer days. Nancy had spoken to his mother of her intent to practice law again. Her grief after losing Ned, her husband of 45 years, had taken a toll on her attitude toward life. Recently, she felt the fog of sadness lifting, accepted that life goes on, and decided to engage more with her world.

Todd's mother had arranged for them to meet, encouraging Nancy to speak to him about the guardian ad litem position she was pursuing. Nancy thought of returning to her previous defense attorney practice. However, representing the elderly, children, and disabled in court by speaking for those who were unable to speak for themselves would give her more satisfaction and a sense of purpose.

Nancy thought her professional history as an appointed federal judge would be an asset to Todd's law firm. The memory of the numerous mishandled cases in her court was still fresh in her mind. The most problematic cases for her to judge were the ones that the detectives and defense attorneys didn't bother to investigate thoroughly, as they were related to elderly deaths and thefts.

"Caring for the underserved seems as unpopular as ever for lawyers like Todd," Nancy spoke aloud, shaking her head. Seething, she expelled a long breath, adding, "Wait until Bess gets a load of this." She continued to fume out loud, tapping her left-hand nails on the steering wheel. "It wasn't as if I was begging for a favor."

Bess, a childhood friend, had moved to the Village a year after she and her husband, Ned, relocated there from the San Francisco Bay Area. Ned's Multiple Sclerosis symptoms began to have more prolonged bouts of immobility issues between remissions, so they retired early and moved to the San Jose Retirement Village four years ago.

They spent their last years traveling, returning home only to plan the next adventure. Finally surrendering to the disease, Ned lost his battle two years ago. Bess had been there for her then, a supportive, entertaining companion and confidant. Nancy couldn't imagine life without her.

Parking in front of the Cup and Vine, Nancy straightened her shoulders, exited the car, and entered the coffee shop-wine bar, heading toward the deck. She was anxious to share Todd's frustrating discussion. Nancy nodded at Stevie, the bartender-barista, confirming the order for her usual Cabernet and searched for Bess.

Surprised, she saw Bess and the happy-hour group gathered on the deck, anxiously watching the activity across the street. Nancy noticed the group was focused on an ambulance in front of the condos. She retrieved her wine from the bar and approached Bess, asking, "What is going on over there? Is someone hurt?"

CHAPTER 2

"Could it be Hilda or Sally? They haven't joined us yet, and they usually aren't late. Since that's their condo building, we are all worried." Bess answered.

Nancy nodded uneasily, watching the activity, hoping Hilda, one of her closest friends, wasn't ill or hurt. She reached for her cell phone and punched Hilda's cell number, hoping to confirm her safety. The call went to voice mail, adding to Nancy's concern.

A black sedan pulled up behind the ambulance. The occupant remained in the car, talking on his cell phone. A navy van with the police forensic team logo arrived. The van driver, backpack slung across his shoulder, joined the man exiting the sedan, and they entered the building together.

As the group watched, tissues in hand and obviously shaken, Sally appeared from the side door of the building, accompanied by one of the emergency responders. Nancy set her wine glass on the nearest table, trying not to panic, and elbowed Bess, "Let's go speak to Sally. We need to find out what's happening. I don't see Hilda." Feeling apprehensive, Nancy left the deck with Bess close behind.

As they crossed the street and walked toward Sally, they were surprised to see the Community Director, Ronald, his assistant director, Marcy, and Hilda's daughter, Lisa, exiting Hilda's front door with the black sedan occupant. Nancy recognized the driver, realizing that the sedan must have been an unmarked police car usually driven by police detectives.

"Uh oh, Bess, that's my daughter's former husband. He's a homicide detective."

Bess said, "Oh, good, maybe he will tell us what's going on."

"Don't count on that; he's not exactly the sharing type. If something happened to Hilda, I want to know why a homicide detective is here," Nancy whispered.

Her intent was evident in her confident greeting. "Hello, Harry. I'm surprised to see you here. What's going on?" Nancy asked.

Harry sighed, shook his head, and greeted her, "Hello, Nancy, I thought this might be your community. I'm glad to see that you're safe. Officially, this is a routine death at-home call. As you know, the department investigates all unexpected home deaths."

Nancy was confused. "Death at home, what do you mean," She asked, wringing her hands, staring at him, eyes wide in disbelief.

"It's my department's responsibility to assure that when a death at home was reported, there was no evidence of foul play." He explained.

Nancy felt her throat tighten as she asked, "Please, Harry, tell us it wasn't Hilda."

Looking at her, he sighed, "I'm sorry if Hilda was your friend; she seems to have died last night." Harry said, his hand gentle on her shoulder, attempting to comfort her.

Tearfully, she whispered, "Oh no, how can this be." Her voice quivering, she asked, "What happened to her? How could she be dead?"

"The forensic tech suspects it was smoke inhalation. It appears that Hilda fell asleep smoking in bed." Harry responded.

Harry explained that they figured she nodded off, dropping her cigarette and catching the gel-foam topper on fire. "The gel in the foam snuffed out the flames, but not before Hilda inhaled enough to prevent her breathing." He shrugged.

Nancy and Bess shared a surprised look. His response didn't convince them.

CHAPTER 3

"But Harry, Hilda would never smoke in her apartment, let alone in bed, especially on that gel-foam mattress!" Nancy said, controlling her voice.

Bess frowned, "She hated that gel-foam topper and never slept on it."

"Again, I'm sorry, Nancy, but it was obvious that she had been smoking on the gel foam topper. The smoldering cigarette had melted the bed linens, and the butt remained embedded in the gel of the topper." He dismissed them gently but firmly.

He wasn't listening to their explanations, Nancy realized. Maybe he thought they were in shock or could not understand his logic. Harry rubbed the back of his neck as he spoke and looked at Nancy.

"I don't know what to tell you, but she had you fooled on both counts; she did smoke in bed, and she did sleep on the topper. End of story."

Nancy thought about the topper. Hilda's daughter was adamant that she use it. She would add it to her bed every time she visited, insisting that it would relieve Hilda's chronic back pain. Hilda wouldn't argue. She would let Lisa think she was grateful for her interest. She told Nancy she felt Lisa was trying to be a good daughter and arguing with her would spoil her intent.

Hilda explained Lisa's reassurances and justification were based upon having read medical journals regarding the gel-foam benefit. But Hilda felt the topper increased her discomfort. Once her daughter left, Nancy, Bess, or one of the community administrative staff would get a call to help remove it. It would be returned to the closet for storage until her daughter's next visit.

Nancy figured that Lisa had visited her mother and added the topper to her bed last evening if she was found lying on it this afternoon. She hadn't called Nancy to help remove it last night but knew Hilda never slept with it on her bed. Shaking her head, Nancy wondered how it could be possible she would be found dead on it.

The van driver approached with the news that they were ready to remove the body. Harry addressed Nancy and Bess, "I am sorry about your friend's death, Nancy. It is unfortunate to meet under these circumstances. Take care of yourself and give Ann my best."

He nodded to Bess as he followed the van driver into the apartment building. Sally had left, likely returning to her condo. Lisa leaned against Ronald, the community director, weeping silently into a tissue. His arm around her seemed to support her while he murmured words of comfort. The assistant director, Marcy, stood beside them, looking at a loss. Nancy approached Marcy, drawing her away from Ronald and Lisa.

"This is so shocking. The whole community will be devastated by this loss. I can't understand how this could happen." Upset, she dried her eyes with a tissue, "How were you notified that something happened to Hilda?" Nancy asked, choking back tears.

"Sally went to Hilda's apartment to walk with her to happy hour. When Hilda didn't answer the door, she called her cell phone. When there was no answer, she was worried and called me. Poor Sally was so alarmed." Marcy explained that she notified Ronald, and he called Hilda's daughter. Lisa wasn't aware of Hilda's plan to leave the condo that day.

Marcy spoke quietly, "Ronald told the daughter that her mother was missing a planned event and didn't appear to be at home. Lisa told him that her mother's car was in the shop. If she wasn't somewhere in the community, something would be wrong."

Sighing, she added, "Lisa made it to the condo just as Ronald used the maintenance key to unlock Hilda's door."

A soft sob escaped between Nancy's lips, "How horrible all this must be for you," reaching out to Marcy, putting her hand on her shoulder. "Is it true that they think she was smoking in bed?"

Marcy nodded, "The place smelled of stale smoke, but it appeared any fire had extinguished itself. From what I could tell, Hilda wasn't even injured, but Ronald said she wasn't breathing. I called the emergency number. It was just awful, Nancy, just so sad!" she sighed, tearful.

Ronald led Lisa away from the condo as the van driver and ambulance attendants helped to transfer the gurney into the van. The two of them appeared to be heading toward Ronald's office, so Marcy took her to leave, drying her eyes with the back of her hand.

"I better see if I can do anything to help Lisa." She quickly followed the couple.

Nancy and Bess walked slowly back across the street to the group on the deck. Nancy was lost in thought and murmured to Bess, "How could this have happened? We know Hilda couldn't sleep on that topper. She complained that it made her back pain worse."

"Everyone was aware of her phobia about stale smoke smells. We all laughed about a smoker who couldn't stand the smell of cigarettes." Bess said, frowning, sliding her arm around Nancy's shoulder.

Nancy sighed, "I just can't get my head around this. It doesn't make sense."

The residents gathered on the deck of the Cup and Vine had been watching the activity across the street and were anxious as Nancy and Bess approached. Multiple questions were directed at them, and Nancy raised her hand aimed at stopping everyone from speaking at once.

"I don't know how to tell you this, but Ronald and Marcy found that Hilda died last night." A collective gasp could be heard, followed by more questions amid a murmur of dismay.

Nancy choked up, her voice shaking, "All we know so far is that it appears the police think she was smoking in bed, fell asleep, and dropped her cigarette, catching her bed linen and topper on fire. They suspect that the gel foam extinguished the fire but believe she died of smoke inhalation."

"How can that be?" Someone from the crowd asked, "Everyone knows Hilda never let anyone smoke in her apartment. We all gathered on her balcony to enjoy our cigarettes. Hilda couldn't stand the stench of smoke on her furniture." One of the women added, "She used to spray the whole apartment with an air freshener after one of our cocktails happy hours on her balcony."

Nancy looked at the crowd, dabbing her eyes with her tissue, "That is the opinion from the forensic and investing team, as unlikely as it seems."

Looking at Bess, who was also drying her eyes, she nodded, thinking, "It certainly seems suspicious."

The crowd continued to ask questions, wondering why the smoke detector didn't alarm anyone and why Hilda would be smoking in bed when she only shared cigarettes on her balcony, never in her apartment. Nancy had no answers, but without a second thought, the question that solved many dilemmas in Nancy's life popped into her head. "What would Nancy Drew do?"

She didn't have to think about the answer. She knew instinctively what Nancy Drew would do to investigate what happened to cause Hilda's death; she would start an investigation of her own. Closing her eyes and taking a deep breath, Nancy cleared her throat, trying to relieve the knot in her chest that tightened every time she thought of Hilda being dead.

Nancy began to ask the gathering crowd questions quietly. She wanted to know when anyone had seen Hilda in an attempt to determine who had seen Hilda last. They all discussed whether she appeared any different, or if she seemed worried about anything, or maybe ill.

Finally, someone asked Nancy, "Why all the questions?"

"Because if we don't believe Hilda was smoking in bed and didn't catch her mattress topper on fire, why is she dead?" Nancy responded.

"Are you thinking that someone else set her mattress on fire?" one of the men asked, "That's ridiculous!"

"Someone could have wanted her dead." Nancy said quietly, "It could be murder."

CHAPTER 4

The following day, Harry found himself wondering, while waiting for his Captain to end the phone call from their Division Commander, what new problem had made him anxious this time. It seemed it was always something. Most often, the problem landed in his department's jurisdiction. As the senior officer, it usually became his problem.

He'd been a detective for almost ten years, having started as a beat cop ten years before that, and twenty years on the force hadn't produced much wear and tear on his lean frame. A little greyer around the hairline close to his temples and maybe the beginning of some flab around the belt line might be evident. At forty-five, Harry kept active with the precinct's baseball team and golfing. If you asked him, he'd tell you he was in great shape for the shape he was in.

He would stop for an occasional beer with his unit but was more of a loner. If it wasn't so early, a beer, or perhaps a glass of merlot, sounded like a good idea about now. Since his recent divorce, wine sipping has decreased. He wasn't drinking much wine without his wife around to make the selection. He felt his mind wandering when he thought of Ann.

"Never a good time to start thinking of beer, wine, or an ex-wife while waiting to respond to a summons from the captain," He mumbled to himself, rubbing the back of his neck.

Shaking off that memory, Harry's thoughts turned to the reason for his summons to the captain's office. He wasn't patient and didn't suffer multiple petty annoyances well. Like being called to the captain's office, he detested those requests. It usually meant extra work, and he and the other detectives had already put in more overtime hours than they liked.

Harry moved forward as the captain replaced the phone receiver," Trouble?" He asked. "Seems that a group of residents at a retirement village think that one of their cohorts has been murdered or maybe it was suicide, but they don't believe that her death was an accident." the captain said.

"This wouldn't happen to be the call I covered yesterday, would it?" Harry asked, scowling.

"It is. According to the Commander, the caller was adamant that we investigate further. The caller stated that Nancy Drouillard, a respectable retired judge and resident of the village, has some suspicions that need to be dealt with." Looking at Harry with a speculative expression, "Seems as if the residents are anxious that there might be a murderer living among them."

Harry shook his head, rubbed the back of his neck, and looked amazed, "Unbelievable, Nancy has agitated the residents, involving you and even the division Commander." Exasperated, he added, "I am aware that the deceased was a close friend to her and a favorite of many of the residents, but suggesting that something nefarious is going on within the 55+ village is uncalled for." Motioning with his upturned hands, he shrugged, "Everything in the apartment pointed clearly to smoke inhalation being the cause of death," Harry's frustration was evident.

The captain, used to Harry's outbursts, hid a smile, "I thought her name sounded familiar, then I remembered she was a defense lawyer during my early days on the force and a fair and effective judge before she retired. I recalled that she also happens to be your mother-in-law."

"A more than likely bored ex-mother-in-law," Harry corrected. He could see where this conversation was headed. Hands in his pockets, "I guess you're going to want me to take care of this, clear up any misconceptions, and calm everyone down?"

"The sooner, the better, Harry. Just don't upset anyone further. I don't want another call from the Commander unless it congratulates us on a timely resolution to this issue."

Harry didn't like it. He didn't care that the captain could see it in his stance, but he knew resisting was useless.

"Yes, sir, I'll see how fast we can resolve this issue." Walking out the door, Harry added, "I will keep you informed."

Harry returned to the 55+ village later that morning., Pulling up to the Cup and Vine Cafe, he planned to visit with the barista. From years of experience, he knew the service providers always have their finger on the pulse of the customers, and in this case, that would be the residents.

In line to order, he noted the unique combination of a coffee-wine bar. The ambiance was one of comfort and community. Groupings of tables and chairs filled the cozy space. Earth tones accented the appearance of outdoor space while still indoors. Screens covered the wide doors, which opened to several decks. The tables and chairs were empty except for a group of men comparing golfing scorecards and a four-top of ladies eating pastries. Harry appreciated the aroma of fresh ground coffee as he watched the barista finish a latte with a rose flourish in the foam.

While ordering a decaf coffee, he was approached by an older gentleman. "Say, aren't you the guy that found poor old Hilda the day she died?" Harry agreed that he was the detective on site that day.

"Whatcha doing back here, now?"

Harry took a second to consider his answer, "We investigate all deaths at home." he responded, "I'm just following up. Some residents seem to feel that Hilda never smoked in her condo."

"Yeah, that's what has all of us scratching our heads." shrugging his shoulders, "Most of her friends knew she couldn't stand the smell of smoke and wouldn't tolerate it in her appointment."

Harry looked at him, "Did you know her well?" he asked.

"No, we weren't close. A few women in the village were, and a few guys who hung out at the wine bar a couple of evenings a week knew her well."

Harry nodded as he sipped his coffee, "Anyone in particular that you think I should talk to," he asked.

"I'd speak with Nancy Drouillard and her friend Bess since they were close. Also, the neighbor, Sally, spent a lot of time with her. Occasionally, some office administration staff would be on her deck with the residents, smoking and sharing cocktails."

Harry had pulled out a small notepad and scribbled, "You say, administration staff?"

"Just the director of the complex and his assistant director, Marcy. Hilda's deck can be seen if you are sitting out front on the wine bar deck. I always look to see if Marcy is present. She's a standout, being the youngest and most attractive." He winked, "If you know what I mean."

Nodding again, Harry seemed to agree, saying, "I think I'll see if I can track down a few of those folks and put this investigation to rest."

"That would be a good thing, detective. We would all be much more comfortable around here without wondering how Hilda passed."

"We at the police department want to ease any fears or suspicions within the village. The sooner we can do that, the better." He thanked the gentleman over his shoulder as he walked away.

Planning to question the barista later, Harry searched for Hilda's neighbor, Sally. Crossing the street, he rang the bell at the condo beside Hilda's. He knocked on the door when no one answered the bell, and still, there was no response.

He remembered seeing some women at a table in the coffee shop, and he thought they might be willing to share their thoughts about Hilda's death. Walking back into the Cup and Vine, he approached the barista bartender and asked if he had seen Sally that day. He pointed to one of the women at the table he had observed earlier. Harry noticed the women all sat up straighter as they watched him approach.

"Good morning, ladies. How are you this morning." His smile included all of them.

"Well, how do you expect us to be after all the distressing happenings," a tiny elderly woman in purple leggings responded. "Such goings on!" she puffed.

"You were here yesterday when Hilda was found, weren't you?" Another somewhat larger woman with caramel skin and bouncing Grey dreadlocks asked. Smiling at Harry, she added, "Don't mind her rude response," pointing at the purple leggings woman, "She's our official drama queen!"

Harry expected the accusation to be refuted. Instead, he was surprised that the first woman seemed to enjoy her title and preened a little at her friend's comment. Tossing her hair back off her shoulder, she sighed.

"Such a tragedy. We all loved her, " she shared, looking at the table for confirmation. Harry noted that all the women nodded in agreement.

He introduced himself, "I'm a detective following up on Hilda's death at home. Do you mind if I ask you a few questions?"

He recognized Sally since he briefly spoke with her the day before. She appeared too upset to give him more than a quick statement yesterday. He was hoping for a similar brief conversation today. Confirmation that she was known to smoke in her condo, at least if not in bed, would remove any need for further investigation.

"So, are you all acquainted with Hilda, then?" He asked the group. As they all nodded again, he looked at Sally, " We spoke briefly yesterday, Sally., As Hilda's neighbor, did you ever see her smoke in her condo?"

"No sir, she wouldn't, never. She hated the stench of old cigarette ashes. Even though she smoked, she was adamant that all her smoking friends weren't allowed to smoke anywhere except on the deck. She didn't even let them smoke close to the sliding doors!"

Harry took a deep breath, shook his head, and asked, "Then how would you explain her being found dead of smoke inhalation in her condo bedroom?" He questioned Sally but looked around at all the women at the table.

The lady in the purple leggings spoke up, looking him straight in the eye, "Isn't it your job to figure that out? After all, isn't that what detectives do?" She added.

He forced a tight little smile, "It is exactly why I am here asking you these questions, hoping that you can help lead me to the answers."

Looking again at Sally, he questioned her further. "You said yesterday that Hilda never slept on the gel foam topper? Is that correct?"

She explained that Hilda always let her daughter put it on the bed to avoid an argument. Hilda said it hurt her back and smelled funny, so she would call Nancy, Bess, or one of the administrative staff to come and remove it.

"I told you all of this yesterday, don't you remember?" she asked, sounding impatient, repeating herself.

"I thought detectives write all the witness statements down in a little notebook, at least they do on television." Again, the purple leggings woman spoke, looking at him from the corner of her eye, obviously disappointed with his interviewing technique.

Ignoring that comment, he turned to Sally, "Suppose it wasn't an accident. Do you know of anyone who wanted to hurt Hilda? When I spoke with her yesterday, her daughter said she may have been depressed."

Harry thought that Sally looked alarmed to be asked to accuse someone of wishing ill of Hilda. Or maybe that look was one of disbelief that one would believe Hilda would contemplate suicide.

"Certainly not, Detective! Hilda was nice to everyone, was liked, and thought well of in this village." She raised her chin and shook her head, insulted by the accusation that Hilda had enemies. "She was one of the community's most outgoing and happy people. Ask anyone!"

Seeing that he wasn't getting any helpful information from this group, he handed out his business card to all the ladies. He advised them to call if they thought of anything that might help him understand how a woman who didn't smoke in her home or allow anyone else to was found dead in bed from smoke inhalation.

The tiny purple leggings lady tilted her head at Harry and suggested, "Maybe it wasn't smoke inhalation that killed her," she suggested, "Nancy could be right; Hilda might have been murdered."

Harry tightened his lips to keep from saying anything he might regret and nodded at the group. He told Sally he may need to speak to her again and thanked all the women for their time and assistance. He left the Cup, and Vine discouraged and none the wiser for meeting with Hilda's friends.

CHAPTER 5

While Harry was busy at the Cup and Vine, Nancy tried to avoid the shock and dismay evident throughout the community as the word of Hilda's death spread. She had called Bess, inviting her to meet for coffee at the French restaurant several blocks from the village.

Having spent a restless night reviewing Harry's description of Hilda's bedroom scene, the evidence didn't add up in her mind. Frowning, she realized that maybe she didn't know Hilda's habits as well as she thought she did.

Attempting to stop thinking about the inconsistencies of Hilda's death, Nancy let her thoughts drift to her discouraging meeting with Todd. She replayed the meeting in her head. His dismissive attitude and insulting comments about her age added to her feelings of inadequacy and insignificance. She sat there, chin resting in her hand, elbow on the table, and sighed.

"What if I am just old and useless?" Nancy thought aloud, blushing as the waiter chose that moment to place her latte in front of her.

He looked at her, eyebrows raised, shook his head, and said, "Even if that were true, at least you're cute." His eyes traveled from her shoulder-length silver hair to her trim turquoise sweater set down to the tips of her matching sandals. Winking, he left her scowling.

"A lot of good being a cute, useless old lady does for one's ego," she mumbled, watching Bess approach the table. She smiled at Bess's typical mused cropped hair, khaki rolled-up ankle pants, and tie-dyed t-shirt. Her trim figure belied her fondness for pastries. She swore the sweets were the reason she was so full of energy, but Nancy didn't buy it.

With a glance at Nancy, Bess knew she wasn't happy. Having grown up together, she and Nancy supported each other through various life challenges. By the sad-half-smile on Nancy's face, her brow drawn and lips taunt, Bess could tell Hilda's death continued to upset her. Bess watched Nancy sit up straighter and tossed her hair away from her face as she approached.

"Good morning, Nancy. Looks like you didn't get much sleep last night," Bess noticed the shadows under her eyes.

"That is pretty much an understatement. After a day like yesterday, I'm not sure how long it will take ever to feel rested again." she responded. "Losing Hilda like that after my meeting with Todd made sleeping impossible."

"Hilda's death is haunting," shaking her head, Bess sighed. "I hope your in-law detective can figure out that mystery. We need to make him see that her death was not caused by smoking in bed." They sat lost in their own questioning thoughts until Nancy corrected Bess, "You mean my former son-in-law?"

Brows raised, Nancy shook her head and scoffed, "He's no more interested in our opinion than Todd was in my potential contribution to his law firm."

"I take it he didn't welcome you back into the fold with open arms?" Bess asked.

Squinting at Bess, "Pretty obvious, huh?" Laughing, "He didn't even entertain the idea for a minute- said I wouldn't be much of a revenue generator, so no interest, period."

Scowling, Bess responded, "Scum!" Just as the waiter appeared at their table.

"Not you." Hand to her mouth, she smiled at the waiter. Ordering an Americano with extra cream, she hesitated before adding an almond croissant, remembering the several donuts she had shared with the village ladies earlier.

"Didn't he realize that with your connections, you would be a real asset to his law firm?" Bess asked.

Looking at Bess, her eyes tearing, "Todd was arrogant and dismissive. He didn't care about those underserved by the legal system, the young, old, or disabled. Nothing but paying for his shiny new office furniture, slick signage, and business brochures."

Sniffing, "When I suggested a guardian ad litem position in his firm, Todd laughed. With my history as a judge, I could advocate for those who can't speak for themselves in court. I would've appreciated the opportunity to make a difference."

"I was so taken aback and disappointed." Nancy continued, "He made me feel so worthless. It brought back memories of being in law school and the chauvinistic professors."

"I remember how angry you were at those professors," Bess nodded, "I recall one you spoke about in particular. He treated all of the women in his class as husband hunters instead of professional law candidates." Bess said, "You were livid!"

"I had several issues with his treatment of me and the other women in the class. It was obvious that he ignored the questions raised by the female students and was attentive and engaged with the male students. I wanted to call him on that and tried to meet with him."

She thought momentarily, seeing the classroom and the professor in her mind's eye. Again, Nancy fell silent, remembering how rude the professor was. "When we finally met, I told him that I noticed he hesitated to respond to questions from the females in the class while taking questions and comments readily from the male students." She frowned.

"He looked at me and admitted that the male students asked pertinent and focused questions, and the females didn't. Instead, they wanted clarification, more detailed explanations, and took up valuable lecture time." She shook her head.

Grimacing at Bess, she added, "He remarked that the men were law scholars, committed to learning, seeking knowledge and justice for the public and clients. He said that those males sitting in his classroom were the future judges and lawmakers of the next generation."

Lost in her memories, "I challenged his lack of trust that one of the few women in his class could be a future judge or lawmaker." Nancy laughed, thinking how absurd his response was 35 years later when several women had been appointed to the Supreme Court. "I reminded him that the female figure holding the scale of justice was blind to the sex of the defenders of the righteous and that regardless of what he believed, both men and women will serve justice." Raising her chin and straightening her shoulders.

"Good point, Nancy," Bess said while picking at the crumbs of her croissant left on the plate, resigned to Nancy's occasional outrage regarding female discrimination.

"He didn't take my response well, though." Looking off in the distance, again, lost in past thoughts, Nancy continued. "He dismissed me, made me feel small and ignorant. He caused me to question my skills and to feel inadequate to fight for justice. It made me doubt if I could become the lawyer my father would be proud of."

Saddened by watching Nancy re-live what she felt was a humiliating experience, Bess could see how her meeting with Todd brought back some of those doubts.

"So, Todd didn't have any suggestions?" she asked, bringing Nancy back to the present.

"Oh, he had plenty of suggestions- golf, tennis, bridge, pickleball. I'm surprised he didn't suggest board games and jigsaw puzzles!" Nancy scoffed, remembering his smug, condescending smirk. "He said I had contributed my fair share in the fight for justice. I had earned a rest and a comfortable retirement. Implying that he and the younger generation would carry on."

"Hey, I enjoy jigsaw puzzles, and there's nothing wrong with card games if the pot is hearty enough," Bess responded, laughing. "I've even been thinking of taking up pickleball if a certain gentleman is a team member."

The waiter smiled at Nancy as he offered to replace her empty latte cup. She nodded in response as Bess cleared her throat and spoke quietly.

"Returning to your *ex*-son-in-law, I wanted to share the latest. He was back early this morning, talking to several of the happy hour group, asking about Hilda's recent frame of mind. "

That startled Nancy, "Nonsense, Hilda enjoyed life. She even corresponded with an internet boyfriend regularly. Her daughter disapproved, but I think they were planning to meet. Hilda didn't want her daughter to know anything about it. Ending her life was far from Hilda's plans."

Bess nodded, "That makes sense. Sally said she overheard them arguing the night before her body was found through the adjoining screen doors."

Nancy was thoughtful, "That must have been when Lisa put the mattress topper back on the bed. She sure was insistent that topper would help her mother's back pain."

Bess agreed and explained that Sally told the detective as much and how often Hilda called someone to help her remove the bulky thing, only to have her daughter put it back on the bed the next time she visited. The detective seemed skeptical about Hilda's refusal to sleep on the topper. Bess said that was when Sally told him that she, Nancy, or the assistant community director were usually called to remove and store it.

"After the detective left, we ordered more coffee and doughnuts. Sally remembered she also overheard them arguing about money at an earlier visit." Bess continued.

"That's interesting. Hilda never shared any disagreements with her daughter with me." Her brow wrinkled, Nancy replied.

"According to Sally, it seems Lisa wanted to know what happened to a large amount of money that Hilda had withdrawn the month before."

Bess added, "Sally reported that Hilda wouldn't tell her even though Lisa argued that it would all be hers someday and she had a right to know where her inheritance was going. Sally added that it was common knowledge that Lisa helped her mother manage her finances and said she wasn't happy that Hilda was withdrawing large sums without sharing where it was going."

"Hilda never mentioned any of that. She led me to believe that she and her daughter were great friends and loving mother and daughter." Nancy looked perplexed.

"Sally made it clear that she wasn't in the habit of eavesdropping, but the sliding doors on both women's decks were open to the screens, so Sally heard multiple discussions on the days when Lisa visited her mother," Bess added with a side-eye look at Nancy.

"She should have told the detective about all that," frowning, she thought that Sally had a shock and probably didn't feel comfortable gossiping with the detective.

Harry was intimidating and might have frightened poor Sally; she was normally anxious, and this crisis must have rattled her. But she wondered about the argument. She knew Hilda thought Lisa resented her because she divorced her father.

Sipping on her second latte, Nancy was lost in thought. Could resentment and blame lead to murder when one's inheritance funds that one believes to be rightfully theirs is disappearing, she wondered.

"Do you think Lisa could have murdered her mother and made it look like an accident?" she asked.

Bess stared at Nancy, her cup stopped midway to her mouth, alarmed by the thought.

Not waiting for an answer, Nancy continued, "We need to find out how heated that discussion about money was and when exactly it happened." She raised her brow and nodded at Bess.

"Umm, really, Nancy," cocking her head at her, "Don't you think we should leave that up to the police?"

"If the police continue to think Hilda's death was an accident, it will be up to us to seek justice for her, ourselves."

Bess lowered her cup, sighing; she realized Nancy was determined to get involved in investigating Hilda's death.

"Well then, we need to find Sally and ask her for more details. I'll call her and see if she wants to meet for tea this afternoon. Poor thing, she probably needs to talk about yesterday anyway." Bess said, checking her plate for crumbs.

Nancy signaled the waiter to bring their tab and agreed to meet Bess at the coffee wine bar that afternoon if Sally decided to talk with them.

CHAPTER 6

As Nancy drove back to the complex, she considered the question of Hilda's missing money. "Could one kill one's mother over money." she wondered aloud, thinking about her relationship with her mother. Nancy's mother was warm and loving. She couldn't think of hurting her in any way, let alone murdering her. Money is usually at the heart of most murder cases, but jealousy, fear, and uncontrollable anger might be other reasons.

Hilda didn't seem to elicit that extreme type of response. Everyone seemed to like her as far as Nancy knew. She frowned as she parked her car in the garage, "I'll have to give this whole murder thing some more thought," she murmured to herself as she entered the house.

In the front room, she was surprised to see her daughter, Ann, sitting on the couch talking on her cell phone. She heard her response to the caller and noted the sound of relief in her voice.

"She just walked in," Ann spoke into the phone, "I told you I would give her your message. I really must hang up." She smiled guiltily at Nancy. Then sighed, "Um, I'm not sure about meeting you later. I have some tentative plans, but maybe some other time?" She paused, "I think that might work, Harry, but I can't guarantee anything."

Nancy thought her daughter's voice sounded strained. Didn't surprise her, however. Ann never liked having to talk with her ex-husband. She slipped off her sandals and watched Ann hang up from Harry.

Nancy smiled at Ann, noting that she had styled her hair differently. It flattered her blond curls and made her look younger. She was slim and dressed in a navy jumper and a short-sleeved blouse. Along with navy loafers, her appearance was professional.

"I take it that call was your ex-husband worried about me with a murderer on the loose in our complex. How nice that Harry is concerned for my safety," Nancy smiled at Ann.

Ann looked at her mother in alarm, "Murder, really, mother. You're the only one believing that Hilda's death was murder. Harry is not concerned about your safety as much as he is concerned about your sanity!"

"He thinks you are about to get involved in Hilda's accidental death, insisting it is treated as a murder investigation. He says you are unnecessarily alarming the residents of the Village related to her death. He wants me to make sure you hear his message loud and clear: cease and desist!" Ann clenched her teeth to keep from raising her voice.

"Ann, it's obvious to anyone who spent time with Hilda that she detested that gel-foam mattress topper and wouldn't be caught dead sleeping on it. Oh, geez, did I just say that!" Covering her mouth with her hand and catching her breath. Dismayed at her choice of words, she felt tears forming, sighed, shaking her head, "I am so sure she wasn't sleeping on that topper!"

Upset at Harry involving her daughter, she walked to her bedroom, grabbed a pair of jeans and a sweater from her closet, then stripped out of her sweater set. Ann followed and stood at the doorway, watching her dress. She couldn't help but smile at her 65-year-old mother. Not as slim as she once was, her mother remained fit and agile as she stripped to her bra and panties. Throwing on an oversized cable knit sweater and sliding her feet into a different pair of sandals, Nancy looked at her daughter expectantly.

"Look, I have to meet with Bess at the coffee bar, but I would love to discuss my thoughts about this murder investigation with you after." Nancy smiled.

"Mother, this conversation is over. There will be no further discussion," Ann insisted, "Your investigation is done!"

"I have to go; I'll see you out." Nancy smiled as she led Ann toward the door, "It's always such a pleasure to have you stop by, Ann. You really must try to do it more often. Oh, and I'm so glad to hear that you and Harry seem to be getting along again, and it is sweet of him to be concerned about me."

Ann looked amazed at Nancy's purposefully implied lack of understanding: "You aren't fooling me, Mother. Harry will not tolerate your snooping around his investigation." She warned, "You know he will be calling me if you don't stop, so please, for my sake, resist this foolish urge to become involved." Nancy had opened the door, waiting for her to leave.

"Don't worry, dear. I won't bother Harry." She said and smiled as she closed the door. She scowled at the thought that Harry was upsetting her daughter.

Her cell phone rang. Noting it was Bess, she answered, "Hey there, are we meeting Sally?"

Sally had agreed to meet with them for tea at three that afternoon. "I think she was happy I called and invited her. She sounded anxious."

"She probably is a nervous wreck and easily intimidated after meeting Harry. Want me to pick you up on the way?" Nancy asked as she watched Ann pull away from the curb. Bess agreed, and she ended the call.

She considered Harry and Ann's interference with her plan to solve Hilda's murder. Neither seemed interested in her explanation of foul play. Both treated her like she was doddering or an interfering old woman!

Again, the feeling of a lack of purpose engulfed her. The fear that she might be wrong was causing her to second-guess herself. What if it were true that Hilda caught the mattress on fire accidentally? She couldn't be wrong, could she? It didn't matter if her daughter and her detective ex-husband thought she was an annoyance with too much time on her hands. Hilda deserved justice, and the murderer wouldn't get away with this crime if she could help it. Straightening her shoulders and raising her chin, Nancy caught a glimpse of herself in the entry mirror. She might appear to be a 65-year-old woman, but she didn't look feeble. She looked determined.

Nodding her approval to herself, she checked her watch, noting she had an hour until she met with Bess and Sally. Walking into her office, she decided to jot down a few notes. She started to list those who could help explain how Hilda ended up on a mattress she refused to sleep on and died due to smoke inhalation from a fire started by a cigarette that she had never smoked in her home. Nancy realized after a brief time that it was a useless activity.

Sighing, she remembered her favorite quote from one of Nancy Drew's mysteries. It was from the *Ghost of Blackwood Hall*. Nancy Drew spoke to her father and said, "She was going to keep working on that case until all the pieces of the puzzle can be made to fit together." That quote became a mantra for Nancy as she sought justice, winning lawsuits as a lawyer and presiding over court cases as a judge.

Sooner or later, the pieces would all fit, but she was still at a loss of means or motive for Hilda's death as she left her office. Grabbing her purse and phone, she headed out the door to pick up Bess.

CHAPTER 7

They found Sally already sitting in a booth at the coffee bar. Sliding into the seat next to Bess, Nancy greeted Sally, who had chosen a selection of treats, "I ordered a couple of scones, sausage rolls, and my favorite crumpets with clotted cream." She admitted, "As well as a pot of Earl Grey tea." Bess was already eyeing the scones, reaching for the blueberry one as Nancy set a crumpet and some lemon curd on a small plate and handed it to Sally.

"Having skipped lunch today, that sounds delightful!" Nancy agreed. Looking at Sally, she asked how she was handling the police inquiry and all the attention related to Hilda's death.

"Well, it hasn't been easy, Nancy. Hilda was a good neighbor, and it is horrible thinking of her laying there, next door, dead." She shuddered, "It's hard to believe that she was sleeping on that mattress topper that she disliked so much, and I never knew her to smoke in her apartment, either!" Nancy poured the tea while Bess added a crumpet to her plate.

"I know it must have been dreadful, Sally," Nancy said as she placed a sausage roll on her plate. "What did the detective say when you told him that?"

Frowning at them, she said, "The conversation with that detective was terrifying. He was so official and didn't seem to care about what I had to say. He made it clear he wasn't interested in what I thought." She shook her head and sipped the tea.

She spread the lemon curd on a crumpet, took a bite, and responded, "This tea service is such a treat. It is nice of you two to be concerned about me during this ordeal."

"What exactly did you think, Sally?" Bess asked in between bites of her crumpet to keep Sally on topic.

"Why, I told him she didn't care to sleep on that topper and that I never saw her smoke inside her apartment. But he didn't seem to believe me. I wasn't the only one to make that claim, either. He acted like we were all making up a story to occupy us and give us something to talk about! I didn't appreciate his attitude, either." She sniffed.

Nancy topped off her cup of tea and asked, "Did you notice any visitors or hear anything that day or night that was odd? Sometimes voices and visitors coming and going are noticeable in the apartment next door."

"I did hear Hilda and her daughter having a somewhat heated conversation., They lowered their voices after a few minutes, and I didn't hear the daughter leave."

"What did the detective have to say about that?"

"He said that mothers and daughters argue all the time-usually about insignificant things."

Thinking he is an expert in mother and daughters, old Harry would know all about pointless arguments. Nancy thought but looked expectantly at Sally and asked her about the argument.

"The latest argument seemed to be about Hilda's daughter's new boyfriend. It appeared that Hilda didn't much care for the growing relationship."

"I didn't know her daughter was involved with anyone; did you recognize a name?"

Sally shook her head and nibbled on a scone, "No, but I know that Hilda was surprised, too. Seemed she didn't like being kept in the dark, either."

Using her napkin to brush off the scone crumbs from her lips, Bess wondered aloud, "They always seemed to get along when I saw them together. I wouldn't have thought they would have a discussion heated enough for you to overhear in your condo."

"Both condo screens on the deck doors are usually open during the day for ventilation, so I can often hear them if they argue."

"Do they argue often?" Nancy asked.

"Not usually, but recently, they were having regular arguments. Last week was about the missing funds in Hilda's bank account." Sally looked toward the ceiling and squinted, "Yep, it was last week, and her daughter was livid. You know she had power of attorney and paid all her mother's bills. Lisa accused her of investing in some sort of money scheme.

Seems like she found that Hilda's account was short, and Hilda wouldn't tell her what she had done with the money."

"Geeze, I wonder if the detective knows anything about where the money went?" Nancy muttered.

"The argument wasn't so much about the money as it was about a strange man, according to Lisa. From what I heard, it seems it wasn't the first time that Hilda gave away money to some strange man, not wanting to talk bad about the dead and all." She glanced uncomfortably at Nancy,

Nancy prodded, "We want to help find out what happened that night, not gossip. You can share what you heard with us. It won't have to go any further."

Sally lowered her voice to just above a whisper. "Well, from what I could hear, when Lisa was younger, Hilda took up with some charmer, and not only did he take a good portion of her late husband's money, but he maltreated Lisa, too."

She breathed, adding, "During that recent argument, Lisa taunted her mother and said it served her right to have lost her inheritance once already."

Sally frowned, "Lisa was angry and laughed at Hilda, kinda nasty, she was. Said something about thinking she should've learned her lesson after that."

Nancy could see Sally was getting upset, reliving that evening and sharing what she had heard. Nancy patted her hand, saying, "I can see this conversation is distressing. Let's change the subject to something more pleasant, shall we?"

Nodding, Sally sighed with relief, agreeing with Nancy. Smiling, Bess asked her about the desserts served at the memorial service. Sally admitted that Lisa, knowing her desserts were among the favorites within the community, had asked her to provide a selection of her baked goods.

They discussed the plans made by those helping Lisa with the Celebration of Life memorial and added a few thoughts to bring to the next planning session. As Sally sipped the last of her tea, she excused herself, "I must look up a selection of recipe suggestions for the meeting. I'd better start looking." Bess reminded her to include her molasses cookies in her selection. Sally nodded at her and patted her shoulder as she left.

Nancy grinned at Bess, "You are shameless when it comes to desserts!" Bess shrugged.

Reviewing their conversation with Sally, Nancy shared her thoughts with Bess.

"It seems, according to Sally, that Lisa was pretty angry, but that was last week, not the night before she died."

Bess said, "It might have taken her a few days to decide how to fake her accidental death. After all, if it was murder, it appears to be premeditated."

Nancy nodded, "We need to talk to a few more people." They drank the rest of the tea in silence while Bess finished the last sausage roll.

She signed the tab for their tea, her hand supporting her chin as she commented, "The past two days have certainly been full of surprises. First, Todd turned out to be a smug, arrogant, money-grubbing idiot. Obviously, with no need for a "seasoned" professional who overestimated her worth. Second, it appears I didn't know Hilda as well as I thought."

CHAPTER 8

Nancy returned to her villa and walked into her office. Mulling over her conversation with Sally, she wasn't confident that Lisa would've killed her mother over past problems. It was evident she needed more information about that mother-daughter relationship. Sitting behind the desk, she picked up a letter opener and tossed it from one hand to the other. She concentrated on what she knew about Hilda's and her daughter's previous life.

Thinking back to the multiple Nancy Drew books she and her mother had shared, she focused on her sleuthing techniques. She remembered Nancy Drew created a plan, studied the facts, and noted details to learn more about the crime. She wouldn't start an investigation without a clear picture of all the players, the victim, and the suspects.

"An investigator needs an array of tools, but the most important is the beginning profile of the victim, according to Nancy Drew." She said, speaking aloud to herself, then smiled at her self-talk. It probably wasn't a good habit to be forming. At her age, others may think she was becoming senile.

She left the office and heated a bowl of tomato soup. As she crumbled saltines into the soup, she sighed. Her thoughts had turned to her meeting with Todd. Her disgust at his behavior and her anger at his treatment of her was fading. She wondered if she was kidding herself by thinking she still had something of value to offer. She even questioned if justice was the motivating factor in the pursuit of Hilda's case or if she was just looking for a distraction from the feeling of being useless.

Running her fingers through her hair, she rose from the table, rinsed her bowl, and loaded it into the dishwasher. She headed toward her bedroom.

"Tomorrow is another day. I need to know what happened to Hilda. I can put my lawyer status on hold until I get a handle on this case," she told herself. "There was no sense worrying anymore tonight." She shook her head and, again, smiled at her self-talk.

With a plan forming to contact the village assistant director in the morning, she decided to call it a night. Falling into bed, she hoped to sleep soundly.

CHAPTER 9

Nancy was thinking about a shower and getting dressed as she added half and half to her coffee. Sipping gingerly, she thought about the plan to talk to Marcy and Hilda's daughter, Lisa. Wondering whom to call first, she decided to chat with the assistant director, Marcy, over lunch. They could casually converse while enjoying a salad in the clubhouse dining room.

She could then meet Lisa for coffee to inquire how she was doing and see if she needed anything. She called the village administration office, and the receptionist answered on the first ring.

Nancy asked if Marcy was available to come to the phone. She was placed on hold and found herself listening to a 1970s Neil Young song, "Entertaining choice," she thought, "definitely a tune from my generation."

"Hello, Nancy. How are you doing after the sad event of the last few days?" Marcy asked.

"Not too bad, considering. How about all of you? It must have been a shock to the staff?"

"Well, yes, we are all so sad to have lost Hilda that way. Dying from smoke inhalation while sleeping, though, is a pretty painless way to go." Marcy answered pragmatically.

"You have a point, as disturbing as that thought is." Nancy sighed, "I was feeling Hilda's loss and thought you might be too. Maybe we could meet for lunch in the dining room to lift our spirits. Are you available?" Nancy suggested.

"How thoughtful, Nancy. It would be wonderful to have some time to visit with you."

"Great, can we meet around 1:00, then?" Nancy asked.

"Perfect, that is my normal lunch hour. See you there, Nancy."

As Marcy hung up, she felt bad for Nancy. Losing her friend must be hard on her. Checking her watch, she noted that she hadn't seen the director, Ronald, yet that morning. He rarely showed up this late unless he had a meeting elsewhere.

Checking her reflection on her computer screen, she patted her hair away from her face and thought about how close she and Ronald had become over the last year. He had gotten too busy to share their meals at the club after they had late evening planning meetings over the last month or so.

He would bring over a bottle of wine on the evenings when they would work at her apartment and would spend the night with her, leaving early so they could arrive separately at the office. Lately, he had been working after hours with the developers for the new pickleball court expansion.

She wasn't involved in the development but understood that the time with the developers left little opportunities for their evenings together.

She believed those intimate evenings would continue once the contractors were selected and the dust settled from Hilda's death. Hilda's daughter, Lisa, would finally be out of the picture, giving him more time to focus on their relationship. Lisa had taken up too much of his time discussing her issues with her mother's finances. Ronald couldn't see she was using him to solve her mother's problems, flirting with him and obviously craving his attention.

Marcy was sure that he was a victim of her manipulations. Now that Hilda was gone, he would realize that when Lisa no longer needed his help, she would lose interest in him. He would have no more excuses for not spending evenings with her.

She knew it was against corporate policy for administrative staff to fraternize with subordinates and was aware their affair needed to remain a secret. Everything seemed safe until Ronald became worried that corporate was asking questions about expenditures from the clubhouse dinners. He said they were questioning the number of meals shared and the charges for wine, so they needed to take a break from meeting outside of working hours. He implied it would be short-term.

Pursing her lips as she thought about the intensity of their relationship, Marcy could see that even though their affair was a secret, she was sure he loved her as much as she loved him. He was possibly scared of commitment and in denial of his need for her. He had often confessed to her that he wouldn't know what to do without her help with the residents, maintenance crew, or kitchen staff.

Now that Hilda was dead, Lisa's fascination with him would pass, and he would be free to focus on their relationship. She nodded to herself. He would come around to see how much he cared and needed her. She just needed to be patient.

Looking at her watch again, she wondered why he was so late this morning. Maybe it had something to do with Hilda's death. She stood from her desk and walked to the window with her coffee cup. Her view of the parking lot was limited, but she noted that Ronald's car was in his designated spot.

She wondered aloud, "Where is he, and what is he doing that he hasn't been to the office yet this morning?" She sipped from the cup and realized the coffee was cold. She tossed the dregs into the wastebasket, decided she needed an espresso, and headed to the coffee bar. At the counter, she ordered her usual, signed her tab, and looked around the room while waiting for her drink. She was surprised to see Ronald with Lisa, Hilda's daughter.

Watching the two of them, she frowned. He seemed to comfort Lisa, holding her hand across the small table. Her head was lowered as she dabbed at her eyes with the other hand. Marcy clenched her jaw, gritting her teeth. It seemed Hilda's death had brought them closer, and Ronald was certainly providing a shoulder for Lisa to lean on.

"Well, that won't last. Now that Hilda is gone, there will be no reason for Lisa to be on-site and distract Ronald from his work." She took her espresso from the barista and walked over to their table.

"Lisa, I am so sorry for your loss; so painful for all of us. I know it will be a difficult adjustment. Please get in touch with us if there is any way we can help you with anything."

Lisa looked up while removing her hand from Ronald's.

"Marcy, Mother always appreciated your visits and felt well taken care of by the entire staff. I will need to contact you over the next few weeks. I appreciate your offer. Thank you."

Ronald agreed, "Anything you need, Lisa, we are here to help you through this sad time." He reached across the table to touch her hand in a comforting gesture.

Lisa covered his hand with hers and smiled tearfully, "I am so grateful for your support, Ronald. I can't think of any way you could be more helpful."

Marcy watched the interchange between Ronald and Lisa. It was as if they had already forgotten she was still present. She smiled sadly at the couple and quietly walked back to her office. Marcy returned to her desk and shrugged. Lisa was not going to be a problem. She would make sure that Ronald knew it was her that he loved. As far as Marcy was concerned, Lisa was history. Once Hilda's Celebration of Life was over, she would be a distant memory.

She realized she was overthinking his and Lisa's relationship; his interest in her would be short-lived now that Hilda was no longer part of the village. He was such a kind man. Being older, he had lots of experience in financial matters and had been spending time with Hilda's daughter to help her manage her mother's money profitably. With those financial concerns of Hilda no longer a problem, she decided Ronald and her relationship would thrive again.

She opened her computer to the Glamping activities folder. Checking her watch, she realized she would have an hour before she needed to leave for the clubhouse to meet with Nancy. She decided to look over the menus the clubhouse chef had planned for the four-day trip. as she drank her expresso.

CHAPTER 10

Nancy showed up at the club a few minutes early, but Marcy was already sitting at a small booth in the corner with a Bloody Mary cocktail in front of her.

"I don't usually drink during a workday, but today is an exception." She grimaced as she waved her hand in the air, "Everyone is upset about Hilda. The camping supplies I ordered for the Glamping trip are delayed, the chef's menu is a disaster, and our receptionist has a medical emergency!"

"Marcy, so sorry about your day. It sounds horrific!" Nancy patted her hand, "If you needed to cancel, I would have understood."

"Believe me; I needed this break." She sighed. "Besides, today's special is their Niçoise salad, my favorite."

Nancy agreed that the kitchen provided an excellent presentation with that particular salad, "Like a full course meal in a bowl, tuna, chilled potato slices, green beans, olives, and a hard-boiled egg. I won't need to fix dinner tonight," she laughed.

Having both ordered the salad, they settled comfortably into the high-back booth in the corner of the dining room.

"I'm so glad you took the time to lunch with me today," Nancy smiled at Marcy.

"It's always a treat to spend time with you." She responded. "I don't get to spend much time with the community's residents, so this is special."

Both were silent momentarily, then Marcy added, "I will have even less opportunity with Hilda gone. Her happy hour deck get-togethers were a great way to catch up with everyone." At Nancy's nod, she asked, "How is Hilda's group coping with the situation?"

In response, Nancy admitted that they were all shocked by her death and confused by the supposition that she was smoking in bed while sleeping on the gel-foam mattress everyone knew she hated.

"If I'm not mistaken, didn't she call you on occasion to help her roll it up to store in her spare closet?" Nancy asked, "I know Bess and I had all taken turns helping to remove it from her bed. It was a bulky bundle for one person, especially for Hilda. She was a tiny lady!"

Marcy smiled and nodded, "I used to get a call about once a month after her daughter had been visiting. Hilda was always so sweet; she would call the office and ask us to send someone to assist with the mattress removal. I would go to her condo and help her. It was an opportunity to visit with her. Hilda always insisted that I share a belt with her.

That's what she called a shot of bourbon with one ice cube." She smiled at the memory and shook her head sadly. "I also wondered why her daughter insisted that Hilda use it. I know she believed it would help her back pain, but every time she visited, the mattress wasn't being used, yet she replaced it before she left. One would think she would get the message that Hilda wasn't going to utilize its healing powers." Nancy shook her head at the absurdity of the placement.

"I know. I wondered about Lisa's insistence on using the mattress topper, too." Marcy agreed.

"They seemed devoted to each other. Her daughter visited almost weekly. Hilda should have told her daughter she wouldn't utilize the topper." Nancy said, "That would have been the end, right?"

"I'm not sure that Hilda and her daughter were that affectionate or that Hilda wanted to upset Lisa. Hilda was very careful not to offend Lisa or seem ungrateful." Marcy observed before taking another bite of the potato. "I know her daughter felt obligated to ensure her mother was comfortable, but I never saw much warmth in their interaction."

"Now that you mention it, I didn't either." Nancy agreed. "Do you think they had issues? For as close as we were, I don't know too much about Hilda's life before Ned and I moved into the Village."

"According to Hilda, she said Lisa had some difficult teenage years. She also admitted that there were some serious resentments of long-standing related to her decision to send Lisa to a convent boarding school when she was 15 years old."

"She sent Lisa to a boarding school. That is a tough age to be changing from a regular high school. Did she share why she felt compelled to do such a disruptive thing?" Nancy wrinkled her brow, trying to justify that decision in her mind.

Marcy appeared thoughtful, then said, "I don't think sharing will hurt. It seems her reason had something to do with a man Hilda was seeing after her divorce." Looking down at her plate, Marcy spoke quietly, "I shared that I had an issue somewhat like that after my dad ran off with his secretary. "

She took a deep breath and explained, "My mom had this guy; she called him *"her gentleman friend,"* but he was no gentleman." Marcy added, "Hilda said she also made a mistake and chose a man over her daughter. Her male friend turned out to be a serial con man who took advantage of lonely women. "

She said that Hilda was tearful when she shared that after sending Lisa to the boarding school and marrying him, she found out that he had taken advantage of several other divorcees and left them penniless.

"By the time she found out about his true character, Hilda told me that she and Lisa were not even talking through her senior year at the boarding school. "

Marcy shared that Lisa refused to move back in with her after graduation. Instead, she and a roommate from the school got an apartment. "Lisa didn't reconcile with her mother until several years later."

A waitress stopped at their table, asking if they needed anything more while filling their breadbasket. Shaking her head, Nancy thanked her and reached for a fresh breadstick. She was surprised by Marcy's revelations and encouraged her to continue, "Wow, I'm amazed that Hilda would confess all that to you."

"Yes, well, while I helped her remove the mattress pad that evening, I could tell she was particularly melancholy, so we passed on our usual single shot and poured a few fingers of her favorite bourbon. She was embarrassed at first until I shared that my mother forced me to move out of her house when I was seventeen because her *"gentleman friend"* was getting too interested in me."

"I shared my experience with Hilda, explaining that my mother caught her gentleman friend kissing me one evening, having arrived home from work early. She was furious with me." Not making eye contact, Marcy continued, "She didn't say a word to her boyfriend; she just called me names and told me to pack my stuff and be gone by the time she returned home from work the next day."

Nancy's fork was suspended between her plate and mouth when Marcy finished speaking, "How horrible for you. What did you do?"

"I packed my stuff and left, moved in with my father and his secretary until I got a job and moved out into my apartment. "

She further explained that episode, telling Nancy that he would routinely kiss and fondle her, telling her how beautiful she was and how mean her mother was not to let her have boyfriends.

"He offered to be a secret boyfriend, and we would sometimes meet in the park across the street when my mother fell asleep. I was young and foolish and didn't know any better." She defended herself.

"After my mother caught us, he apologized for the misunderstanding, said he didn't mean any harm, was just teaching me about life."

"That was a pretty harsh lesson," Nancy said, patting the back of Marcy's hand.

Laughing bitterly, Marcy added, "I thought he loved me, being a naive 16-year-old. The irony is that Mother married him only to divorce him after finding him in their bed with the neighbor lady."

Taking a deep breath, she found it painful to remember the humiliation, "I explained to Hilda that my mother and I forgave each other and eventually got along. I shared that Lisa would eventually get over their disagreement, too." Marcy smiled sadly at Nancy, then continued to eat her salad, avoiding further eye contact.

Sensing her embarrassment, Nancy said, "I'm so happy you and your mother have become close again."

"We had several good years together until she developed an intense drinking problem," she said, "She died just before I moved to California."

"Oh, I'm so sorry to hear that." Nancy reached across the table to pat her hand again.

"It was an accident. She fell down a stairwell and broke her neck," Marcy explained, shrugging her shoulder.

"How awful!" Nancy said, wondering at the lack of emotion in Marcy's response.

"At least she didn't suffer," Marcy said. "At any rate, I have found a man that recognizes my true value and loves me." Looking askance at Nancy, "It's been tough being single and only meeting young men who think they are a gift to women."

Nancy shook her head, "I wouldn't know about that. Having been married to my high school sweetheart, I didn't spend much time with other boys."

"Exactly, they all seem like high school boys," nodding at Nancy, "My older man appreciates a woman, cares for her, treats her special. My guy adores me."

"An older man?" Raising her eyebrows, she asked, "Someone who lives in the Village?"

Giggling, Marcy shook her head, "Certainly not. Corporate wouldn't allow it, but then again, what corporate doesn't know won't hurt." She laughed out loud at her last comment while Nancy wrinkled her brow, not understanding the joke.

Shrugging her shoulders, Marcy turned the conversation to happier thoughts and plans for an upcoming outdoor concert. She related a funny story about the new yoga instructor and the problems with refurbishing the tennis courts to add a new pickleball court.

Marcy said the planned "Glamping Trip" scheduled for next month has become a chore. "The glamping group was demanding about the menu, sleeping provisions, even the linen and mattresses they would be sleeping on, was an issue." They laughed about that, and after discussing caloric intake, they decided to split a molten brownie dessert anyway.

As they parted, Nancy had one last question, "So you do think that Hilda fell asleep smoking and it was an accident that she died?"

Marcy answered, "Absolutely, unless the coroner finds she had a heart attack or something." She thought for a moment longer, then shrugged, "Or maybe her daughter's resentment and anger got the best of her, and she caught the mattress on fire before she left."

CHAPTER 11

Having left the Clubhouse, Nancy passed Hilda's condo and recognized Lisa's car in the driveway. When Nancy knocked at the open door, Lisa was sorting through what looked like bank statements and checkbooks on Hilda's desk. Lisa looked up and signaled to enter.

"I saw your car parked outside and thought I'd stop by and check on you," Nancy said.

"Oh, Nancy, thank you for stopping. I'm trying to figure out where to start with Mother's finances. Her death was so unexpected. It wasn't as if she had been ill."

"I know it is hard for all of us to realize that she is gone," Nancy agreed. "When you are done here today, why don't you stop by my villa? I have a new favorite winery and a delightful red blend. We can open a bottle, and you can let me know what I can do to help."

"That's an offer I won't refuse. I will need a drink when I finish organizing the clutter on her desk. Who knew it would be so difficult to figure out her finances?"

"We are all feeling confused by the situation. We enjoyed Hilda's entertaining happy hours, sly remarks, and sense of humor. She touched so many lives in this community over the years." Nancy added.

"Yes, she loved this little community. I would appreciate your review of the guest list for Mother's Service, but I'll probably be at least another hour before I'd be ready for that glass of wine. It appears mom drank the last of her supply before she fell asleep that night," Lisa responded.

Nancy nodded, "No worries, I planned on being home the rest of the day. Stop by when you finish here."

As she gazed around the condo one last time, the only changes she noted were dishes in the sink and the financial papers out on the desk. There was nothing suspicious in view. Maybe it was an accident, as impossible as it seems, Nancy thought as she drove home.

Her thoughts returned to her conversation about Lisa and her mother's relationship that she had with Marcy. She wondered if Marcy was right about their lack of affection for each other, as she had noted a sort of reserve but not coldness when they were together.

Lisa arrived at Nancy's villa closer to two hours later than she predicted. "I lost track of the time, trying to pack up all her things. It will take me another day to sort through kitchen items, shoes, and her clothes," Lisa said as Nancy led her to the sofa.

"Were you able to find all her financial papers? I know she had some stocks she was particularly fond of?" She asked Lisa. "She always had good advice for our resident happy hour group, keeping us informed on the stock market fluctuations."

"Too bad she didn't have the same skill in choosing men," Lisa mumbled. Nancy raised her eyebrows at that comment as she filled a wine glass and handed it to her. Lisa gratefully took the glass and sighed. "Thank you. I never thought about her dying. She was so full of energy and life. I hadn't realized there are so many little details to figure out."

"It must be hard; you and your mother seemed close. It will be sad for us to miss her at our gatherings. I can only imagine the void in your life." Nancy said.

"Our relationship wasn't that great. I'm starting to regret that I wasn't a more caring daughter."

"How can you say that? You visited most weeks, and she looked forward to your visits and enjoyed seeing you. You were so concerned about her back pain." Nancy said.

Lisa dismissed Nancy's comment, "You must be talking about my insistence that she sleep on that gel foam topper to ease her back pain." She shook her head. "I didn't realize until talking to the detective that she disliked the mattress topper." Sipping the wine, she didn't meet Nancy's eyes.

"Every visit, I would find she had removed it from her bed. I would put it back on, making noise about how beneficial it would be. I would go on about how her back would feel, her range of motion would increase, and she would rest better."

"That sounds like you were being a concerned and caring daughter," Nancy commented, confused.

"In subtle ways, she would try to discourage me from adding it to her bedding, but I guess she didn't want to upset me by complaining or refusing to add it. She was afraid of offending me. I had read articles about how it would relieve pain; it was an attempt to try to be a more concerned and caring daughter. We have had our differences." She sounded as if she regretted their past relationship.

Raising her chin as Nancy refilled her wine glass for a second time, she said, "I was often petty and childish." She shrugged. She drifted into a reflective mood, sharing that her mother had changed after her father passed. He was from a wealthy family, and the settlement was substantial as his death was caused by an industrial accident.

"I was an only child, and over the years, she grew sad and lonely. She seemed to crave attention, and although I did well at school, she never really seemed interested in me. She cared so little for me; she sent me to an all-girls school run by nuns."

Reinforcing her tale of exile to the convent boarding school, Lisa shared that she was a sophomore and active in numerous clubs. Popular in high school, a cheerleader, a good student, and a class officer, she enjoyed a pleasant and supportive relationship with several of her teachers. Lisa said her life was perfect at school but not at home.

"I had a good-looking but somewhat nerdy boyfriend and enjoyed going to movies and hanging out with a bunch of friends, you know what I mean, right? My mother was so busy with her men that she never really engaged in any of my school activities." Sipping more wine, she continued.

"One night, I was home alone when Mother's latest lover stopped by. Mother hadn't returned home from her ladies' auxiliary meeting yet, but I didn't see any harm in letting him in the house to wait for her." As Nancy added some more wine to Lisa's glass, she continued to relate what led up to her removal to the convent boarding school.

"It was a Friday; we had our first pep rally for the football team. I was wearing my cheerleading outfit, and he commented on how cute it was and made some remark about never dating a cheerleader when he was in high school." Lisa recounted, not looking at Nancy.

"He grabbed me around the waist and slipped his hand under my short skirt, saying he had never kissed a cheerleader before. He made some sick reference to cheerleader porno movies and tried to kiss me. I was surprised and struggled to free myself when my mother came in the door." Lisa stared at the lamp on the coffee table before her, seeming lost in thought.

"How awful for you! Lucky your mother came home," Nancy exclaimed.

"It got even more awful. My mother told her gentleman friend that he needed to leave, and after his departure, she turned on me. She accused me of trying to seduce him instead of supporting me." Lisa continued in a quiet and subdued voice, "As soon as he left, she called me names and slapped me when I tried to defend myself. The next week, I was shipped off to boarding school."

Nancy could understand Lisa's bitterness and could tell she was still hurt and resentful of her mother.

"Did she confront her gentleman friend?" Nancy asked.

"She married him two months later!" Lisa answered. "He swindled most of my father's inheritance from her. I'm afraid she didn't learn her lesson, either."

"That seems like a harsh punishment and an even worse outcome!" Nancy said. "What do you mean she didn't learn her lesson?"

"She recently withdrew 100,000 dollars from the account I manage for her and wouldn't tell me what or who it was for." Lisa answered, "We argued about it, but she wouldn't budge; that's why I think she had gotten involved with another man again."

Nancy waited for her to continue her thoughts about the money, but instead, she returned to her original story.

Lisa took a moment to sip her wine and then shared more of her boarding school experience. After the hasty wedding, Lisa was expected to spend holidays and school breaks at the convent school with those who had no close families or those whose families didn't desire or weren't available to care for their daughters.

As a teenager, Lisa stated, "I felt not only rejected but disposed of," according to her, "As if I was garbage."

After her third refill of wine, Nancy noted that a sad and resentful woman replaced the devoted, grieving daughter. Lisa appeared conflicted about the loss of her mother. Sorry, since her anger and shame were never resolved, and now, with her mother gone, there was no hope for genuine reconciliation.

"She did try to make it up to me, but I found it impossible to forgive her. Our relationship remained shaky; now it's too late." Looking at Nancy, "It's done." She sighed, shrugging her shoulders.

Nancy sensed that the hurt of being abandoned fueled Lisa's conflicted feelings and, as she mentioned, discarded. Shaking her head, "It just doesn't sound like the woman we all knew and loved here in the Village," Nancy said, frowning.

"Yeah, sorry, I didn't mean to sully her reputation. I guess grief overrode my pride." She shrugged again, "I'm not in the mood to talk about her memorial service anymore," she said with a slight slur.

She finished her third glass of wine and rose to leave, a bit unsteady, "Let's talk about it tomorrow when we meet with the others."

Sadly smiling, she walked to the front door, "Thanks for listening to my teen angst story. It was a difficult time, but I survived."

Nancy offered to call a cab or one of the driving services to take her home as she drank several glasses of wine, but Lisa refused, saying she needed to stop at the Director's office before leaving the Village.

"Mother did try to make it up to me. It was just too little too late." She said as she left.

Nancy reviewed her conversation with Lisa as she cleared the wine glasses and took them to the kitchen. Drying the wine glasses before storing them in the cupboard, it seemed that Lisa's actions and her mother's acceptance of having earned them had been the foundation of their relationship for years.

What could've changed to drive Lisa to the final act to avenge her hurt and anger by killing her mother? Nancy wondered. She had difficulty accepting that a daughter might be vindictive enough to want to kill one's mother. Nurturing a decades-old grudge could be a motive, but what would be the deciding factor or stimulus to act now?

If it was murder, Nancy realized, there must be more to this story. Thinking again of Nancy Drew's instinct for clues, she asked herself, what was she missing? Remembering the *Brass Bound Trunk Mystery*, Nancy Drew explained, "*One should not keep guessing; one needs to find the facts.*" It looked like she had to speak with Harry. The detective might not appreciate her help, but she needed more information if she was going to solve this mystery.

CHAPTER 12

Harry was on the phone when his coworker advised him of a female visitor. He looked through the blinds in his office and sighed. He waved her in, ending his conversation as Nancy joined him. He had to admit that his ex-mother-in-law had an undeniable presence.

Granted, it wasn't every day an older woman walked into the precinct with an air of owning the place. That was most likely due to her reputation as a force to be reckoned with when she sat on the bench as a presiding judge. He stood up from the desk to greet her.

"What a surprise. I didn't expect to see you in my office. What can I do for you?" he asked.

"Good morning, Harry. I've come to discuss your investigation of Hilda's death." She responded.

"There is not an ongoing investigation of her death, Nancy. We are still awaiting the coroner's report, but it is pretty evident that she died of smoke inhalation as a result of smoking in bed and catching her mattress topper on fire."

"I do not doubt that her death was the direct result of her gel-foam topper catching fire, but there is circumstantial evidence contrary to the fact that she never smoked in bed or routinely slept on that dreaded topper," Nancy stated as if speaking to a child.

Shaking his head, Harry thought she always had the power of her convictions; he had to give her that. Against his better judgment, he gestured to the chair across from his desk, and as she sat down, she pulled a manilla folder out of her oversized handbag and proceeded to hand it to him.

"I've been talking, informally, of course, to Marcy, the Assistant Director of the community. Also, Lisa, Hilda's daughter, and I shared a bottle of wine the other evening, and she also shared insight into their mother-daughter relationship."

Harry interrupted her, "Speaking of mother-daughter relationships, didn't your daughter tell you that I had specifically asked that you stop your intrusive investigation, hoping that you would stop agitating the community residents and not harass Hilda's grieving daughter?"

"That investigation related to the supposedly grieving daughter is why I am here," Nancy responded.

"Why would you use supposedly, her mother is dead," Raising his eyebrows, "Obviously, she is grieving."

"I haven't seen much evidence of grief, and there is no real remorse either, mostly regret." Nancy sighed, "It is a sad situation that needs follow-up."

"Why are you looking for remorse, Nancy? Her mother died unexpectedly; one wouldn't expect remorse. After all, it's not as if she had anything to do with her death." Harry looked at her.

"What if she did?" Nancy paused, "What if she killed her mother?"

"Nancy, you are being absurd. What motive would she have? She visited her mother frequently and looked after her well-being. It appears that Hilda listened to her when her daughter requested that she try to use the gel-foam mattress to protect her from pain, unlike some mothers who don't seem to listen to their concerned daughters." He responded.

Nancy sighed, "I wish you would stay on topic, Harry. You are determined not to take me and my concerns seriously. Why won't you even consider that she could be a suspect?"

Looking at her, she seemed agitated, unlike the Nancy he knew as his ex-mother-in-law. Losing Ned, after being married all those years and having watched his slow loss of energy and eventual death, seems to have taken a toll on her.

"Look, Nancy, I understand that Hilda was a good friend to you and your happy hour group, but I think you are looking for clues to justify her death, and the fact is that she died of smoke inhalation. He stood up and, walking around his desk, put his hand on her shoulder. "She fell asleep while smoking in bed and caught her mattress topper on fire," he repeated. "Luckily, it was extinguished before it involved her condo or complex. You need to accept that." Stroking her shoulder gently, he added, "I know you are still grieving for

Ned; death is hard to accept, but we have no evidence of foul play in this instance. You need to let this go."

She listened to Harry silently but felt her chin rise at his mention of Ned. She realized he was trying to label her investigation of Hilda's death with an emotional reaction to Ned's death two years ago. She didn't like him touching a nerve, but she could see that her desire to blame someone else for Hilda's death might be interpreted as the injustice surrounding death in general. She turned her head to look at him, her expression free of emotion,

"Harry, I'm going to leave these notes with you. Please agree to read them. If you see no merit in them, I will consider your request to quit my inquiry. That is the best I can offer."

She stood to leave, patted the manilla folder she had placed on his desk, "And by the way, Ned's death does not play a role in my pursuit of justice for Hilda," she turned to leave, "Death is often not fair, but it is inevitable. We will all die, even you, but murder is a crime, and you, of all people, realize that justice must be served. "She paused before closing the door behind her, "Goodbye, Harry, we will talk soon." She was gone before he could respond.

He watched her leave the department through the blinds in his office and turned his attention to her folder. He flipped it open to see several pages of neatly outlined notes. Closing the folder again, he shook his head, thinking this should be an open and closed case of accidental death at home. Thinking of Nancy and his relationship with her daughter, he wondered how easily life gets complicated.

Looking back on his marriage, as hard as he tried, he couldn't feel the earlier resentment in those months before the divorce. He hadn't seen Ann in some time, and he remembered how much he enjoyed just being with her in the past. That was on his mind when he phoned her and requested she call her mother off the hunt for Hilda's murderer. He found himself not wanting to end the call. Instead, in his attempt to listen longer to her voice, he asked her to meet him for a drink. Playing with a paperclip, he frowned; that was probably a foolish attempt to reconnect with her. It probably wasn't the best timing, especially after pointing out how out of control her mother was.

He moved the file to the top of his "look at later pile" just as the forensic pathologist walked into his office. That didn't happen often, so she had Harry's full attention.

"Glad I found you in your office. I would have left this report if you weren't here with a message to call me after you read it." She handed the file to Harry and waited for him to open it before continuing.

"You'll notice there isn't any evidence of smoke inhalation mentioned in the cause of death." She commented as he read.

"How can that be?" Harry looked up from the report at her.

Raising her eyebrows, the pathologist said, "If you read further, you will see the cause of death was hypoxia, lack of oxygen, not smoke inhalation. The opposite, no inhalation at all."

"How do you explain that?"

"I have some ideas," she answered." But I'd like to examine the gel-foam topper first, though."

"Why would you want to do that?" he asked, annoyed at the turn of events.

"Some gel foam is highly flammable, and others are the opposite. Once the flames ignited the gel, the fire was slowly extinguished due to the oxygen in the room being consumed by the flames. No oxygen is a problem, and in this case, the victim suffocated."

"Wouldn't the victims notice, gasp for air or something?"

"Possibly, but this victim had taken some strong sleeping pills before retiring, and she had elevated blood alcohol, too. I suspect it was a perfect storm of complications that led to her death."

"But it was still an accident, right?" Harry asked.

"I believe so, but I want to check out that mattress topper, look at the burn pattern, and analyze the amount of burned gel by assessing the damage done to the topper. The victim could've been drinking and passed out after being drugged by her sleeping pills."

She continued, thinking aloud, "Once unconscious, someone could've laid her on the topper and set one of her lit cigarettes on it. I will need to examine the cigarette butt too," she said thoughtfully, adding, "They could've shoved the lit cigarette into the topper and waited until the flames started before leaving her alone in the room. As long as the windows and door were closed, she wouldn't have any oxygen to breathe."

"Are you saying it might not have been an accident?" Harry asked.

The pathologist shrugged, "Maybe, maybe not. It could've been murder."

Leaving the file on Harry's desk, the forensic pathologist turned to leave the room, "Besides the gel-foam topper, I'd like access to the linen and anything else found at the initial burn site." She said.

"I'll check with the evidence team. I believe they have already removed the police tape from the door and allowed the daughter back into the apartment," Harry said.

"Good. Tell the evidence guys to leave both in my lab when they can. I'll let you know what I find." She said as she left.

Harry re-read the report, shaking his head. He thought that this wouldn't decrease Nancy's interest. Looking at the file she had left him, he opened it and read her notes.

The detailed notes outlined Hilda's daughter's multiple long-standing issues with her mom. Adding the loss of $100,000 from Hilda's bank account, Lisa, who had a power of attorney, had a right to know where the money was spent. The fact that her mother had taken it out of her IRA without conversing with Lisa would be upsetting, but murder seems rather extreme. He wondered what happened to the $100,000, especially since it disappeared so close to Hilda's death.

Nancy had laid out a convincing plot with Hilda's daughter being the chief suspect. The daughter certainly had the means, being the principal advocate of the mattress topper. Nancy provided the opportunity part of the equation by noting that neighbors heard Lisa arguing with her mother the night before she was found dead.

According to Nancy's projections, the long-term resentment and the missing money, part of the daughters' expected inheritance, could have been the absent motive.

"I guess I should have a conversation with the daughter after all," He muttered as he left his office while contacting her on her cell to see when she would be available. She answered his call on the third ring.

"Hello, Lisa, this is Detective Higgins. We met at your mother's apartment. I have a few questions to ask you. Do you have any time to meet me today?"

"Are you available to meet now?" She said, "I have plans to discuss Mother's memorial with a few of her friends at the Village coffee shop in about an hour. We could connect there before I join them."

"That would be doable. See you there in 30 minutes?"

Lisa agreed, "I will look for you then,"

CHAPTER 13

Walking into the Cup and Vine, Harry was greeted by the barista, Stevie. "Hi, detective; what can I get you?" He asked.

"I recall I had an excellent Americano here the other day. I'll take another one of those and whatever the young lady walking in the door wants, too," he added as he watched Lisa approach them.

"Hi Stevie," she said, "A Latte would be perfect. Thank you, Detective." As they sat at a table for two, she asked, "You say you have some questions for me?"

"I wondered when was the last time you saw your mother, Lisa."

She answered, cocking her head in thought, "Around 7 o'clock the night before Sally found her."

"And was the mattress topper on the bed when you left?"

"Yes, I had just placed it back on her mattress after putting clean sheets on the bed." She added, "She was sitting in her favorite chair, with a magazine, drinking the glass of wine I had poured as I left."

"You didn't drink any of the wine with her before you left?"

"No, it was from one of her favorite vineyards, but I was late for another activity," Lisa said, thanking Stevie as he brought her latte, looking suspiciously at Harry.

"Did you see anyone or notice anyone who could verify the time you left?" He asked while sipping coffee.

"No, but I don't understand why you're asking me these questions. Surely, you don't think I had anything to do with her death!" She asked, "She died of smoke inhalation. These questions seem immaterial."

Harry shook his head, "These are merely routine questions. I'm trying to establish whom Hilda had seen the day before her death, what her state of mind may have been, that sort of thing."

"Well, she seemed much as she always was. Maybe somewhat distracted, even a tad sad. I suspected she was romantically involved with someone and didn't want me to know anything about him."

"How did you get that impression?" He asked.

"Because, as her power of attorney, I reviewed her monthly bank statements and noted that her IRA account had decreased by $100,000 last month." Lisa sounded frustrated. "There was not an invoice, check stub, or receipt to enable me to track such a large sum, and she refused to share where it went, if you must know." Clenching her jaw, she continued, "My mother had a bad habit of investing in manipulative relationships."

Harry was surprised by the animosity he heard in Lisa's voice. Hearing her resentment that tended toward hostility, he questioned her further, "$100,000 is a lot of money, and you have no idea where it could have gone?"

"Mother, although not extremely wealthy, had a respectable amount of money due to multiple inheritances, first her parents', a brother's, and then my father's." Shaking her head, she said, "He never bothered to change his beneficiary after the divorce, so she was fairly well off." She answered. "She also was a poor financial manager."

"Do you think your mother had gambling debts or maybe was an investor in a company start-up? Did her interests lie in stock purchases or commodities?"

"None of those options would be likely. She had a slight interest in stocks or commodities. She did attend the stock club meetings occasionally, and there were always stock market discussions with her happy hour group, according to her." She explained to Harry that several months ago, her mother attended a stock club meeting that a group in the community had planned. "I never knew her to gamble."

"I usually transfer money from her IRA to her checking account for mother's monthly expenses," Lisa informed Harry that Hilda met a financial planner in the Village and took his advice to cash in a low-performing stock in her portfolio and set up a mutual money market fund where the money would continue to earn interest yet was available for monthly withdrawals for her expenses.

"According to mother," Lisa further explained, "She would then be able to handle her finances and wouldn't need my help."

That revelation raised Harry's brow, "How did that make you feel," he asked.

"I was skeptical since one investment she made was marrying a scoundrel several years after her divorce and allowing him access to her savings." She replied.

"What did the financial planner have to do with the missing $100,000?"

She explained to Harry that Hilda received over $170,000 from her IRA and invested it all in the money market fund. Hilda told her that he said it would last at least the rest of her life. Hilda believed the financial planner when he said her IRA would gain income value by not having monthly withdrawals and associated fees.

"It made sense, and after the first statement, I could see that the account was in her name only and was legitimate. Until last month's statement when $100,000 had been withdrawn, and Mother would not tell me where it had gone!"

"How did your mother respond to your questioning her about the money?"

" How do you think," Lisa's chin rose in defiance, "She told me to mind my own business, leave her affairs alone."

"How did you respond to that?" He asked.

"I told her I didn't appreciate her attitude; I was just trying to make sure she wasn't making another mistake and putting her livelihood at risk."

"I take it from your tone of voice that wasn't well received either. Did you argue about that?"

"We had some heated words. She accused me of only being interested in the money, not her. She implied that my only concern was my inheritance."

"That was hurtful?" He asked.

She denied any pain, "It was just her being her nasty self. Occasionally, her old mean streak would return. I was used to its appearance every once in a while." As Lisa watched her mother's friends enter, she continued, "Her meanness never surfaced with her friends in the Village. Speaking of which, Mother's friends are here to put the finishing touches to our plans for her Celebration of Life. I need to join them."

"So you think another man is taking advantage of her? Any idea of who that might be, perhaps someone here in the Village?" Harry detained her.

"I'm not sure if it is someone local. To whomever or whatever she gave that sum, it appears to have been a cash deal. There is no money trail at all." He noted, once again, the frustration in her voice.

"One more question: did you argue about the money the night before she died?"

Lisa took a deep breath, stood up from the table, looked him straight in the eye, and answered, "As a matter of fact, we did argue it is not the best memory of one's last meeting with one's mother. I worried that she had taken up with some man again, and the last thing I did as I left her that night was to call her a foolish, lonely, old woman."

He looked at her standing next to the table, "I didn't mean to upset you, but we are investigating her death as suspicious."

Wide-eyed, catching her breath, she looked at him and continued, "You don't think she died of smoke inhalation?" Startled, she said, "I am not proud of the last conversation I had with my mother. I will have to live with that final scene for the rest of my life, but I had nothing to do with her death,"

"It appears the cause of death was from the mattress catching on fire. We think someone set the mattress topper on fire using the cigarette. It was intentional, and we are leaning toward murder."

Lisa slowly dropped back onto her chair, "Who would have wanted Mother dead? Everyone loved her."

Harry shook his head, "If our conclusion is correct, obviously, not everyone."

"If it wasn't smoke inhalation, how did she die? What killed her?"

"According to the forensic pathologist, it was a combination of alcohol and sleeping pills but ultimately the lack of oxygen."

"That sounds like carelessness, not murder," Lisa said.

"Was your mother given to careless behaviors?"

She sniffed, then sighed, "Only when it came to men and her generosity with her money."

"I'll be following up as we get a better understanding of what happened in that apartment the night before she was found. I will stay in touch as I might have further questions,"

"No worries, Detective, but please keep me informed." Rubbing her forehead with her hands.

"Before joining the ladies, tell me where you went after leaving your mother?"

Startled, she stood up from her chair again, "Seriously, you think I need an alibi? I had a date; I didn't murder my mother!" She spoke quietly so as not to be overheard.

"I need to know the name of your date, please." Harry waited patiently as she rolled her eyes and sighed, "I went to the Chamber of Commerce fundraiser with Ronald, the Village Director."

Nodding at the table of women helping to plan her mother's memorial, she said, "They will be appalled. They won't believe it was murder, either." She said.

He followed her gaze, seeing Nancy conversing with the neighbor, Sally. He nodded in the gathering ladies' direction, "Let's not alert them yet. We don't want them alarmed."

She shrugged as she turned toward the others, "Whatever you want, perhaps it would be better if we wait until after the memorial service."

As she approached her mother's friends, Lisa smiled at them while covering a sense of dread, thinking that the detective was looking for a motive for her to have murdered her mother.

She wondered what he knew of their relationship. Did he know how conflicted her relationship with her mother was, how much she blamed her mom for her lost teenage years? Joining the women at their table, she greeted them, burying those disturbing thoughts for a later time.

Harry, on the other hand, was perplexed. He couldn't get a handle on Lisa's emotional state. Watching her join her mother's friends, she seemed genuinely determined to be considerate of the community's feelings for her mother. Although she appeared saddened and shocked at the apartment when her mother was found, even tearful and unsteady as the Director of the Village supported her, today she seemed unmoved by her death.

He wasn't even sure she cared much for Hilda, especially hearing the disdain in her voice when discussing her mother's relationship with men. But he did wonder about that $100,000. When did it leave her mutual funds, and where did it go?

That seemed to be his new focus. Looking over at Nancy, he hoped she didn't learn too soon about the change in the status of the investigation. He didn't want her getting involved and mucking things up. With any luck, Lisa would heed his advice and not share their conversation, and he would be able to keep Nancy out of his hair for a few days more.

Maybe he should call Nancy's daughter and inform her of the investigative progress, hoping she could warn Nancy away from interfering. Besides, he missed Ann, as hard as it was to admit that fact. He didn't think the divorce was a mistake, but maybe they could have remained friends if they had never married. Grinning, he knew he was kidding himself; perhaps they could have stayed lovers. This investigation and its involvement with Nancy reminded him of his life before the divorce. Hopefully, it would be settled soon, and he could go back to his life of denial and not be reminded of his loss on a daily basis.

CHAPTER 14

Opening the Cup and Vine door to join the planning meeting for Hilda's Celebration of Life Memorial, Nancy was surprised to see Harry and Lisa conversing at a separate table. Neither appeared happy. She wondered if he was sharing her suspicions with Lisa. Hopefully, he didn't reveal their previous discussion, which would make further interaction between her and Lisa uncomfortable.

Nancy greeted the other ladies at the six-top table, sat next to Bess, and left the opposite chair for Lisa. She joined in their conversation. Bess was nibbling on a figgy scone and pointed to the Americano she had ordered for Nancy.

"Thanks, Bess," she said, "I appreciate you ordering for me; I desperately need this," as she sipped the coffee.

"No problem," Bess replied, "I forgot my wallet, so you will need to settle our bill before you go."

Nancy, brows raised, commented, "Of course, Bess, how unfortunate to leave your house for a coffee and pastry date, forgetting your wallet!"

Bess grinned sheepishly, "I am so forgetful; seriously, I didn't forget it on purpose!"

"No bother," Nancy grinned at her, "I will gladly cover you again," she answered, emphasizing the last word. "It was considerate for you to order for me since I'm paying!" she laughed.

The other ladies smiled at their interplay. They all enjoyed Nancy and Bess teasing each other. Sally told them Lisa would buy them coffee and pastries for agreeing to meet with her so there would be no need to argue over the tab.

The conversation turned to Hilda and her death. The grief surrounding her surprised passing was sincere, and it was evident those at the table were fond of her and that she would be missed. Sally was teary at the table as she spoke of their neighborly connection.

"She was such a kind and generous neighbor; you couldn't ask for better."

Adie, the woman beside Sally, spoke of having financial issues after an unexpected inheritance from a distant relative a few months ago. Hilda introduced her to a financial advisor who had newly moved into the village. Her dreadlocks bounced against her neck as she added, "I can't remember what country he was from, but he helped me invest my money in a money market." She shared that he had a delightful accent, grinning sheepishly.

"Shame on you, Adie. If you weren't blessed with that flawless mahogany skin, I'd swear you were blushing!" Bess grinned.

Ignoring Bess, "I could use a financial advisor; you say he lives here in the community. What's his name?" Sally asked.

Adie answered, "Enrik Againi, he lives in the back arch. Very polite, knowledgeable, and pleasant to look at, too!" She smiled just as Lisa joined the group.

"Sorry to keep you waiting, but the detective had a few more questions," she explained.

They all nodded and expressed their condolences again. Having lost one's mother is an emotional strain, they all agreed, and having strangers asking questions was distracting.

The discussion then revolved around when the memorial would take place, the best time of day for her friends, and who would be invited. Eventually, a consensus was agreed upon. Sally asked Lisa if there was anything else she or the other women could do to help.

"I haven't given that much thought yet," Lisa responded. "Thanks for the offer. Maybe later today, we could go through her closet and decide what to donate and what to pitch if any of you are available." Sally agreed to help.

"I would like to help with that, too," Bess offered, "The women's homeless shelter downtown always needs items. If you donate her clothes, I could take them for you."

"Great, are you both free around 3:00 later today?"

As everyone stood up to leave, they both agreed. Lisa touched Nancy's arm, "Can you stay for a minute?" "Sure, no problem," Nancy answered as she sat back down, watching Lisa pay the tab, her mind wandering.

She worried during Lisa's meeting with Harry that he told her Nancy suspected she murdered her mother. That was going to be a difficult conversation. Or he could be questioning Lisa because he thought she might be right in her assumptions.

That seemed unlikely, too, she mused to herself. So, what were they talking about? Sighing, she watched Lisa make her way back to the table and smiled expectantly, thinking maybe I could lead her to tell me as Lisa took her seat again.

Lisa nodded at the others as they walked out the door, "My mother sure had a great group of friends. I wonder if she appreciated how much you all cared for her," She took a deep breath and shook her head.

"Everyone seems to have such fond memories of her, and they have such kind things to say about her, too. It just doesn't seem to resemble the woman I grew up with." Lisa added.

"Lisa, she was very kind to all of us and generous with her spacious deck where most of us often gathered before dinner at the club or after. She was a very considerate hostess and a friend to everyone."

"Those gatherings are what I want to discuss with you," she admitted.

Nancy, frowning, questioned, "What concerns you about the gatherings? They were pretty innocent, primarily retired, and quiet community members. No drunken, noisy parties."

"I wondered if Mother had a particular interest in any men that hung out on the deck? Did she seem, you know, involved with anyone?"

Smiling, Nancy laughed, "Your mother was pretty picky. Bess and I used to laugh at her descriptions of some of her want-to-be- suitors. She didn't pay much attention to them except to tease them about their clothes, hair, or lack of, or taste in music. Even their sports teams weren't off limit. But I don't think she cared about any of them, romantically, I mean."

Thinking for a minute, Nancy followed up with her own question. "Why are you interested in her relationships, if I can ask?"

"The detective I met with earlier asked me about the money that is missing from mother's bank account. It was that $100,000 that I thought she could have given it to some man."

"As I shared with the detective, she had a habit of making bad decisions regarding men. It wouldn't be the first time she invested in a money-making scheme from some gentleman friend."

"That's right; you mentioned that she took a financial loss with her second husband. She never shared much about her life before moving here." Nancy admitted.

"It was a nightmare most of the time. Like I said, we didn't speak for some time, then after the divorce, she was a wreck and needed my help." Lisa shared.

"She was lucky you were there for her; sometimes mother-daughter relationships are difficult to manage," Nancy said, thinking of her daughter.

Lisa stated defensively, "She wasn't difficult; she was impossible at times. I slowly grew to resent all the time and energy I spent supporting her emotional and financial neediness. For a time, our relationship became one of mere duty."

Nancy shook her head sadly, "That sounds like a difficult position to be in." She was thinking about how much she cared for her mother and still missed her.

"It got a lot better after the surprise inheritance from a childless brother she hadn't spoken to in years," Lisa explained. Unbeknownst to them, Hilda was his only beneficiary. He had quite a lot of money in the stock market, and those funds, along with her first husband's settlement, have kept her mother comfortable for the last few years.

"I had been taking care of her finances since the divorce, but a couple of months ago, she met with a financial planner in the community here, who advised her to sell a particular stock and invest in a money market fund, which gave her cash flow ability a hefty bounce."

"Was that where the $100,000 came from? " Nancy asked.

"That and another $70,000 more," Lisa answered. "I asked her what she planned to do with the money, and she said, somewhat loftily, that it would cover her living expenses for the rest of her life."

Lisa repeated to Nancy much of the same conversation that she had with Harry. She focused on how secretive her mother was being. She added the increasing anxiety she felt as it brought back all these memories of being abandoned by her mother for a worthless lover. "I was extremely upset at the missing $100,000, but she wouldn't tell me where it went!"

"How did she respond to your anxious questions?" Nancy asked.

"She shrugged her shoulders at me." Lisa demonstrated, shrugging on her own.

Nancy sat silent for a while; she could see that Lisa was angry, but she sensed an underlying hurt. She couldn't pinpoint the source entirely, though. There was the pain of her mother's distrust, but maybe she feared that, once again, her mother was placing her future and that of her daughter's inheritance in the hands of a strange man.

"If you want, I can help you determine where the money went." Nancy offered, patting her hand lying on the table.

"With the shock of her death, I'm not even sure where to start looking for the recipient. Planning the memorial and emptying her apartment, I am beginning to feel overwhelmed." Lisa looked at Nancy hopefully.

"I can help. What was the name of your mother's financial planner?" Nancy asked, reaching for her phone to type in his name.

Lisa realized that she didn't know his name but was sure it was in her mother's financial papers in the apartment. She was meeting the others there that afternoon. She assured Nancy she would find his name and contact information and text it to her. Getting up from the table to leave, Nancy reassured Lisa that everything would work out. Lisa nodded and watched Nancy leave. Frowning at Nancy's back, she rubbed her hand across her forehead, weary and remorseful.

Returning to her villa, Nancy saw that Lisa had left the Cup and Vine through a side door and was walking toward the office. She supposed Lisa had details related to Hilda's death that needed to be handled by the staff. The director, Ronald, met her in the office parking lot. Nancy was surprised to see him pull Lisa into his arms into a passionate embrace and lingering kiss. As she watched them kiss, it didn't look like a comforting encounter. Interesting, she thought as she walked home.

Walking in the door, she wondered how long Ronald and Lisa had been romantically involved. After her discussion with Lisa, it was evident that she had solid and resentful feelings surrounding her mother and her perceived abandonment. But if Hilda was murdered, it seems it was premeditated, not an act of passion. Nancy wasn't sure that Lisa would be capable of that. But if Ronald was involved, that could be a different story.

The two of them could have planned it without much difficulty. Being the Village Director, he could move within the various buildings without question. He could've assisted Lisa in arranging her mother's death and then helped her sneak away. He might even have killed her himself to gain favor with Lisa. She imagined Harry's response if she shared that theory with him. Laughing out loud, she thought maybe she would share it just to see his reaction. She wasn't even sure he thought Hilda had been murdered, let alone be pleased that she would provide two suspects!

Sitting at her desk, Nancy decided the next step was to find the resident financial planner. He had to be relativity new to the community since he was unknown to her.

She recalled the morning conversation at the coffee shop.- Didn't Sally ask someone there for the name of a financial planner?

Distracted by Harry's presence talking with Lisa, Nancy didn't pay attention to the answer to Sally's inquiry. Thinking it might be the same consultant that Hilda had met with, she called Sally. Answering her cell on the second ring, Sally texted the contact information that had been shared at the coffee shop. He was Enrik Agani; according to Sally, many widows in the Village appreciated his financial suggestions. He had quite a following for a short tenure in the community.

Nancy had never met Enrik Agani. That wasn't much of a surprise, though, as she hadn't been active in the community in the last few years. After Ned's diagnosis of MS, they decided to travel to all the places they had planned on visiting after they had retired. Moving into the villa in the 55+ community was their home base while on the road, so they hadn't become very active members. After Bess moved into the Village, she kept Nancy informed of the activity and especially the gossip regularly but hadn't mentioned a financial planner.

.

Once Ned couldn't travel comfortably, they were pretty much homebound. After his death, it was too hard to socialize without him, but she had become close with Hilda. Bess talked her into meeting with Hilda's happy hour group most weeks. She was familiar with the members of that group, but not all the residents were participants. Without a current network of the larger community outside of Hilda's group, she would need to find out more about the financial planner.

Nancy figured there were several ways to investigate his past and present. She could ask Marcy about him; as the assistant director, she would know his history. She would need an excuse for visiting Marcy again. Maybe she could pretend to be looking for a missing package delivery. That would be a problem that would require her to visit the office. "But how do you get more information about what kind of financial planning services he provides?" She asked herself.

Running her fingers through her hair, she thought maybe Sally could make an appointment with him to learn more about what his work for Hilda entailed. Shaking her head, she realized Sally was too timid to carry that ploy off.

Sitting up straight, she realized that she could consult with him about her own financial needs and see if he was legit. Picking up her cell, she called the number Sally had given her. Heart racing in anticipation, she realized she was enjoying this detective activity. He didn't answer, but after the 4th ring, he asked to leave a message in a slightly accented voice. She left one saying that she was seeking a financial advisor; he had been recommended, and she would like to make an appointment to discuss her finances.

CHAPTER 15

Waiting for a return call from the financial planner, Nancy decided to stop in the Village office to find out what Marcy knew about him. Walking in the door, she asked the receptionist if a package had been delivered by mistake to the office. While the receptionist checked the mail room, Nancy stood at Marcy's door, waiting for her to look away from her computer. Marcy glanced at the door, surprised to see Nancy standing in the opening.

"Hi, Nancy. I didn't hear you come in. Did you need something? " glancing at her computer, hesitant to be distracted from her work.

"Just thought I'd say hello, as I was here checking on a package delivery." She added, "But if you have a minute, I've been speaking to other women in the community about finances, and someone mentioned that an Enrik Agani might be a resource right here in the Village." Marcy nodded, glancing regrettably at her computer; she stood and walked toward Nancy.

"He's relatively new here, moved in at least six months ago. He did one of the monthly information meetings sponsored by the Village stock clubs."

Surprised, Nancy said, "I wasn't aware of any stock clubs in the Village."

Nodding, Marcy said, "There are several groups of 10-12 members in each group; they meet monthly and quarterly. The groups meet for a presentation and share insights. Enrik presented at the last one a few months ago."

"I don't think I've met Enrik. Do you know anything about him?" Nancy asked.

"The members seemed divided on his recommendations." She laughed at the memory, "The various groups argued for days when they met at the coffee shop or the bar, even on the golf course, about the validity of his strategy."

"I'm not sure I want to discuss my finances with him if he was so disruptive." Nancy looked thoughtful, her hand to her cheek, smiling.

Marcy agreed that one needed to be careful with one's investments, "I've heard he had some gambling debt from betting at the local casino." She said, laughing.

"Do you know if he has any Village clients I could speak with?" she asked.

"I'm not sure, but I think that SueLi Smith might have met with him. Perhaps she could provide some insight into his abilities." She answered more seriously.

"I know SueLi. She and her husband used to join us at happy hour until he had his stroke. I haven't seen her in a while. I wonder how her husband is doing?'

"According to SueLi, he is just as ornery as ever," she grinned. "She said his orneriness attracted her to him in the first place, but she added that his army uniform didn't hurt either." Nancy smiled, "I had forgotten they met in Vietnam. "

Marcy nodded, following Nancy to the door, "I'm sorry to have interrupted you, but thanks for sharing." She smiled as she waved and left the office.

The receptionist shook her head as Nancy walked past, "No packages left here for you, Nancy."

"Thanks for looking." Nancy smiled at the receptionist as she left.

Walking back to her villa, she checked her cell phone. Still no call from Enrik. Thinking about her next step, she decided to walk past SueLi's villa and see if she was available to give a reference for her financial planner and maybe share if she knew if Hilda was meeting with him, too.

As luck would have it, SueLi was in front of her villa trimming her bougainvillea hedge. Waving at her, Nancy walked up the drive and watched SueLi remove her ear pods. Nancy was always surprised at SueLi's youthful appearance. She was sure that her straight bob, minimal silver among her jet black hair, and flawless skin gave her a much younger look than most women in the Village.

"Hi there, Nancy. I was just listening to my favorite podcast and didn't hear you come up the drive."

"So many new and enlightening podcasts available these days; who are you listening to?" Nancy asked.

SueLi smiled sheepishly, "It's a yoga class. I don't do yoga, but I always feel so much better after listening to the instructions on moving, and the instructor's voice is so charming and serene." She laughed as she shared her thoughts.

Nancy laughed, too, "I'm glad I walked this way. I will have to find a yoga podcast to enhance my serenity." Smiling, Nancy added, "It might help me with my search for a financial advisor, and I heard that you might know one to recommend?"

"Oh yes, Enrik is so patient and kind when explaining all the financial options. I never had much talent for figuring out the money details; I let my husband do all the investing. Since his stroke, he isn't interested in our financial position at all, so it has been a big learning curve for me. Enrik has been such a blessing."

"I'm glad you found someone you can trust. Having faith in one's adviser, especially regarding one's livelihood, is so important," Nancy said.

"Well, some of the stock club members thought he was too progressive with his recommendations, but my neighbor next door convinced me to contact him. As neighbors, Gary and David, the couple next door, are so thoughtful. We play cards together every Wednesday. They tell the most amazing stories of their travels; it amuses Dick to hear their banter." She chatted.

"I met them at Hilda's happy hour gatherings. They are a couple of entertainers, for sure." Nancy agreed. " Well, they disagreed about Enrik's financial plan. Gary thought it was innovative and eager to learn more, but David thought it was risky." Grinning, she added, "They always seemed to enjoy arguing, but Gary won David over this time. The next thing you know, they are bragging about Enrik's wisdom and encouraging me to meet with him, too." SueLi shook her head, laughing.

"After meeting with him, I felt confident. He is so charming, too, and, like I said, kind. I had spoken to several other financial advisors, and they tried to intimidate me and hard sell their brands. One guy even tried to scare me into signing up with them so they could care for me, as if!" Indignant, SueLi frowned, adding, "They just wanted to care for my money."

"I think I will have him look at my holdings and see what his thoughts are." Nancy said, "Did you invest any money with him."

"He went over all our investments, and my husband and I decided to have him manage our money market fund. It seemed convenient to invest with him." She added, "He had some good suggestions about still earning interest on the funds in the money market while allowing our investments to grow without withdrawing from the profits."

Nodding in agreement with his thoughts, Nancy changed the subject. Admiring her array of flowering plants, Nancy remarked that she must have a green thumb.

"No, I struggle to get these plants to bloom prettily every season." She said, " I do love my garden. It distracts me from the everydayness of life and gets me outside, moving my bones!" Looking around proudly at the beauty surrounding her, she smiled.

"You, of all people, know the heartache of watching your nearest and dearest deteriorate before your eyes." Sighing, she added, "Gardening is a distraction, providing a brief escape from the reality of things we can't control. It's an opportunity to feel a peaceful sense of accomplishment."

Nancy nodded and patted her shoulder, "Appreciating the wonder of nature is soul-affirming,"

They were silent for a moment, each with their thoughts. Finally, SueLi offered to text her Enrik's contact information. Nancy thanked her and continued to walk home. She was quite pleased with herself. She had a credible referral source to share with Enrik when he returned her call. While she waited for his call, she might as well explore the community director's relationship with Hilda's daughter. Then, wondered what the best approach would be.

She had a habit of squinting when deciding between options for action and found herself engrossed in the alternatives. She thought Marcy might have some insight into the relationship. Then again, Sally overheard Hilda being upset with Lisa over a man she was involved with. Maybe she knew more than she mentioned. As she arrived at her home, Nancy realized that the best solution would be to address Ronald, the director, himself.

Nodding to herself, she thought if one were seeking answers, he would be the best respondent. She would have to approach the question of his relationship with Lisa carefully. Prying into one's love life, especially a casual acquaintance, would appear intrusive. In the four years she lived in this community, she had only had a personal conversation with Ronald after Ned had died. How could she approach this topic when there was no common ground? Searching for common ground, she thought property management was his responsibility, and she owned property.

Now that she was single maybe using the need to downsize would be an excellent excuse to meet. She could enlist Bess to talk with him about the two of them sharing a different villa now that Ned was gone. She thought either of those ploys would work and planned to meet Bess to discuss how they would approach Ronald about his romance with Lisa. As she pulled her cell phone out of her pocket to call Bess, it rang. She saw her contact file identified the caller as Enrik. Smiling, she answered, "Hello, this is Nancy."

The charming voice she had heard on the answering machine responded, "Hello, Nancy," he replied with the slightest of accents, "This is Enrik Agani. You left a message for me to call you related to your finances.

"Enrik, thanks for returning my call. I spoke to SueLi Smith about some financial questions, and she recommended I contact you for help with my future planning."

"Certainly; what help are you needing?" he inquired.

"Having lost my husband two years ago, I realized that I probably need to reevaluate my future earnings and make sure I'm making the right decisions for whatever my future may bring." She responded, surprised by the quiver in her voice.

Even after two years, she still found it hard to talk about Ned being gone; his death left such a void in her life. They spent most days together during the last year of his life, and as his illness progressed, each moment was precious. Nancy cleared her throat and continued, "I'd like to make an appointment to discuss my financial options." She said.

"Do you have a financial advisor currently?" He asked.

"Yes, but he was used to working with my husband, not me. My husband and I were two different people. I believe when discussing money, one needs to be on the same page as one's adviser, don't you think?" she asked.

He agreed. "When would you be available to meet?" he asked.

She wanted to meet as soon as possible to see if he was indeed Hilda's financial planner and if he knew what happened to the $100,000. "When is your earliest convenience?" she asked.

He explained that his schedule was open for the coming week due to the University where he taught being on break. She agreed to meet at the coffee bar at 11:30 a.m. the next day, relieved that he was available so soon. But that meant that her evening would be spent reacquainting herself with the details of her portfolio. Shrugging acceptance, she walked into her villa.

Her thoughts returned to wondering if Bess would be willing to join her in her plan to approach Ronald about his relationship with Lisa. She concluded that making an appointment for both she and Bess to discuss relocating to a joint villa would be a believable option. She thought Bess would be eager to join the investigation. Nancy planned to invite her back to her villa after their afternoon Tai Chi class.

CHAPTER 16

At her villa after class, Nancy explained her plan to Bess, who was eager to do anything with her. She hadn't been able to involve her grieving friend in many village activities, and she was delighted to see her so engaged in this investigation.

Bess suggested that involving Ronald in assisting them to find new living quarters would give them an excuse to ask if he knew what Lisa's plans were now that her mother's condo was free. Once Lisa was brought into the conversation, they could ask about seeing them together and determine how long they had quietly been an item.

Nancy decided to call and see when he was free while Bess was with her so they could decide on a mutual time. The receptionist put her call through to Ronald, and he agreed to meet them the following day at 9:30. Hanging up, Nancy smiled at her co-conspirator, sipping on cups of herbal tea, they devised a story of wanting to conserve money and share the burden of one villa instead of two.

Bess suggested they should ask if he was aware of any larger villas they might tour. Nancy wondered why she would want a tour.

"I'm just nosy; I like to see the insides of other homes—you know, compare and contrast," Bess admitted.

Nancy snorted, "At least you admit to being nosy, but I'll pass on the tours." Satisfied, they parted company, planning to meet at Nancy's villa again the next day, half an hour before meeting with Ronald.

Nancy sat at her desk and added Ronald's and Enrik's appointments the next day to her calendar. She was satisfied with the progress she was making in identifying suspects. Her next thoughts were wondering what type of financial issues she should present to Enrik. "One doesn't meet with a financial planner if one doesn't need help formulating a financial plan," she thought aloud, then smiled as she realized she was talking to herself again.

She pulled out her portfolio from her financial advisors and began to look for appropriate questions to ask. An hour later, she had developed four major issues and would question him about her taxes, inheritance income responsibilities for her children, and what he thought she should do about the passive income royalties the estate received from a textbook Ned had written. That ought to give him something to research; she nodded, smiling in anticipation of their meeting.

CHAPTER 17

Nancy was up early the next morning and brewed a pot of coffee before she and Bess left to meet with Ronald. She had one of Bess's favorite croissants waiting for her arrival. They rehearsed their story one last time and enjoyed making up different scenarios. When it was time to leave for their meeting, they both realized at the same time that this was serious. All humor aside, they needed to know if Ronald assisted Lisa and was somehow involved with Hilda's death.

Ronald greeted them at his office door. He was an attractive man. The slight graying hair at his temples spoke to middle age, but he was tall and slim, moving easily to welcome them into his office. His suit fit him well, and his Oxford shirt and pastel tie gave him an air of sophistication. Nancy had been aware of the discussion some of the Village women enjoyed, wondering about his love life. Everyone knew he wasn't married, but Nancy couldn't recall any gossip about him taking up with any of the Villagers.

Bess was immediately interested in the sculptor of an eagle in flight. Ronald explained that he had inherited it from his older brother, who was an avid collector of wildlife art. Nancy asked if the wooded forest and rocky creek running through the beautifully framed picture behind his desk was also a gift from his brother. He responded that it was a picture from the same brother currently living in Vietnam, as well as some smaller nature-inspired art pieces throughout his office. He directed them to a side table, and they seated themselves comfortably while he asked what he could do to assist them.

Nancy explained that she and Bess were contemplating moving in together to decrease their living expenses, thereby allowing them more discretionary income for travel. He appeared somewhat surprised, looking first at Nancy and then at Bess.

"Neither of you are having financial difficulties, presently?" he asked, appearing concerned.

"Not at the moment, but we want to make sure that we remain that way," Bess answered.

Nancy added, "It seems foolish to have two houses remain unused while we travel when we could share a jointly held villa."

"I suppose that makes sense, but we would be very disappointed to lose you as members of our community." He said. "We are in conversation with the property owners adjacent to the tennis courts, hoping to reach a purchase agreement. The plan is to build an assisted living complex so our current residents could continue to age in place." Looking at them, he nodded, "But we are also discussing the development of individual smaller concept villas, complete with the latest technology to enable our independent members to remain functional for as long as possible."

Both Nancy and Bess denied their desire to leave, explaining they weren't looking for smaller space, "We thought you might know of any open villas, a bit larger than Nancy's for us to purchase."

"Since Hilda's death, I think I would feel better living with someone else in my home." Bess sighed.

"Yes," Nancy agreed, "We hear the police think her death might not have been an accident!" They both nodded their heads.

"Oh, come now," Ronald scoffed, "You can't believe that."

"Well, Lisa seemed upset after meeting with that detective," Bess added, followed by more head nods.

"Didn't you think she was upset when you met her after the meeting?" Nancy asked.

"What meeting are you talking about," he asked, looking again, first at Bess and then quickly at Nancy.

"One to two days ago, after our memorial planning meeting, we saw you comforting her. It seemed you two are extremely close," Bess mentioned.

"It certainly didn't look like the first time you embraced and kissed," Nancy added, smirking knowingly.

"Were you two spying on us?" he asked indignantly, his hands grasping the chair's arms, knuckles white.

"Of course not. We just happened to see the two of you embracing each other in the parking lot and thought it odd. We were surprised to observe such a romantic attachment between you two as we hadn't known about it."

Her chin raised defensively, she added, "This is a tight-knit community; things like romantic liaisons are usually a source of gossip or at least community interest. Were you two keeping your relationship a secret?" Bess turned her head, giving him a side-eye as she raised her suspicions.

"This is none of your business, Bess. We weren't being secretive. As you must know, Lisa and I have been seeing each other for several months. There was no need for our relationship to become public knowledge." He seemed more embarrassed than defiant.

Nancy shared that Lisa seemed distressed after she met with the detective, and during her last visit with her mother, they had argued. She asked Ronald if he knew what they argued about. He admitted that Lisa was upset with her mother, but she was sad that the last time spent together ended with a heated exchange.

"When I picked her up that evening, she was still upset with Hilda." He admitted. "We were at a Chamber of Commerce fundraiser I had agreed to help sponsor, but she wasn't enjoying herself, so by 10:00, I finished my duties, and we left early."

Nancy wondered, silently to herself, where they went after they left the fundraiser. Could they have returned to Hilda's apartment and staged the death scene?

"When was the last time you saw Hilda?" Nancy asked.

He looked at Nancy, confused. "What is with all these questions? I have already spoken with the detective and answered these same inquiries!" Looking first at Nancy and then Bess, "You're acting like I'm a suspect in Hilda's death." He added, "I thought you were here to discuss housing options, not accuse me of murder."

Nancy attempted to calm him down by nodding at Bess, "She's just being nosy. She likes to know everything that is going on in the community. We think that Hilda's death was an accident, but we wondered when you saw her last if she seemed depressed or anything?" Nancy reassured him. "We don't want the community to think Hilda took her own life. Hilda would hate that."

"She was fine the last time I saw her." He answered without further clarification.

Nancy returned to their previous discussion regarding the scarcity of larger homes in the gated community. Bess, too, returned to the reason for their meeting, discussing the cost of living on the outskirts of Santa Barbara and the advantages of shared housing. He calmed down and provided them with several options. As they were leaving his office, Nancy thought she would have to ask Harry if he had a time of death for Hilda.

CHAPTER 18

After returning home, having discussed Ronald's conversation with Bess over coffee at the Cup and Vine, she gave Harry a call.

"Higgins, here," Harry answered.

"Hi, Harry. So glad you are in. I won't keep you but for a minute." Nancy said.

"Always good to hear from you, Nancy." He rolled his eyes at the lie.

"I'm wondering, did the pathologist decide on smoke inhalation as the cause of Hilda's death?" she asked.

She could hear him sigh, "As a matter of fact, she died of hypoxia," he answered.

Confused, Nancy scowled into her cell phone, "Seriously?" pressing the speaker button on the phone, needing both hands to make a cup of tea, she asked him how that could be possible,

Harry explained what the forensic pathologist had shared in the updated report. She had found that the cigarette hadn't been smoked, there was no nicotine stain through the filter, and they couldn't isolate any separate fingerprints on the butt.

"Not even Hilda's?" Nancy raised her brows and looked expectantly at the phone on the counter, waiting for his answer. When he hesitated, she added,

"So someone wanted it to look like an accident, but it wasn't?" Nancy asked, thinking that surely those plans appeared well thought out and Hilda's death was premeditated. Removing the tea bag from her cup, she again directed a question at Harry,

"What was her time of death?" Nancy asked.

"They think sometime between 8 and 10:00 pm," he answered without thinking. Then, immediately, he was sorry to have given her more fodder for the investigation he had demanded she quit.

While Nancy thought about that answer, Harry, although unhappy with her involvement, thought she might have some insight into the mother-daughter relationship.

"I think you might be on the right track with the daughter being involved with her mother's death. I was planning to meet with Lisa this afternoon. There is something suspicious about their relationship."

"I wouldn't bother," she responded, "she was at a Chamber of Commerce fundraiser from around 6-10 with Ronald, the community's director. According to him, he spent last night comforting her, as she was upset after your discussion that morning."

Harry gritted his teeth; frustration was evident at her continued involvement in questioning his suspects.

"How do you know her whereabouts on the night her mother was murdered?" he asked, sounding terse.

Nancy cringed; she could tell he was angry by the way he clipped off the end of his words.

"I was merely talking to Ronald. He mentioned that he and Lisa had attended the fundraiser and spent the night together." She answered.

"Nancy, I specifically asked you not to get involved in my investigation." He added, "Any further involvement will be considered an attempt to impede my investigation and will not be tolerated."

Nancy decided that now would not be a good time to tell him about Enrik and her appointment with the financial advisor. She thanked him for sharing his information but stopped short of agreeing to stop interfering. She also resisted the urge to remind him that she only agreed to cease seeking justice for Hilda if he found that her death was accidental.

At the end of the call, Nancy checked the time and realized that if she didn't hurry, she would be late for her meeting with Enrik. Heading toward her closet, she wondered what one should wear to meet a financial advisor murder suspect. Examining her choices, she smiled, somewhat amused, thinking Bess's suggestion would be to accessorize with handcuffs and mace. Removing white pants and a mauve linen shirt from her closet, she thought the outfit would be flattering yet present a business casual look. Not too much business, but not too casual either. He had sent a message requesting that she bring her investment financial records to the meeting, and she had collected her income statements in a manila folder.

She slipped on her signature kitten-heeled sandals, grabbed the folder, and headed out the door to walk to the Cup and Vine in time for the meeting. She was surprised at how tracking down suspects was an interesting experience. If she weren't attempting to find Hilda's killer, she would enjoy this excitement that brought purpose to her day.

She sat at an outside table under the awning, protected from the afternoon sun but still able to enjoy the slight ocean breeze. Nancy didn't often take the time just to sit outside, surrounded by the beauty of her Village. Today, having ordered an iced latte from Stevie, she felt grateful to be in such a serene community. Not far from the big city of Santa Barbara, close to the ocean, and yet secluded from the crowds and bustle of tourists. She remembered that Ned and she thought long and hard before even considering a 55+ community. They wanted active and engaged neighbors but worried they would be embroiled in constant Homeowners Association (HOA) disagreements and community governance issues. Several of their friends in Napa Valley shared nightmare HOA scenarios that made them wary.

Finding a beach city eleven miles from Santa Barbara was perfect, though. It was established and named for the carpentry shops in the former settlement of Mishopshno, the area's indigenous tribe. Early on, the area was noted for the quality fishing boats that the men constructed, using the natural local tar pools as a source of sealant. Eventually, the San Jose El 55+ residential village was conceived and started by the local carpenters' union for their retiring tradesmen, an offshoot of the original boat tradesmen. Nancy sighed, remembering how she and Ned appreciated the heritage of their new home. In the beginning, there were two apartment buildings, a restaurant, and a deli that served alcohol, coffee, and light snacks. Available parking areas and a park-like setting, with acreage for further development, made the area attractive.

They learned that, eventually, a developer bought the property and several more acres surrounding the apartments. He added a golf course and a clubhouse next to the restaurant and refurbished the cocktail lounge into an imported coffee, tea, and an excellent wine bar. Cocktails were still served, as well as pastries and snacks. He added three concentric arched streets of villas- each half-circle had only five styles of homes. They were multi-colored in desert tones of brown, beige, and sand shades. There were thirty in the first row, smaller and compact; the second row had fifty homes, and most had three bedrooms and a single garage sharing space with the golf cart. The third row had larger lots, only forty homes, three bedrooms, and a free-standing casita-one bedroom, bath, and sitting room detached from the main home. Those homes had a garage with a door and space for the golf cart.

All were landscaped tastefully and groomed weekly by the landscape company. Palm trees, bougainvillea, various cacti, and multiple trees adorned the common spaces and surrounded the various parking lots throughout the village. She noticed that Bernie, the handyman and gardner for the non-residential properties, was hard at work watering the flowering plants around the pool. He was always around early in the day to complete his yard work and returned in the evenings to remove the trash from the various containers placed in strategic areas around the Village. She smiled and waved at him when he walked across the street to the doggie dumpster. He stopped to wipe his brow, smiled, and nodded in her direction.

Thoughts of Ned sitting by the pool and visiting with their new friends in the Village caused a sigh to escape. Thinking of him and his loss squeezed her heart. Maybe the act of retrieving the investment files brought on a sense of melancholy. Shaking off thoughts of Ned, Nancy realized she hadn't paid any attention to the accounts since his death except to file the monthly summaries when they arrived. It might be good to have fresh eyes on them since Ned had handled that part of their financial life. When he realized that his disease was progressing, he hired an old friend from his firm to be responsible for handling any transactions, and Nancy didn't have a reason to change that arrangement.

Sighing again, she sipped iced coffee, turning her head toward the door as a distinguished-looking gentleman entered. Nancy was pleasantly surprised as she had prepared herself to meet a disreputable sort. Shouldn't a man who would sink so low as to defraud an innocent older woman look somewhat sleazy? Instead, she seemed to be meeting a nattily dressed man, short in nature but powerfully built, appearing to be in his mid-sixties. He had a full head of frosty snow-white hair and wore a golf shirt, snug beige slacks, and sock-less loafers. She thought he appeared to be the type to be more comfortable wearing turtlenecks and tweeds, possibly even smoking a pipe. He stopped to talk to Stevie, and she watched him look in her direction and approach her table.

"Hello, Nancy. Stevie directed me to your table," He smiled at her while reaching out to shake her hand, and she again noted a slight accent as she nodded assent.

"Enrik, good to meet you." She shook his outreached hand before he sat to join her.

Setting a leather-bound journal on the table in front of him, he removed a pen from the holder in the journal and prepared to take notes. Stevie approached with the Americano that he had ordered and served Nancy a second iced latte. Enrik proceeded to ask questions and listened carefully to the answers. Nancy found herself sharing the story of Ned's diagnosis and his eventual limitations, leading to decreasing his responsibilities related to the functioning of their household. She explained that Ned always handled the financial affairs, and she never paid much attention to their investment portfolio. Nancy tried unsuccessfully to stop her voice from quivering while explaining that as his endurance decreased, he deferred the management of their monthly finances to her. She cleared her throat and added that Ned thought it best to retain their accountant to manage their investments.

"After Ned's death, I continued to manage my monthly expenses. I am ashamed to admit that I haven't been following our investments closely."

Shrugging, "I'm not sure that future gains will be adequate for me to maintain the lifestyle I have become accustomed to." She implied, faking a worried expression while handing him the manila folder.

"I am sure it has been hard losing your husband, Nancy. One cannot blame you for taking time to grieve," he said, taking the folder and patting her other hand on the table. "It is understandable to neglect those things that seem to be taking care of themselves."

He opened the folder, assured her every page was complete, and confirmed the name of her accountant in case he was required to contact him with questions. Enrik nodded at Stevie, indicating he would like a second Americano.

"Is it your plan to have me look at each of these investments and ascertain their long-term viability?" he asked.

"SueLi Smith explained her interaction with you when I spoke with her. I believe that was the idea," Nancy answered.

As he sipped coffee, Enrik explained that he would look at her holdings and estimate the time needed to review them. At that point, he would call her with an estimate of the cost for him to analyze their worth and viability. He also explained that he might find alternate investments that could provide better returns, adding that it would be entirely at her discretion.

As he closed the folder, he smiled at her, "I will contact you tomorrow with an estimate."

"Thank you, Enrik. I already feel relieved," she said, smiling gratefully, remembering her purpose in meeting with Enrik.

"When SueLi recommended your services, I realized we had never met. It seems odd, being that we are a small community and a good number of us socialize together." She said.

"I have been busy with classes and orientation at the University, having been hired as an adjunct professor. That did not leave much time for socializing. I have only been part of the Village for several months and am just getting to know some members." He said. "It's not hard to meet people here; one just needs time to be out and about in the community. Do you or your husband golf or play tennis?"

She explained that she used to golf and enjoyed a challenging game of tennis, but when they sold their home in San Francisco, Ned's health was already deteriorating. She added that they had moved here to have a home that was secure, enabling them to travel safely.

"Participating in golf or tennis would have involved team membership, which would be difficult when traveling as often as we did. Ned didn't have the endurance to continue with either sport, and I was busy making travel plans and taking care of him." She explained, "We were only here for three years before he died. Are you interested in joining the golf league or tennis club?"

Enrik stated that he was an average tennis player and missed the exercise when not playing. He said that back at his family home in Croatia, he was ranked in his post-college days but now played for fun when he found the time.

As they drank their coffee, the conversation turned to the weather, and Enrik compared California with his homeland of Croatia. "My family owns a vineyard there, and my son manages it with my elderly father."

Nancy smiled, noting that he became more animated as he discussed his family wines. She commented that it must be difficult to be far from family and an enterprise that one seemed to enjoy. "I left Croatia almost 30 years ago and am content traveling and living in the United States."

Having finished their coffee, they left together. Nancy left to walk to her villa, and as Enrik approached the parking lot, he looked back at her as she walked away. He thought how pleasant their short visit was. She certainly was charming and engaging. Smiling to himself, he thought he would enjoy helping her with her finances.

Nancy entered her home with some of the same thoughts. Surprised at how one's expectations could be so misdirected and how delightful it was to sit in the sun and visit with a new acquaintance. She realized that since Ned's condition deteriorated and following his death, she hadn't done much socializing except with her usual happy-hour friends. It was becoming evident to her now that she had avoided meeting new people because she resisted sharing her status as a widow. That always seemed to lead to a discussion about her deceased husband and made her sad and uncomfortable.

Talking about Ned in the past tense was painful, and thinking about her future without him made her miserable. So, conversing with new people was awkward. Enrik was different. Perhaps it was because they met to discuss business, not as a social engagement; it was less personal that way. At any rate, she marveled at her enjoyment, humming as she entered her office. She stopped suddenly in mid-stride, realizing that Enrik was a suspect in Hilda's death.

Squinting at her reflection in the office mirror, she thought all that charm and delightful conversation was probably how he lured Hilda into giving him that missing $100,000. Looking steadily into her reflection, she voiced, "Well, he isn't going to fool me with all that foreign charm." She nodded at herself as she sat down at her desk.

She always felt productive when sitting in her office. Pulling the notes she had copied for Harry out of the folder, she sighed. Trying to make sense of Hilda's murder was difficult. Enrik didn't meet the profile of a scamming conman, but that didn't eliminate him from being a suspect, either. Seriously, she thought, how would I know a fraud from a respectable man who wanted to help an older woman manage her money?

Nancy Drew would know; she would use her deductive reasoning and would have found the murderer by now. Laughing out loud, she thought of how much her mother would love the sleuthing she was involved in. When hard decisions needed to be made or difficult problems needed to be resolved, her mother would nod sagely at Nancy and ask, "What would Nancy Drew do?" Rolling her eyes and sighing in frustration, the teenage Nancy would stomp off, losing her patience with her mother's continued obsession with the girl detective.

Her mother had a difficult pregnancy and spent the last two months confined to bed. Nancy's father bought all the Nancy Drew books available to entertain her mother and give her something to read while stuck in bed. Smiling, she remembered how her mother would tell anyone who would listen that she adored the Nancy Drew mysteries, so much so she named her newborn daughter Nancy. Her favorite memories of childhood were of her mother reading a chapter from one of the books every night at bedtime and their attempt to guess the endings.

Remembering her mother's comments made her think about Nancy Drew's attitude. Not only did she never give up until she solved the crime, but she also always kept her eye on the big picture. If Enrik wasn't to be trusted, she needed to find out. Not just for Hilda's sake but for the other women like Ann. Smiling at her memories, she returned to reviewing the notes and tilting her head. She asked out loud, "I wonder whom Nancy Drew would think was the most likely suspect?"

CHAPTER 19

The next morning, Nancy's thoughts were still on her meeting with Enrik as she prepared her first pour-over coffee of the day. It was easier for her to imagine that Lisa and Ronald teamed up to plan Hilda's death than that Enrik would have murdered her for the missing $100,000. That thought brought her up short. Blinking in surprise, she wondered at her defense of Enrik. She had known Lisa and Ronald over the last several years and only just met Enrik. His slight accent was charming, and he did have a reassuring manner, but that was no excuse to trust him. In fact, it might be the best reason to distrust him.

Her confusing thoughts were interrupted by her cell phone ping. Looking at the screen, she noted it was a message from Bess. She clicked on the message of a cheerful greeting.

"Hey, let's have a snack after yoga class today, and you can catch me up on your encounter with the mysterious Enrik Agani," Bess had texted.

Looking at her desk clock, Nancy realized that she needed to leave for class soon and sent an emoji thumbs-up agreement to snacks, as she hadn't eaten breakfast yet. She walked to her bedroom to change clothes and shook her head. Lost in thoughts of Hilda, she had forgotten about her routine yoga class. Yoga practice was almost a meditative activity for her, one in which Nancy always felt a sense of serenity and relaxation. Attending class three times a week and walking every evening was Nancy's therapy after losing Ned.

Moving her limbs and getting in touch with her body and its need to stretch helped her focus, and her walks gave her time with nature to breathe and absorb the beauty that was a daily part of her life. Even the saddest days could be tempered by feelings of gratitude for her friends, her healthy, flexible 65-year-plus body, and the beauty in her life.

As she walked into the yoga studio, Nancy felt relaxed as she nodded to her friends and rolled out her mat next to Bess. Forgetting all about Hilda, murder, and suspects, she smiled as Bess chatted about snack plans.

"I'm already famished," Bess said as she took her place on her mat.

Enjoying the movement and soft-spoken directions of the yoga instructor, she soon completed the savasana or corpse pose, the last movement of the weekly practice. Nancy felt relaxed and energized. The ability to lie completely still took practice and the skill to be fully aware yet unattached from the present moment allowed her release from the constant mental babbling in her head, letting her just be.

Standing and silently rolling up her yoga mat, she looked at Bess, snoring gently on her mat. Toeing her with her bare foot, Nancy woke her.

"Hey there, you're not supposed to fall asleep," she quietly laughed as Bess stretched.

Yawning, Beth responded, "That's what happens when you are starving."

They left the studio together, discussing lunch options and deciding on a Mexican restaurant. Bess begged to ride with Nancy in her Mustang convertible. Nancy slid behind the wheel, and Bess laughed out loud when she lowered the top as they secured their seatbelts. She explained to Nancy that she always enjoyed the stares and comments from the other drivers as they passed. Nancy smiled and agreed that the auto received its share of attention.

At Delgado restaurant, they were immediately seated. Bess ordered the Chile Verde Bean Dip as an appetizer, and they decided to share a Fiesta Platter and lemonade. As soon as the waiter left, Bess cross-examined Nancy about her meeting with Enrik. Nancy reported that he was pleasant and pointed out that he was attractive and had a charming accent that would lend itself to impressing most women. She added, "He is from Croatia, he has taught business courses at the University of California, at Berkley, for several years, and had recently relocated since retiring from full-time teaching."

"Do you think he did it? I mean, did he appear capable of murder?" Bess asked.

"Well, he didn't look and sound like a man who stole their money, murdered his women victims, and absconded with a fortune if that's what you mean. Seriously, Bess, we met for about thirty minutes, not enough time to form an opinion or judge one's character." Nancy responded.

While scooping chips into the bean dip, they spoke of Hilda's planned memorial, which led to the discussion of Lisa's and Ronald's relationship. They both were surprised to learn that the two were a couple. Bess wondered if anybody else knew, and Nancy doubted it was common knowledge. Bess was sure that the gossip circuit would be in full force if any of the residents knew about their romance. The waiter brought the bill. Once again, Bess did not have her purse with her, leaving it locked in her car at the yoga studio. Nancy just shook her head and handed the waiter her charge card.

"You are going to owe me a fortune if I keep having to pick up the tab every time we go out." She laughed as Bess grinned and shrugged her shoulders without any sign of embarrassment.

While waiting for the return of her credit card, they sipped lemonade, and the conversation returned to Enrik. Bess was curious about Nancy's plan during her next encounter with Enrik. Nancy shared that it would depend upon Enrik's review of her investments and his suggestions. Leaving the restaurant, the conversation continued without an exact plan being developed.

Dropping Bess off at her car, Nancy drove toward home, thinking about meeting with Enrik again. With several scenarios running through her head, she decided to just wait and see what developed. She noticed her daughter's car in front of the house as she drove up the driveway into the garage.

Grimacing, she straightened her shoulders and walked toward the front door. She had forgotten about her conversation with Harry. He must have called her daughter again to complain of her continued interest in Hilda's murder. Entering the villa, she found Ann selecting a bottle of wine from the rack beside the bookcase.

"The Portuguese red blend is a nice afternoon pour," Nancy said as she watched her select a bottle. Startled, Ann turned quickly, almost dropping the bottle she had just retrieved.

"Mother, you shouldn't sneak up on people like that. You frightened me!" Ann responded.

"Well, you shouldn't be sneaking around, stealing wine from your mother without her knowledge. If I knew you planned on visiting, I would've been home to offer you a glass myself."

Handing the bottle of wine to her mother, Ann looked somewhat sheepish as she explained that she hadn't planned on visiting but was in the neighborhood and took a chance that she might be home. The raised eyebrow directed at her from Nancy as she uncorked the wine bottle caused her to sigh. Glaring at her mother, she tried to excuse the obvious lie.

"Okay, you know why I'm here. Harry called, and he was extremely put out that you continue to interfere in

Hilda's murder case," she admitted. "I tried to explain that you were close to Hilda and were the first to suspect that she hadn't died of smoke inhalation, so of course, you would be interested in his investigation. But he is worried that you will inadvertently become a victim yourself if you continue to snoop around," she added, looking worried.

Nancy poured them both a glass of wine and tried to control her frustration. It was outrageous that Harry would ask Ann to intervene, especially since it was obvious she was being helpful to his case.

"Harry's just afraid that I will solve the case and make him look bad," Nancy stated firmly, scowling at Ann. "He should be grateful for my so-called interference, not tattling to you!"

Ann looked at her mother, sensing her determination. Noting the heated defense of her actions, she wondered if there wasn't something more to her desire than justice for Hilda, something personal. "Mother, what is it about Hilda's death that has you so determined to ignore Harry and pursue this course?" She asked.

Nancy looked at her, slowly crossed the room, and sat on the couch. She thought for a few minutes, staring at the wine she swirled around in the glass. She looked up at Ann, who had joined her. To both of their surprise, tears were forming in Nancy's eyes. "I'm not sure what is driving me to follow up on the clues to Hilda's murder. I just feel compelled to solve this mystery." She said.

"This isn't about the 'What would Nancy Drew do?' factor, is it?" Ann asked quietly, trying to understand her mother's sudden melancholy.

Nancy shook her head, smiling, and answered slowly, "Ah, I can see how you would wonder about that. After all those years of my mother using Nancy as a role model as you were growing up, how could you not? But this fight for justice for Hilda isn't really about modeling Nancy Drew. It is more about finding a sense of purpose in my life."

She brushed the back of her hands across her eyes and continued, "Since your father died, I have been feeling more and more insignificant, merely going through the motion of living. Coffee with friends, yoga and book club, happy hour with the usual crowd, all fun and entertaining but in the end just filling in the hours."

Ann tried to reassure her mother that she had worked all her life and deserved her leisure time and space to relax and enjoy fewer pressures.

Teary-eyed, Nancy shook her head at her daughter. She tried to explain that although she was still willing and able to contribute to her community and others, no one really needed her. "There were lots of volunteer groups, many organizations to join to occupy one's time, but not any that I feel particularly passionate about."

Ann lowered her glass to the side table and put her arm around her mother's shoulders. Nancy leaned into her daughter's embrace and sighed. They sat together like that, comfortable, until her cell phone rang. Sniffing, Nancy left

Ann's side to retrieve it from her purse. Seeing it was Enrik, she sent the call to voice mail.

"Darn, spam alert again," she grimaced at Ann. She reached for a tissue from the box on the end table and dabbed at the corner of her eyes.

Finishing her wine, Ann stood to take her glass to the kitchen and returned to hug her mother. Looking at her sternly, she admonished her to be careful and stay out of Harry's way if she was determined to follow up on pursuing Hilda's murderer. Adding, "He isn't going to like the idea that I couldn't do something about my interfering mother's investigation," she shrugged and allowed he hadn't been happy with her for a while, anyway.

Nancy watched Ann leave, feeling a bit smug that her daughter, while not necessarily supporting her investigation, was not going to get in the way. Picking up her unfinished glass of wine, she sat back on the couch and scanned her phone to the voicemail message from Enrik. Listening to his soft accent, she smiled at the whimsical sound of his voice over the phone.

From his message, it appeared he had reviewed her holdings and had a few questions regarding several entries in the last year. He wished to discuss the discrepancies and offered to meet at the same place at whatever time would be convenient for her. Thinking that it was highly unlikely that there was any problem with her investments, she was suspicious about his motive to discuss a problem.

She had thought if he had taken Hilda's money, he would entice her to invest her money with him. Wondering if this was his next move to lure her into some sort of scam, she pressed the call-back button on her phone. When he answered, she agreed to meet him in an hour at the Cup and Vine once again during happy hour. Ending the call, she walked to her office to review her notes on Hilda. She thought she might do some research on Enrik, too.

She would start at the University. Faculty usually have resumes or curriculum vitae. At the least, she should be able to find out his educational background, qualifications, previous experiences, and employers. She had an hour before their meeting. She might as well get to know him better before then.

CHAPTER 20

While preparing to meet Enrik, Nancy continued to think about his faculty bio. She spent the hour reviewing Enrik's faculty information. She learned that he had earned his Economics and Business Ph.D. at the University of Rijeka. His first degree, Business Management, included studies in project management, business administration, investment practices, finance, and marketing. Following that, he received an MBA in Global Finance. His resume listed the family vineyard Gargac Family Winery, among other entrepreneurial experiences. He held faculty positions in several countries and joined the University of California 10 years previously. He had some serious educational credentials for a potential conman.

She decided that if tricking women into giving him money was his con, having an expert understanding of finance would be necessary, as well as being charming, and he did have a certain charm. Standing at her closet, she decided on a turquoise tank top and beige capris. Slipping on a pair of turquoise beaded sandals, she dropped a notebook into her bag and threw the bag over her shoulder. Looking at the time, she would be late if she walked, so she decided to take her golf cart and headed to the Cup and Vine.

Upon entering the coffee-wine bar, Stevie caught her eye and nodded toward the outdoor patio. Nancy saw Enrik sitting at the same table where they had met previously. Seeing her, he smiled and stood as she approached. She returned his smile and greeted him warmly. They both sat, and Stevie brought the happy hour list of wine selections and reminded them that small plates and snacks were available on the back of the wine selections.

"Do you have a favorite wine selection?" Enrik asked.

She admitted that she usually just chose the house red during happy hour.

Enrik nodded and pointed on the menu to a Portuguese red that he thought she might enjoy.

"As a winery owner, I will bow to your knowledge and try the Portuguese red," she said. When Stevie arrived, Enrik ordered two glasses as well as a charcuterie board to accompany their selection. While waiting for Stevie to return with the wine, they engaged in small talk. Enrik asked Nancy how long she had lived in San Jose's community, and she explained that Ned's diagnosis and decreased activity tolerance led to the purchase of the villa five years ago.

Nancy asked, "What led you to settle here?"

"The proximity to the campus, I enjoy the small town lifestyle, and yet we are close to the larger city of Santa Barbara." He said and added, "I also appreciate that San

Jose's 55+ community is a collection of individuals with a vibrancy that I find invigorating."

Stevie arrived with the wine glasses and charcuterie tray, and Enrik raised his glass,

"Here's to a continued sound financial future. Zivjwli, Cheers!" He added as they touched the rims of their glasses.

"Agreed, Cheers!" raising her glass to his, "Was that a Croatian toast?" she asked, inhaling the aroma of fruit and cedar while swirling the wine in her glass.

The ruby color spoke to a fruity blend, and the swirl revealed strong legs coating the inside of the glass and disappearing into the next swirl. But it was the aroma of berries, mild spices, and the hint of earthiness that held Nancy's attention. Sipping, she was surprised at the smooth finish.

"This is delightful, Enrik," swirling the wine again, enjoying the vision of the wine legs coming and going, then inhaling the aroma when taking another sip.

"Ah, I had hoped you might like it." He nodded. Smiling at her, he reached into his letter satchel to retrieve her manila folder. "Let's look at the results of my study of your investments, shall we?"

"You are right. As delightful as enjoying a glass of wine, some excellent cheese, and a lovely sunny day is, we need to get down to business and discuss your research results."

Again, he smiled at her over the rim of his glass, "Perhaps I could introduce you to a selection of Croatian wines that we could enjoy during less business-like discussions. Possibly over dinner sometime, when we could get to know each other better instead of working on finances?" He suggested.

Nancy was disconcerted by his remarks and surprised by her response. "Um, that. . . . would um . . . .be lovely," she answered. She was finding it hard to catch her breath. She coughed a few times, covering her mouth with a cocktail napkin. She took a deep breath and said, "Excuse me, I must have gotten a cracker crumb stuck in my throat."

Enrik watched her, concern on his face, unable to discern her reaction to his suggestion. He hoped the cracker and not having dinner with him caused her distress.

Nancy took another careful sip of wine, taking time to regain her composure. For a moment, his suggestion of wanting to spend more time with her was flattering and pleased her, immediately followed by being flustered by her initial response and a sense of guilt. She wondered at that reaction but had no time to consider it when Enrik spoke again,

"Perhaps this weekend, Friday or Saturday night?" He asked.

Looking at him, she saw and sensed his sincerity. "I'll check my calendar when I get home and let you know which night I might be available," she said as if she was ever booked on a weekend evening.

"Good then. With that settled, I have a few questions related to these investments that puzzle me." Enrik opened the folder with her portfolio and his notes.

She sat forward, straining to view the contents. Enrik noted her straining, stood up, and moved the folder and himself to the chair next to her rather than opposite so she could readily view his notes. Nancy found herself in close proximity to him and felt somewhat overwhelmed by his focus and intensity related to the papers in front of them.

On the other hand, she noticed how his white hair shone in the bright sun and the tan skin around his eyes creased under his reading glasses as he perused the figures. Shaking her head to concentrate on what he was saying, she looked at the dates he was questioning.

"How long has this company managed your investments?" He asked.

"I can't quite remember when we started to work with them," she answered, " but they worked with Ned's firm and were part of his benefit package for at least the last 15 years. When he left due to his illness, we just stayed with them."

"Did he leave the firm about four years ago?" He questioned her.

Wrinkling her brow, Nancy thought for a moment, "No, it was more like six years ago that he retired, but it was four years ago when we met with our financial planner, Rob. He began to provide oversite of the investments since Ned was worried that there would be a time when he would be unable to manage them himself."

Enrik explained that it appeared that about two years ago, there seemed to be an investment strategy change. He related that it might be coincidental in relation to her husband's death but suggested that she look into the newer approach to investment. She questioned him further about the changes, and he rubbed his forehead, obviously confused by the spreadsheets in front of him.

"There are multiple questionable trades, selling off solid stock to buy risky commodities with hefty brokerage fees. It appears that you have been incrementally losing money invested with the commodities, but the loss is being concealed by the gains in your profitable tech stocks." He explained. "Not only are you taking a loss in the commodities, but it is costing you in broker fees, too, as they are bought and sold."

Pointing at the figures on the spreadsheet, Enrik showed her what he was describing. It did seem odd that she wasn't informed of the new strategy, if indeed there was one. She recalled the last in-person meeting with Rob. She knew they spoke of keeping the investment plan low risk at this point in her life. The profit and loss statement produced by Enrik's spreadsheets was highly suspicious. Either her portfolio was being mismanaged, or Enrik was misrepresenting it.

"What do you suggest I do?" She asked him.

He suggested she make an appointment with her brokers and ask them to explain the discrepancies. Shrugging, he said there might be an adequate explanation for the strategy change. Nancy thought he looked doubtful.

"What if there isn't a good explanation?" She asked. Frustrated, she continued, "Then what would I do."

He responded that he had other brokers he could recommend, but she should wait to see what hers had to say first. He closed the folder, replaced it in his leather satchel, and turned to her.

"It is too pleasant of an afternoon to waste discussing this situation further." He said as he signaled to Stevie for another round, tilting his head to smile at her.

She tried to be miffed that he didn't ask her if she would like another glass of wine, but looking at his handsome face and smile, she decided to pass on, mentioning the inconsideration. Besides, she enjoyed the new wine and would appreciate a second glass. Complementing him on his wine choice, she asked about his preferences. He tilted his head back to look at the clear blue sky and remarked that a fine glass of wine was like beautiful music or art. Confused, she looked at him, and he added,

"It speaks to one's senses, delights one's appetite for all the beauty that surrounds one." He smiled unapologetically.

She laughed at the poetic description, "I never thought of wine as an art appreciation tool."

Enrik smiled at her, "Appreciation of good wine involves much more than taste and aroma-it encompasses all the senses."

They continued their discussion of different wines while finishing the cheese tray. But the conversation returned to her finances. Nancy agreed to call her advisor and set up an appointment to meet.

"And you will call me to discuss which night you will be free to have dinner with me?" He reminded her. She nodded.

Smiling at him, "On that note, I'm afraid I should head home."

She asked what she owed him for his research. When he resisted any payment, she attempted to at least pay for the wine, but again, he refused. He explained he had enjoyed sharing the happy hour with her. As she stood to leave, he stood too and escorted her to the door.

Waving as she drove off in her golf cart, she was thinking of how pleasant sharing a nice wine and conversation was with Enrik. Those thoughts led to her amazement that she had agreed to have dinner with him, and she immediately felt guilty. She wondered where the feeling of guilt came from. After all, she was unattached and free to have dinner with whomever she chose. As she parked the golf cart in the garage, she realized that it wasn't the thought of having dinner with Enrik that was bothering her. It was the thought of being unfaithful to Ned's memory.

Closing the garage door and entering the house, she decided it wasn't fair to blame Ned for her feelings of guilt. He would want her to enjoy life. Frowning, she put those thoughts away, noticing it was almost closing time at her brokerage. She scanned through her phone's register, found the agency number, and placed the call. A receptionist answered and explained Rob wasn't available. Nancy asked for an appointment, requesting the earliest possible. The receptionist said he had a cancellation for ten the next morning and scheduled her to meet with him then.

She slipped out of her sandals and walked into her office to retrieve the original copy of her investment portfolio. Sitting behind the desk, she found the pages that had caused Enrik to be concerned. It did look as if there was an unusual amount of activity in the past two years compared to the previous years. It seemed even more unusual as the timeline coincided with Ned's death. Thinking back to phone conversations with Rob, she couldn't recall any changes in strategy being discussed. Tilting back in the desk chair, she decided to review all her holdings before her meeting with him tomorrow morning.

CHAPTER 21

Nancy arrived at Rob's office five minutes before her appointment and was shown to a small, comfortable conference room. Rob joined her within a few minutes and took her hand in his.

"It is a pleasure to meet in person instead of our biannual phone conversations. You are looking well." He said.

"It is good to see you, too," she said, "It is nice of you to meet with me on such short notice." They hadn't met in person for several years, but his rounded shoulders, rimmed glasses, and uneasy smile hadn't changed, she noticed.

Still holding her hand, he asked how she was coping without Ned, hoping that the need for a personal meeting wasn't due to financial difficulties. Bracing for the quick squeeze around her heart she felt in response to the caring concerns from others when Ned was mentioned, Nancy assured him that she was adjusting daily to being on her own,

She removed her portfolio from her shoulder bag and opened it to the most current profit and loss statement. Rob followed by opening her file and found the same statement. She looked pointedly at him and casually asked him to explain the losses.

"It does appear that you have sustained various setbacks in your trades, but your profit line remains solid related to your tech stocks." He nodded, smiling at her, having shared what he thought to be a good outcome. She returned a thin smile, but the raised eyebrows left no doubt that she wasn't reassured.

"What I am concerned about is the trades. They seemed unusual choices and appeared risky at best. Selling them for a loss to trade for other low-performing stocks doesn't seem like a profitable act either."

Pointing at the bottom line of her itemized trade list, she added, "Looking at the result of those actions seem to be contrary to our previously agreed upon risk-averse retirement plan."

Rob looked hurt, "My dear, we at this firm understand that success requires the ability to recognize and discard outdated solutions in order to generate truly innovative ideas and exciting new directions." Looking over his glasses perched on the tip of his nose, he smiled reassuringly.

"Your innovative ideas and exciting new directions don't seem to be generating success for me," Nancy pointed to the line item listed as broker fees, "It appears that the buying and selling of these low-performing stocks has a price that your firm tacks on to my portfolio management fee. Can you explain the extra fees? They are considerable throughout the last two years."

Rob stated, "It is standard industry practice for brokers to have marketing agreements with various product suppliers, for example, mutual funds, annuity and insurance companies, and occasional limited partnerships."

He added that clients should understand that the firm may charge their customers fees related to revenue sharing or marketing fees, sales commissions, markups or markdowns trailing fees, or general service fees in connection with those purchases. "After all, our clients have all agreed that they have read and signed our management consent forms." He added, starting to sound defensive.

According to him, the fees charged for the annual portfolio management plan are for the plan only and do not include additional compensation that may be earned by the financial consultants or brokers for implementing the trades.

"Occasional exceptional opportunities fail to perform to expectations, but continuing to pursue our goals by accepting the challenges of those occasional losses provide further growth opportunities for unimaginable success." Shrugging with hands extended in the air, Rob reassured her.

Nancy didn't appreciate his condescending attitude. "Those fees are understandable if they are charged above and beyond the portfolio plan, Rob, and agreed to by your clients." Shaking her head, she added, "What I don't understand, though, is why these fees have only shown up in the last several years." Nancy said.

"Up until that time, Ned was making his own decisions and trades. Eventually, he couldn't keep up with his health challenges and asked me to take over your investments," Rob explained.

"I am aware of the history, Rob. I'm interested in the recent history and the future." Nancy claimed. "You and I have had bi-annual conversations regarding the portfolio," Nancy pointed out, "we never discussed the losses."

"Your total tech stocks income and dividends compensated for any losses, commissions, or fees, so the portfolio continued to show consistent gains." He answered.

"I wasn't aware that you would be interested in the details as long as your income remained intact. I only discussed the investments with Ned, and as he trusted us to manage your finances while he was alive, he would have expected you to trust us after he passed." Rob raised his chin, saying, "I'm hurt that you would doubt our integrity."

He sat across from her, hands folded over her file, and Nancy looked at him, trying to decide if he was sincere. It was true that the investment value remained the same, but as Enrik had pointed out, the commissions and fees ate into her gains, money that would still be in her account if not wagered on poor-performing entities.

Looking Rob in the eyes, she asked him, "Are you aware now that I am interested in details?" Head cocked to one side.

Nodding, he agreed, "I believe you are making that clear. How would you like to proceed?"

"I am not willing to lose the money I made on my tech stocks on occasional exceptional offers in sell-offs, commissions, or fees," She said, " I believe that I should be emailed any suggested trades or purchases, and all purchases should be approved by me before any action to acquire is taken."

"Even if the market is in a negative free-fall?" He asked.

"Especially if the market is tanking!" She responded, looking at him with brows raised again, challenging him to try to change her mind.

Looking somewhat aggrieved, he nodded in agreement, "Going forward, we will contact you for approval of any changes in your investments."

He apologized for any misunderstanding and assured her that her portfolio would remain in low-risk status. He thanked her for meeting to resolve her dissatisfaction and hoped she would contact him at any time with questions, patting her hand reassuringly.

Nodding while freeing her hand, she said, "I will look forward to hearing from you." Nancy stood and gathered her folder and bag.

CHAPTER 22

Leaving the office, somehow, Nancy wasn't surprised that Enrik was right about the profit and loss statements. She just wasn't sure what to do about trusting him. Maybe if she asked him to manage her investments, she could trap him into trying to scam her.

It was so difficult. She rather liked him, and it didn't feel right to try to prove he was a murderer. Thinking to herself as she slipped into the car seat, "What kind of a woman finds a possible murderer agreeable company and thinks his offer to take her to dinner an appropriate, harmless date?"

Shrugging, she grinned at herself in the rearview mirror, buckled the seat belt, and lowered the convertible top. Checking her phone before heading out of the parking lot, she saw a missed call from Bess. Clicking on the recall button, Bess answered after the third ring through the car speaker. She had been on an overnight bus trip with her travel group to Mission Santa Ines.

She was calling first thing upon her return as she couldn't wait to catch up with her sleuthing activities. Laughing, Nancy agreed to meet her at her villa, " I'll fix lunch, "she offered, anxious to see Bess's response to her progress with the investigation.

Pulling into her driveway, she noticed Bess's golf cart out front and saw her sitting in one of the front garden wicker chairs, scrolling through her cell phone. Following the walk to the door, she entered the passcode to unlock the door and called Bess to follow her in.

Nancy went to her office to drop off her bag and file her folder while Bess checked for leftovers in the fridge.

"Why don't you have any Styrofoam boxes full of mysterious parts of past lunches or dinners sitting around in your fridge, like a normal person?" She asked.

"Salad, fruit, and baked chicken tenders are in the veggie drawer. We can make up a salad while I catch you up on what I have been doing in your absence. I'm going to change my clothes into something more comfortable." Nancy answered as she headed to the bedroom.

Having changed into baggy capris and a tee shirt, she joined Bess in the kitchen. The bag of Caesar salad mix sat on the counter, as well as a peach, strawberries, blueberries, and a Tupperware container of chicken tenders.

"Why do you have so much fruit, and are these those healthy chicken strips you're always trying to get me to make?"

"These chicken strips are quick, not cooked in grease, but taste crunchy like they were fried. It's about making healthy food choices, obviously something not a priority in your life." Nancy laughed, reminded of Bess's fondness for pastries.

Cutting the chicken strips into bite-size pieces, she spread them over the salad mix and added poppyseed dressing, a hint of barbecue sauce, and a handful of blueberries. She set one of the plates in front of Bess, who immediately stabbed a chicken strip while looking at Nancy, one brow raised.

"I am dying to know what has been happening while I was gone," Bess said between bites, "But I'm starving, so just tell me everything. I'm too hungry to take the time to ask questions!"

Nancy laughed, "As you know, I was waiting for Enrik to call to discuss my investment portfolio. He did right after our yoga class lunch. We met later that afternoon."

She told Bess about the discrepancies he had found, adding his suggestion that she discuss them with her broker and financial planner. Having just returned from a meeting with her broker, she shared her disappointment that a business associate of Ned's would take advantage of his carte blanche investment empowerment. "Ned trusted him, so I had no fear in trusting him, too." Sadly, she shook her head.

Nancy didn't mention that she and Enrik met over a couple of glasses of wine during happy hour but did share that she planned to seek his advice about what to do next. Bess asked when she would see him again and was surprised that Nancy hesitated over her answer.

"I think I will probably meet him tomorrow evening to review the information from Rob, my broker."

"Saturday evening?" Bess was startled, "Why Saturday evening?" She added between bites, with an emphasis on the word evening.

"We may be going out to dinner that night; at least, I think we might." Bess noticed that she wasn't making eye contact, which was unusual for Nancy.

"You think?" Again, Bess was startled. "Honestly, Nancy, what is going on? Do you have a dinner date with Enrik?"

"Kinda," with a side eye at Bess, she said, "Well, I wouldn't call it a date." Nancy shrugged her shoulders, "He asked me. I haven't agreed yet."

Bess hesitated, surprised that Nancy would agree to a date since she was still so grief-stricken over losing Ned. She was even more concerned with the identity of the proposed date. Ironically, Bess questioned, " Do you think it wise to be dating a murder suspect?"

Nancy was quick to respond, "I repeat, it's not actually a date. It is more like a chance to see if he is a crook and scam artist, taking advantage of older women and stealing their money."

"So you're thinking that if he tries to trick you into investing your money, he might have done the same to Hilda?"

Nancy nodded, "When she realized what he had done, she confronted him, and he killed her."

"Ahh, I see. You're not dating; you're setting a trap!" It was Bess's turn to nod unconvinced.

Nancy did look somewhat guilty, "Not exactly a trap, more of a morality check."

A second skeptic nod, "I see, not a trap, a test?"

Losing patience, Nancy said, "Aren't all dates a test? Isn't the purpose of a date a test of compatibility?"

Bess agreed, "Yep, that's what dates are for, but you just said this wasn't a date!"

Sighing, Nancy admitted to Bess that she was struggling with the idea that dating felt like a betrayal of her relationship with Ned, even though he had been gone for two years. She also had a hard time misrepresenting her intentions to Enrik.

Bess became suspicious of Nancy's concern for a possible murderer and thief and inquired further, "Tell me more about this Enrik." Giving Nancy an innocent glance. Nancy confessed that they met during happy hour, and he introduced her to a different wine than her usual happy hour red. He was charming and very professional when reviewing her financial holdings. While exchanging small talk, he invited her to dinner this weekend to taste wine from his home country on condition that they did not talk business. She believed, though, that she could slyly introduce the topic, and he would follow her lead.

"How old is he? When did he move here? I don't know him, and I usually make it my business to know everybody!" Taking a breath after the rapid succession of questions, Bess finally asked the most important one, "Does part of his charm rely on his appearance? How handsome is this guy, anyway?" She tried to sound innocent but failed miserably.

Squinting, Nancy responded to the questions in the order they had been asked, "I guess he is about our age." She gave Bess a detailed description of his average build, full head of snowy-white hair, expressive face, excellent manners, and delightful faint Croatian accent.

"It sounds like he'd make an interesting dinner date." Looking pensive, she thought if he weren't a murderer and thief, it would be nice to see her best friend abandon some of her grief. "I'd take him up on the offer." Nodding, Bess added. Then distracted Nancy by asking, "So what does one wear on a dinner date with a possible murderer?"

Nancy grinned at her, "Only you would see the humor in that question!" Shaking her head, she cleared the dishes from the table and loaded them in the dishwasher.

"Maybe we should go to the mall and shop for the perfect outfit to be murdered in," Bess said. "Something to die for?"

Nancy groaned at the gallows humor, "I'll need to call him first and agree to dinner on Saturday."

While she called Enrik, Bess went home to grab her purse. Nancy had agreed to drive and planned to pick her up in 15 minutes.

Scrolling for Enrik's number, Nancy smiled, anticipating not only another step in solving the mystery of the missing $100,000 but also in finding justice for Hilda. Dialing, she surprised herself by guiltily admitting that she also was anticipating dinner with an attractive and charming man, dismissing the part about a possible murderer.

CHAPTER 23

Nancy had just finished brushing her hair and sliding on her sandals when Enrik arrived. She agreed to wait to discuss the meeting with her broker until after they had dinner, as Enrik was adamant no business would be discussed during dinner. She wore a pale mauve linen peasant skirt, a sea-foam green short-sleeved top with a matching mauve, and a green gauze scarf. Her kitten-heeled sandals were decorated with miniature seashells. Opening the door to Enrik, it was evident that he approved of her appearance.

"You look lovely this evening, Nancy." He said as he entered, smiling.

Nancy thanked him, noticing how well his casual open-necked white shirt and navy sports jacket suited him. She smiled at his bare ankles and leather loafers. She never got used to the trend of men not wearing socks. "You don't look bad, yourself." She said.

She slid her phone into the new purse she and Bess had found that afternoon during their shopping trip. Grabbing her matching sweater from the back of the chair, she joined him at the door and pulled it closed behind her, flipping the lock as they left. He opened the door of a silver-blue Tesla, and she slid into the passenger seat.

"Nice car, Enrik, very comfortable. Is it as fun to drive as it looks?" she asked as he slid in beside her.

He explained that he bought it for its lack of environmental impact but admitted that he enjoyed the sporty handling as well as its economy. He added that the silver-blue color reflected the sunlight and decreased the air conditioning fuel consumption.

"Plugging it in at home in the evening saves on fuel costs, too," he added.

She smiled at Enrik's enthusiasm for his auto's environmental consciousness and asked the name of the restaurant where they would be dining. He explained that Toma's Restaurant had a delightful cocktail bar and charming bartender, and the owner has been known to wander Croatia's coastal wine country in search of the perfect blends.

He explained, "The bar is surrounded by a larger dining area, but the restaurant is still small compared to the Village clubhouse."

"I like the intimacy. The owner bought a couple of cases of Croatian wine, so we can share a bottle and pretend the waterfront is that of the Adriatic. I will be anxious for your appraisal." He grinned at her.

She laughed, "I will probably enjoy your wine, and the restaurant sounds charming."

They pulled up to the front of a terra cotta building with knotty vines climbing the outside walls and onto the roof. A large lighted sign stood above the large oak doors.

Enrik shared that he was fond of this family-run restaurant. It reminded him of the importance of sharing the workday with those one loves the most: family. As they were shown to the bar to await their table, Enrik offered Nancy a seat.

The bartender welcomed Enrik back, glad he was home safely from his trip to Croatia. He greeted Nancy with a broad grin, tilting his head toward Enrik, he said, "He's like family. We miss him when he doesn't show up every week!" Looking at Enrik, "I believe you drink your bourbon, neat?" He smiled again at Nancy, "What can I fix for you?" Nancy requested Grey Goose Vodka, up, very chilled, with two olives. The bartender nodded, "The woman knows what she likes, Enrik, be careful. She could be demanding," he winked at Nancy. She smiled at Enrik, admitting she hadn't known about his recent return from his visit to Croatia. She asked about his family still living there.

Enrik looked down into his drink and sighed, "Yes, my son, ex-wife, and her husband operate the family winery." He added, "My father, and his father before him, loved the rugged vineyards of the coast and toiled for years to make the small winery profitable. When my father passes, my son will carry on that tradition."

As the bartender served Nancy her martini, she sympathized, "It must be difficult, living so far from family."

"Once my wife and I divorced, it was better that I left. My father and my ex-wife's new husband were strong Croatian influences on my son. They taught him to care for the land and respect the vines. He has grown to love the land and the winery."

Running his finger around the rim of the glass, "I am proud of my ancestry, but the Vintner is usually a viticulturist who assesses the growth of the vines, monitors the maturity of the grapes to ensure quality, and determines harvest dates. That was not my forte."

Nancy looked at him, doubt evident in her surprised comment, "From our earlier discussions about the wines of Croatia, you seemed to be an expert!"

Avoiding looking up from the glass, he said, "My ex-wife married our Vintner, allowing our son to be raised at the vineyard and watched over by my father. It was better that I left, and it worked out well. My son is now the Director of the winery. My reduced University workload allowed me to spend three weeks with him. It was good to see how well he is doing." He looked up at her with a sad smile, ending the conversation as the hostess approached.

She led them to their table, where a wine list was located at Enrik's seat. Changing the conversation and distracting Enrik from the regret she heard in his voice, Nancy looked around the dining area.

"What a delightful place, Enrik. It's so elegant but still has the comfort of a bistro." She smiled at him. The crisp white table linen and gold-trimmed china were accented by floral napkins, and a candle glowed warmly in a delicate metal holder. A waiter filled their water glasses, offering a menu to both. Before Nancy could even glance at the appetizers, the chef approached them, holding his arms wide and calling to Enrik.

"Welcome back, man; we have missed you!" He said, patting Enrik's shoulder while smiling broadly at Nancy. "Who is this lovely woman you have with you?"

"Nancy, this is Luca, the chef of this fine establishment." Grinning, he added, "Luca, this is my friend, Nancy. I promised her a glass of the finest Croatian wine only available at the finest restaurant in Santa Barbara."

"If he has lured you here with the promise of exceptional wine and food, you will not be disappointed." Reaching for her menu, he removed it from her hand and placed the menu and her hand near his heart, "You will not need a menu. If you have no allergies or sensitivities, I will choose our finest delicacies." Looking over at Enrik, he released her hand, "For you also, I know what you are fond of and will choose for you since you brought such a lovely companion for me to cook for."

Both Enrik and Nancy were amused by Luca's enthusiasm and grinned at each other. A basket of warm crusty rolls was placed on the table, along with a bottle of Vinarija Dingac Postup wine. Enrik explained as the waiter uncorked and poured the wine that was imported from the Peljesac Peninsula in Croatia. Dingac was the most well-known of the Croatian wine varieties.

He added that wines bearing the Dingac name come from the southwest-facing slopes on the steep Adriatic coastline between the small villages of Trstenik and Podobuce. Dingac continues to define the Plavac Mali-based reds, and wine aficionados make up the bulk of the tourist traffic along the coastal areas.

"I was unaware that Croatia wines inspired such devoted followers. Actually, I didn't know Croatia imported wines, " Nancy admitted.

"Croatians have been producing wine for over two thousand years. Viticulture was introduced to us by the ancient Greeks," there was a note of pride in his voice as he explained further.

"The Plavac Mali is the name of the small blue, tough-skinned grape that is a varietal of Zinfandel and Dobricic, an ancient Croatian variety." The sommelier poured a sample into Erik's glass. He swilled it, checked the color and scent, then sipped.

"Ah, that will be fine," he nodded while Nancy's glass and his were filled, "Nazdravlje, Good health! " He tapped their wine glasses together in a quiet toast.

Nancy stumbled over repeating Nazdravlje, and laughed embarrassingly, "To your health." She added as the waiter delivered a charcuterie platter filled with salami, prosciutto, and several cheeses.

The waiter identified the meats and cheeses, named each, and gave a review of their age and region of origin. He returned with a platter of bruschetta, explaining that the bread was freshly baked this morning and the olive oil was from the chef's family's olive orchard in Italy. The tomatoes and basil were picked fresh today from the restaurant's gardens. Nancy, surrounded by all the food, thought it felt like a picnic.

Just as Enrik finished warning her to pace herself on the appetizers to have room for the entrees, Luca appeared at their table again. "I see you approve of the bruschetta," he noted her half-eaten crust of the olive and tomato-soaked bread, "and the antipasti met your expectation, Enrik?" Both nodded as Luca began to refill their wine glasses.

He cocked his head at Nancy, "Toma is known for their calamari and our uniquely flavored stuffed squash blossoms. They are served with preserved lemon, pine nuts, and goat cheese, finished with shelling peas and tangerine citronette. They are tasty, but for you, I think a more adventurous selection would be our grilled Spanish octopus."

He explained that it was served with Romanesco fregola pasta garnished with gremolata- chopped parsley, garlic, lemon zest, and a smoked tomato remoulade. Smiling at Nancy, he added with no attempt to appear humble, "It is exquisite!"

She smiled back, "How could I say no to an adventure in dining?" Luca turned his attention to Enrik, who shrugged and ordered the calamari. Focusing his attention back on Nancy, Luca offered his opinion of her main course choice.

"For your main course, I think you will like the grilled Skuna Bay Salmon." Seeing Nancy nod, he explained it was served in a classic puttanesca style with fresh clams, white polenta, tomato, and pearl onions, accompanied by capers, olives, garlic, and anchovy.

Turning to Enrik, he shrugged, "For you, it will either be the rack of lamb or your favorite braised beef short ribs. Which would you prefer tonight?" Luca asked. As Enrik finished his bruschetta, pressing his lips to his napkin, he turned to Nancy to explain his fondness for Luca's beef ribs. He described how the beef was nestled in the red onion confit and lemon garlic olive oil.

Raising his hands in the air, he said, "I should've guessed!" Luca said as he headed toward the kitchen.

Enrik laughed as Luca left and asked Nancy if she had ever had octopus before. She admitted she had shared and enjoyed a portion at a restaurant in Portland, Oregon, at the Mediterranean Exploration Company, once at a conference. She added, "It was the first time I had tasted octopus. They prepared it charred. It was delightful."

Shaking his head, he said he wasn't fond of octopus but enjoyed most other seafood. He admitted he had never had a reason to visit Portland. They spoke of other meals and realized that they had visited many of the same dining establishments in several cities and even other countries.

Nancy spoke of how she and Ned took frequent trips to Italy, and especially her fondness for Tuscany's food and people. The waiter brought the appetizers while Enrik shared that she must go to Croatia sometime to see the Adriatic coast and enjoy the beauty and culinary experts there. "They love visitors and are proud of the land." He added as he forked a calamari tendril. She sipped her wine between bites of octopus and enjoyed hearing Enrik talk about his homeland and his family's winery.

Luca arrived at the table, this time accompanying the waiter. Topping off their wine glasses again, he announced with a flourish, "Your dinner is served; enjoy!" He waited as they took their first bites. The aroma of both entrees was intoxicating. Nancy's first taste was heavenly. The seafood was fresh and immersed in the lightly lemon-seasoned shrimp reduction, and the pasta was excellent.

Enrik and Luca watched Nancy as she marveled at the superb tastes. Enrik nodded and smiled at her obvious pleasure as he started to eat his meal. In between bites, they talked of other favorite Italian meals. Nancy shared a story about a tiny bistro in Italy where she and Ned had been stranded during a wicked rainstorm. "We spent hours there, eating, drinking Chianti, and listening to a local trio playing jazz and also traditional tunes," she smiled, remembering that evening, "And tunes made famous by Italian American performers like Frank Sinatra, too."

Enrik smiled, too, "If you like to listen to music, there is a nightclub down the street from here that features a jazz trio. They come here to eat occasionally before going on stage." He added,

"I have stopped in to listen. They have a nice mellow sound."

"I haven't listened to live music in years, except for the community concert band provided at the activity center." She tilted her head in thought, "Guess that wouldn't compete with a nightclub's jazz trio for skill, but the community members are generous entertainers if lacking in professional execution." She raised her eyebrows, grinning at him.

Enrik laughed, "Having not heard the community band, I will withhold judgment, but we could walk down to the Castillo Inn Lounge for your appraisal of the trio." As she looked hesitant, he added, "You will want a short walk after the dessert. I am sure Luca will serve us."

Changing the subject, Nancy wondered how Enrik had made such a good friend in Luca. He told her their friendship started with a competition for regional wine. Luca thought his Italian Puglia vineyards produced the best red wines in the whole world, while Enrik favored his family's grapes and had several cases delivered to Luca. They spent several memorable nights testing each other's theories, to no avail, as neither would budge on their favorite.

Nancy found herself sharing a story of getting a case of expensive imported Italian wine from a suspected drug dealer as a bribe when she was a judge. She admitted that they drank it but also said he was found guilty anyway. "After all, it was the jury that decided the guilt, not me!" She shrugged.

The waiter removed the dishes from the table and swept crumbs with a tiny brush into a tiny crumb tray, then reappeared with a silver pot and began to set up a coffee press. This time, Luca himself brought two desserts to the table.

He presented Nancy with a phyllo dough concoction of a raspberry mousse stuffed pastry in a pool of berry sauce, surrounded by ripe strawberries, "The finishing touch to the freshness of the berries is the delightfully light whipped vanilla bean cream." He said and served Enrik, "One of your favorites, I believe. This citrus Olive oil cake was baked fresh this afternoon, and the tangerines peeled just moments ago."

He slipped the cake in front of Enrik while reaching for the coffee. Pouring a cup for Nancy, he watched her as she took a bite of the cake. She sighed. "This is the best dessert I have ever had the pleasure to taste!"

"My mamma's recipe, as you fall asleep tonight, it will give you sweet dreams." He winked at Nancy as he left the table. She and Enrik sat quietly, sharing their desserts, and sipping the remains of their coffee.

"It is still early; would you care to walk down the street to listen to the trio at the lounge?" Enrik asked, "Having met the keyboard player here one night, I was interested in hearing his music, and, as I said, I have wandered down to listen a few times after dinner here. If you are a jazz fan, you will like their sound."

Nancy agreed that a stroll would be ideal after their dining experience, especially the dessert. "I haven't been to a club in such a long time." She said, at the same time wondering if it was wise. After all, the plan was to discuss her finances, not be entertained. As Enrik spoke with the waiter while paying for their meal, Nancy excused herself to visit the ladies' lounge.

As she reapplied fresh lipstick, Nancy felt conflicted about visiting the nightclub. Shaking her head at her image in the mirror, she thought she was enjoying herself way too much to consider this time spent with Enrik as investigating.

CHAPTER 24

Nancy watched the steaming water circulate around the filter of her cup as the fresh brewed aroma of Guatemalan grind filled the kitchen. She woke up later than usual, and as she completed her morning yoga stretches, she thought about the night before. Slowly, the pleasantness of the evening in her memory began to dim. The awareness of having forgotten the investigative nature that the time with Enrik was supposed to be, led to feelings of guilt and then remorse. Preparing her pour-over coffee provided her with time to reflect on the evening.

Taking the cup outside to her deck, she tried to examine where all these conflicting emotions were coming from. She wondered how a plot to uncover a possible murderer turned into an enjoyable dinner with a charming man. Did that then constitute a date, as Bess questioned?

That made her feel more guilty. She didn't want to be dating. She was still grieving losing Ned, and dating sounded like one was searching for a replacement. Ned was not replaceable. Looking for perspective surrounding these conflicting emotions, Nancy thought about the reason she and Enrik were together that evening. After all, she was investigating him as a possible murder suspect. There was nothing wrong with enjoying a great meal while getting to know your suspect, right? Detective work didn't need to be boring and unenjoyable. After all, Nancy Drew seemed to take pleasure in her adventures.

Finishing up the last of her coffee, Nancy sighed; she was probably overthinking the whole thing. Staring at the open refrigerator a minute later, she realized that she couldn't remember what she was looking for, causing concern for her mental state. A sure sign she needed to organize her thoughts before plowing forward in further pursuit of solving the mystery of Hilda's death.

While making a second pour-over, Bess appeared on her backyard deck with a knock on the sliding door. Nancy was glad to see her, as she might be able to help sort out all the confusing thoughts. Waving a bakery bag in the air, Bess said, "Let me in. I come bearing gifts!" Nancy laughed as she invited her in. "Enter, please; what do you have in that bag?"

"Apple fritters and a bear claw from the Lucky Llama coffee shop, and a Latte for me!"

"Great, I was trying to decide if I had enough fruit for a breakfast smoothie. Problem solved!" She said while taking the bag from Bess and plating the goodies.

Bess sat down at the snack bar that divided the kitchen from the dining area. "I'm dying to hear how your non-date went last night," she said, biting into the bear claw.

"I'm not sure anything was accomplished last evening regarding Hilda's death," Nancy admitted, reaching for the apple fritter. "The purpose of sharing dinner was to discuss my meeting with my broker, but we never really got around to discussing my finances."

Sipping her coffee, she avoided looking at Bess. Although Bess was busy pulling her pastry apart, enjoying small pieces at a time, hoping that the flavorful, flakey morsels would last longer, she noticed the avoidance.

"So, what did you talk about during dinner?" she asked, neglecting her last pieces of pastry, looking pointedly at Nancy.

Nancy explained that they spoke of their careers and his life in Croatia. She shared with Bess that they talked about his vineyard history and favorite Croatian wine, his faculty position at UC Davis University, and working at the Santa Barbara campus. Nancy could tell that Bess wasn't satisfied with those details and squirmed in her chair, beginning to feel defensive.

"Seems pretty much like the conversations one would have on a first date?" Bess speculated.

Resigned, Nancy admitted that her reflection this morning pretty much agreed with Bess's observation. "The evening was so relaxed, the atmosphere comfortable, and the food was exquisite. It had been so long since I was so indulged; it was gratifying. I just didn't want to spoil the evening."

Squinting, she rubbed her forehead, "Enrik was so attentive and entertaining. I don't know what I was thinking!"

"You were thinking it was pleasant and enjoyable and just let it happen without further thought." She reached across the coffee bar to Nancy's hand, patting it, "It's okay; you deserve a night out, being pampered and pandered to."

Nancy looked at her, still not totally convinced it was right.

"Besides, now you have him where you want him," Bess announced as she swallowed the last of the bear claw pastry, "He'll think you were enchanted by his attention, call you to meet to talk about your investments and then take your money. You'll have trapped him after all into trying to scam you!" She reasoned.

Nancy wasn't so sure about that. After their dinner last night, still refusing to call it a date, she had her doubts about Enrik being a crook. But Bess could be right; he might pamper all his victims into trusting him. The idea that he saw her as vulnerable to his charm irritated her. She needed to make certain of his intent. If he was looking for an easy target, he had the wrong woman.

"You may be right, Bess," she said. Holding her cup of cooling coffee in both hands, she thought, "We need a plan to flush out his motive."

They discussed various scenarios, deciding against Nancy calling Enrik. Instead, they both felt that if he were intent on trying to get Nancy's money, he would call her. They decided that Nancy should be hesitant but easily persuaded if he tried to elicit her capital so he could invest it for her. The plan was to notify Harry once she was sure that Enrik had taken Hilda's money and let the police handle it from there.

That being decided, Bess left for a pedicure appointment while Nancy changed into a pair of old cut-off jeans and a faded Half Moon Bay Pumpkin Festival tee shirt. The weeds lining her entrance walkway were interfering with her pansies' growth, and the gardener seemed to be neglecting the Mexican bush sage at the corner of the house. A trim was needed. Getting her tools from the potting table in her garage, she headed toward the fuchsia plants that surrounded her hummingbird feeder.

Having thinned them out, she realized her shrub rose bush was blooming and went back to the potting table to retrieve her pruning shears. Thinking the roses would add color and a light scent to the coffee bar, she snipped three buds from the bush. With them held gingerly in her gloved fingers so as not to bruise the stems, she laid them on the potting table. Taking her tools back to the garage, she carefully retrieved the roses and turned toward the house. Looking up from the rose buds, she almost bumped into Enrik.

"Oh, I didn't see you there," she said, surprised.

"I was on my way home planning on calling you when I saw you in your yard." He said. "I thought I would stop instead of calling and see if it would be convenient for us to chat about your conversation with your broker."

"I am just finishing some yard work, but come in if you want."

Realizing she must look a mess in her muddy gloves and grass-stained cut-offs. She carefully handed the roses to Enrik, "Be careful with the thorns," she warned as she removed the gloves and ran her hand through her hair. Leading him in through the back door, she took the roses from him and sat them in the sink.

"Why don't you go out to the deck through the sliding door? I will join you once I wash my hands and put the roses in water." She smiled at him. "I have iced tea freshly made this morning; would you like to join me in a glass?"

'The iced tea would be welcomed," he answered. While he waited for Nancy to return, Enrik took a seat on the deck and noticed her manicured yard and trimmed hedges. He wasn't sure he would ever get used to the resort-like settings one found in retirement communities. The amenities made life extremely convenient; golf, tennis, and the recent attraction of a new pickleball court kept a majority of the members busy.

He appreciated the fully equipped gym and the occasional community-sponsored musical entertainment. The monthly lunch meeting, sponsored by a group of men and women who had financial backgrounds and shared their insights with the members of the various stock clubs, was interesting and occasionally informative.

He entertained the idea of checking out the list of books the book club had been discussing to see if there was anything he might be interested in reading and discussing. Having just recently moved into the village, he still felt like a visitor, but he was feeling more comfortable getting to know more of the other residents.

Shrugging his shoulders, maybe he could learn to appreciate the area. Being so close to the ocean reminded him of home. Having recently returned from his Croatian visit and the vineyard of his youthful past, Enrik realized that his future didn't lie there. Restless, he stood and wandered around the deck to look at the flowers at the back stoned fence.

He noticed an array of garden ornaments, flamingos peeking out of tall grasses, and Gnomes staring around the rocks strewn about the fuchsia surrounding the hummingbird feeder. He smiled at the frivolous, playful display.

Nancy approached carrying two glasses of iced tea and the manilla folder. Handing one glass to him, "I see you've found my garden creatures; I find planting surprising curiosities provides some childish joy. They make me smile." She grinned at them, "I have my notes from the meeting. Let's sit down, and I'll share his response to my questions." She waved the manilla folder toward the deck table and chair he had recently left.

Sipping his tea, he watched her sit and open the folder. He moved the chair from across the table to her side and sat down. Distracted by that move, she took a deep breath and turned toward Enrik, finding him much too close. Quickly returning her gaze to the folder, she cleared her throat,

"It seems that he might have been skimming money from my account by charging brokerage fees for stock purchases." She explained. "The stocks weren't producing revenue, so he would sell them and purchase others, again charging brokerage fees."

Flipping the pages, she showed him the broker had done that multiple times. She said she didn't notice the losses or the number of fees paid because, foolishly, she merely gazed at the year-to-date total. The bottom line grew in small increments in her monthly portfolio email because, in essence, her tech stocks gains covered the losses just as he had predicted.

Enrik looked at the pages she showed him and shook his head. "I thought as much," he said, "I think you need to find a new broker."

She looked at him, cocked her head, and asked, "Do you know of one?"

He smiled at her and said he could suggest a few, "You don't want to do anything rash, though." He then asked about the conversation with her broker after he revealed the multiple fee charges. She explained that she told him that only approved buys were to be completed and that she would be watching her monthly statements closer for any unapproved activity.

Enrik nodded and asked, "You didn't threaten to take your portfolio elsewhere?"

"No, I didn't think that would be wise until I thought about the situation less emotionally and discussed my next steps with you." She said.

He looked again at her portfolio and asked her questions related to her risk tolerance to discover how aggressive she wanted to be in her investment strategy. Thoughtfully, staring into the distance for a minute before turning toward her, he suggested that she leave the majority of her portfolio where it was currently invested. He then recommended that a portion be invested more aggressively in an attempt to regain the monies lost by the brokers' fees scheme.

"How large of an investment are you thinking, Enrik?" She asked.

He responded that it would depend on her comfort level. Removing his phone from his pocket, he said he needed to do some quick calculations. Watching him click on his phone app, she stood and, reaching for the empty glasses, offered to refill them and headed for the kitchen. Putting the glasses on the snack counter, she retrieved the tea from the refrigerator. Pouring, she noticed her hands shaking.

Surprised at the physical evidence of her anxiety, she hesitated to pick up the glasses. Confused by her emotions, she had hoped all along that Enrik would offer to take her money, confirming her fears that he was a thief and stealing from Hilda. Yet, somewhere deep inside, she had hoped she was wrong. But the thought of him betraying Hilda's trust and possibly murdering her caused Nancy to realize that finding out what happened the night Hilda died was what really mattered.

She stood up straighter, filled the glasses without trembling hands, and headed for the deck. She could feel her heart beating faster in anticipation of Enrik's response to the size of her investment.

CHAPTER 25

Returning to the deck, Nancy set the glasses on the table and looked at Enrik expectantly. He cleared his throat and pointed out the stable nature of her low-risk portfolio but added the downside to low-risk was a decrease in maximum growth compared to sustainable maintenance of the funds.

"You probably won't run out of money, especially since you also have an annuity," he stated, " but you could look at purchasing additional higher-risk growth funds to optimize profit to protect against future downturns in the market."

Nancy said, "Maybe I'll look into that. Any suggestions?"

"I have three favorites. The initial buy-in of all three is less than $100,000. An investment of $100,000 would provide an estimated 13-15% rate of return but on higher risk options."

"The advantage of betting on those growth shares would provide greater wealth. I'm not sure I see the value in increasing my risk." She responded.

"Over the course of the next five years, that would cover any negative inflation or market value decrease of your existing portfolio and assure your ability to enjoy the lifestyle you have become accustomed to." He smiled. "I'll write down the websites of the three funds I recommend. You can research them and let me know what you think. We can go from there if you wish me to invest the money for you." He offered.

Watching him print the names and websites of the growth funds, Nancy thanked him for taking the time to assist with her portfolio. Enrik assured her that it was what he did when he wasn't teaching and that he enjoyed helping others to manage their incomes most effectively.

"So, did Hilda invest her $100,000 in growth funds, too?' She asked.

Startled, he frowned at her for a moment. Relaxing, he admitted that he and Hilda had several discussions related to investments but that conversations between his clients were confidential. "Just like our discussion today, I wouldn't share your confidences with others," he said.

"So, Hilda was a client, though?" She asked.

"I didn't say that she was. I merely stated that my consultant discussions are confidential." He corrected her, frowning.

"What exactly were you discussing?" she asked, "Did you take the money her daughter says is missing from her account?"

"I fail to see what concern it is of yours." He responded, pushing his chair back and standing up from the table, preparing to leave.

Thinking quickly, Nancy decided to suggest that Hilda told her that she had given the money to Enrik to invest. "There is no need for you to get agitated. Hilda told me about a new venture that she had invested $100,000 into, and I wondered if you had introduced her to that opportunity. That's all," she responded.

"I find it hard to believe that Hilda shared her investment in her new venture with you or anyone else for that matter. " Enrik appeared to become increasingly annoyed.

At that, Nancy stood up from her chair and, standing across from him, stated, "You know what I find hard to believe?" Nancy asked, "I find it hard to believe that Hilda is dead under suspicious circumstances and $100,000 of her savings is missing! No one close to her knows where it went!"

Enrik, extremely irate, demanded, "What are you implying, Nancy?" Looking at her incredulously, "That I tricked her out of her money and then murdered her by setting fire to her mattress in the hope that she would die of smoke inhalation?"

Raising her chin, she lied to see his response, "She told me she gave you the money."

"I very much doubt that, Nancy." Squinting at her, after a moment, he quietly asked, "Was the object of the meeting to discuss your investments and having dinner with me merely a ploy to find out if I was involved in Hilda's death?"

She looked at him defiantly. Shaking his head at her, he turned to leave. "You are playing a dangerous game, Nancy. Watch your back," He warned as he walked from her yard,

"Chasing murderers is not for the faint at heart. You could be the next victim."

Nancy watched him leave and dropped back into her chair, wondering if that was a threat or a promise. She found it difficult to believe the charming dinner companion of last night was warning her to cease her pursuit of justice for Hilda. The implied threat was scary, too.

Leaning back into the chair, she sighed, acknowledging that her ruse didn't go well. She realized she needed to tell Harry about their conversation and Enrik's threat. It was Sunday, and she knew he probably wouldn't be at the station. Her next thought was to call her daughter and ask for his cell number. She was confident Ann had her ex-husband's personal contact information. After all, he had called Ann to pressure Nancy to quit prying into Hilda's death.

Entering Ann's name into her cell, it rang only twice before Ann picked up. "Hi, Mother. Are you calling to tell me you found the killer," Ann joked.

"Ann, don't be flip," she said, "but I might have, so I need Harry's cell number."

"You can't be serious. Tell me you are joking, Mother!" Ann responded, worried, she began to pace. "What have you done? You know he will be livid to hear from you on his day off, especially any discussion related to Hilda's death!"

Nancy agreed, "I realize that, but it is Sunday, he is not at the office, and I need to get in touch with him."

"Mother, it is his only day off, and you have been a royal pain in the neck for him. Can't it wait until Monday?" Ann asked.

"I know it won't make him happy. But I think I have discovered the murderer," Nancy answered, recognizing a need for her daughter to cooperate and give her his number. She added, "But I've been threatened."

"What do you mean you've been threatened?" Ann replied, alarmed. "What kind of threat?"

"I was warned that I might be the next victim," Nancy shared.

"Who threatened you and why?" she asked, even more alarmed.

Nancy had hoped she wasn't going to ask that question. It was impossible to answer without intimidating herself.

"There was $100,000 missing from Hilda's savings account, and I think I know who took it and then murdered Hilda. I need to share that information with Harry." Nancy dodged the question.

"Really, Mother, he will probably still be angry with you. It's his golf day with his club members." She tried to discourage Nancy. "You can try his cell, but he will remind you that he told you to stay away from Hilda's case."

She sent Harry's contact information to Nancy's phone and pleaded with her to stay out of Harry's way. "Take care of yourself, Mother. Don't take any chances and listen to Harry for a change!" Ann said, feeling relieved that Harry would know of the threat, in spite of the fact that he would be extremely angry at Nancy.

She hated it when Harry nagged her about her inability to control her mother. As if that were even possible, she thought to herself while hanging up. After disconnecting from Ann, Nancy dialed Harry's number.

He didn't pick up. "Damn," Nancy thought, wondering in the two seconds she had before the voice asking her to leave a message would disconnect if she should hang up. Deciding the importance of the threat made it necessary that she stay on the line.

"Harry, this is Nancy. I need to talk to you about Hilda's missing money." She spoke quickly and left her number before adding, "Don't be mad. Just return my call. You can yell at me later."

Clearing the still-full iced tea glasses from the table, Nancy walked back to the house. Loading the dishwasher, she was tempted to pour herself a small glass of wine to quiet her nerves. While she considered that option, her phone rang. Taking a deep breath, anticipating Harry's anger, she saw the phone screen show it was Bess calling.

She answered, "Bess, I'm glad you called," sounding relieved.

"You sound agitated, Nancy. What's wrong?"

"I questioned Enrik about Hilda's money, and he got angry and stormed off." She said.

"That doesn't seem the act of an innocent man. "What did he say when you questioned him?"

"He stated, in so many words, that it was none of my business and questioned my implication," Nancy responded.

"You mean he thought you accused him of taking her money?" Bess didn't sound surprised.

"Exactly, not only taking her money," grimacing at the phone, she said, "but also killing her!"

"Wow, that must have upset him," Bess responded with a low whistle.

"He was so upset he threatened me!' Nancy said.

"Threatened, what do you mean?" alarmed Bess asked.

"He said I was playing a dangerous game, and I could be next!" Nancy said.

"Geeze, Nancy, that is frightening! What are you going to do?"

Nancy said, "I left a message on Harry's phone. Ann thinks he might be golfing, though."

Bess suggested she not be left alone and offered to let her stay at her villa. When Nancy refused, she suggested she stay with Ann.

"My daughter wouldn't appreciate me being bait for a killer and requesting to stay with her." Nancy laughed, "Never mind, Bess, I will be okay on my own."

"Do you want me to come there and stay with you?" Bess continued to urge Nancy not to be alone. "He might hesitate to assault you if there was another witness present."

"I doubt that would make a difference," Nancy laughed again, "Besides, the more I think about it, his comment was more of a warning than a threat. I don't think he is planning to harm me."

"But Nancy, if I were staying with you and something did happen, I could at least call the police or ambulance-which ever was needed!"

"Very generous of you, but no!" Running her hands through her hair, she said, "Please, just quit!"

Bess agreed, exasperated, "Fine!" she said, then changed the subject. "Didn't the assistant director, Marcy, say that the women liked Enrik and his investment suggestions while the guys didn't trust him?"

Nancy explained that Marcy had mentioned how he seemed to impress the women and upset the men. She explained to Bess that Marcy seemed to feel that the men were just jealous of the female attention he was getting.

Some of the men appeared to have followed Enrik's suggestions at the monthly meetings and seemed to be rewarded with significant gains. She said that SueLi seemed to enjoy his company and shared that her neighboring couple, Gary and David, recommended Enrik after they followed his advice.

Nancy wondered aloud, "Bess, do you think Enrik had taken any of the other women investors to his favorite restaurant and took them dancing?"

"Wait, you danced with him?" Bess was incredulous. "You thought he might have murdered one of your best friends, and you danced with the man? Geeze, Nancy, what were you thinking?"

"I wasn't thinking about Hilda at the time. I was thinking about how pleasant the music was and how much I was enjoying my martini. I was thinking how long it had been since I had an opportunity to dance." Sighing, "It wasn't just the dancing. It was more about being held like I was precious. I told you the man is a charmer."

"Do you really think he has charmed others in order to fleece them?" Bess responded.

Enrik's activities with other women, according to her conversation with Marcy, didn't seem out of line. Nancy was trying to remember exactly what she said about his relationship with the Stock Club members. She recalled that Marcy was vague but did say the women found him knowledgeable. Nancy smiled at that. She bet they replaced charming with that term.

Nancy decided she needed to talk to SueLi again to check on her opinion of him. Perhaps he tried to steal money from her, too. "I'm not sure about anything regarding Enrik at this moment, but I think I should visit SueLi Smith and ask her what she thinks of him. Want to come along?"

Nancy could hear Bess's excited response through the phone, "I wouldn't miss it for the world," she said, "let me know when you arrange to meet, and you can pick me up on the way over there."

"I will, but I will tell her I'm bringing you to see her amazing flowers. So be ready to be impressed by her flowers. " Hanging up from Bess, she found SueLi's contact information and clicked on her cell phone number.

Answering the third ring, SueLi agreed to show Bess her flowering garden and invited them to stay for tea after viewing the flowers. They planned to meet in her front garden in a half hour. Nancy notified Bess she would stop by to pick her up in 20 minutes.

Arriving at SueLi's villa, they could see SueLi trimming some wilting blossoms from her hydrangeas, "You caught me trying to tidy up before you got here," she laughed. Bess didn't have to pretend to be impressed with the array of flowering bushes of multi-colored flowers. "SueLi, your display of flowers takes my breath away. I had no idea you were an expert gardener. Did you take a master gardener course or something?"

SueLi shook her head, "Merely learned by my mistakes, setting plants too close together, watering too much or not enough. You might say I learned the hard way."

While they wandered around the yard, with SueLi pointing out various plants and providing amusing narratives about their origin and her procurement, Nancy waited for an opportunity to discuss Enrik. It wasn't until they had spent a good part of an hour admiring her handiwork that Nancy was able to broach the topic.

Sitting outside on SueLi's deck, with cookies and iced tea offered, she casually mentioned that she had met with Enrik. "By the way, I took your advice and contacted Enrik," Nancy said. "He seemed extremely knowledgeable about investments related to strategies, brokers, and different options."

"He seems to have a comprehensive knowledge of finances, but he should; after all, he teaches finance at the university." SueLi agreed.

"His recommendations of growth options seem sound. Did he suggest any particular stocks for you to purchase?" Nancy asked.

"He presented several and provided me with the pros and cons of each stock purchase. They were a bit higher risk than I was initially comfortable with, but after our discussion, I chose one of his recommended growth groups." SueLi nodded.

"I'm thinking about moving some of my current low-risk investment money into a growth fund, and he recommended $100,000. He said that even a five-year investment at my age now would provide a guard against inflation ten years from now." Nancy shared.

"He told me the same thing," SueLi said. "$100,000 felt like a large sum to move, but the spreadsheet showed a good five-year return with a move to safer investments later."

She further explained that the men at the stock club thought it was risky to invest now at our age to hedge against future inflation, but Enrik disagreed with them. She said that several of the men argued with Enrik about the accuracy of his spreadsheet math, but he defended his stance.

"Wow," Bess said, "I need to know more about this. Did you give him the money to invest, or did he recommend a broker?"

"It was wonderful. Enrik handled it all. I just had the bank transfer the money to his firm, no problem at all." SueLi said.

"How much of a profit have your statements shown?" Nancy asked.

"Well, I haven't gotten a statement yet. The statements are posted every three months, and I only invested with his firm about a month ago."

"I guess your husband liked the proposal as well, or did he need convincing like the other members of the club?" Bess asked.

"Since his stroke, he hasn't been very involved in decision-making. He just doesn't seem to want to be bothered trying to figure things out." SueLi sighed.

"So sorry to hear that. It must be hard having to be responsible for all the planning." Nancy was able to relate, "It's been a real learning curve for me since Ned passed."

"That's why I appreciated Enrik. He took his time discussing my options, brought me gardening magazines, and even that rose bush over there was a gift from him. He just made me feel special again. Like he enjoyed visiting with me, and he really seemed to like my flower garden." She said, sighing again.

They sat in silence for a moment until Bess reminded Nancy that she needed to be home as she expected a delivery. Nancy thanked SueLi for the tour of her garden and the iced tea as they took their leave.

Once in the car, Bess shared her pleasure in viewing the garden but inquired of Nancy what she thought of the investment conversation. "I think Enrik knew exactly how to get SueLi to invest in his firm, and I bet he talked Hilda into the same thing," she admitted quietly. She remembered her conversation with Marcy, too. "As a matter of fact, he may have a gambling problem," Nancy said.

"What are you talking about?" Bess questioned.

Nancy explained that when she was asking about Enrik at the community office, Marcy had hinted at a gambling problem, saying that he had paid off his debt there before leaving town last month.

CHAPTER 26

Having dropped Bess off at her villa, Nancy was pulling into her drive when her phone rang. Noting it was Harry, she answered quickly. "Hello, Harry. Thanks for returning my call."

"It's Sunday, Nancy. Obviously, whatever you have your nose into now can't wait until a workday when I am in my office. Of course, I will return your call." She could tell by his tone that he was being sarcastic.

"Harry, I think I know who murdered Hilda. He had motive and opportunity. I'm not sure about the means part, tho'." She responded.

Silence, followed by a long breath, exhaled loudly, "Nancy, I told you to leave this case alone. You are interfering with an ongoing investigation. I could arrest you for that."

"But I'm sure he conned Hilda out of $100,000. She figured out the scheme and wanted her money back and threatened to report him, so he killed her." Nancy spoke rapidly before Harry could interrupt her.

Sighing, "Who is this guy, and what makes you think he swindled Hilda out of her money?" he asked, resigned to her continued involvement but worried about her interference.

"His name is Enrik Agani. I'm sure he conned Hilda because he's been charming other vulnerable women in the community. They succumb to his charms and find themselves giving him $100,000 to invest for them in risky growth funds." Again, speaking rapidly.

She shared what SueLI had told her about the frosty reception of his investment insights by the community's stock club. Explaining that Enrik recommended higher-risk investments for a short period to assure adequate protection against inflation as they aged.

"Most of the male members found it poor advice." She said, informing him of how Enrik charmed and convinced his female potential investors. Nancy also shared her suspicions that he had a gambling problem.

"Don't you think all those circumstances aren't somewhat suspicious?" She asked, looking at her phone as if she expected to see him nodding at her.

"I'm not going to agree to that, but I am interested in who the vulnerable women are," Harry asked, thinking he might need to ask them some questions.

"I'll text you SueLi Smith's contact information, but he follows a pattern. The last time I met with Enrik, he suggested I invest in risky growth groups with his firm, too." She said, relieved that he was taking her seriously.

"Wait, you met with him more than once? Was that before or after you suspected that he was a murderer?" Harry didn't try to hide his irritation. "Are you insane, meeting and setting up a possible murderer?"

"Well, we weren't ever alone until we met today at my house. He came by to recommend financial investments. That's when I knew he must've been responsible for Hilda's death."

"You knew because he offered you financial advice?" Again, frustration was noticeable in the tone of his voice.

He seemed to be focusing on the wrong thing. "It wasn't that, Harry. I knew after he threatened me." Nancy was getting impatient, as it didn't seem that Harry was following her conversation very well. He seemed to be focusing on the wrong thing.

"What the hell, Nancy? What do you mean he threatened you?" He shouted over the phone.

"Maybe it wasn't a threat after all, merely a warning." She answered thoughtfully in an attempt to calm him. "After I confronted him about stealing Hilda's money, he said I was playing a dangerous game and that I could possibly be next."

"You accused him of being a thief and a murderer? What were you thinking?" His quiet question worried Nancy more than his shouting. "Do you realize the danger you could be facing?"

Trying to sound reasonable, she replied, "Of course I do; that's why I called you."

"And what do you expect me to do?" he asked, evidently frustrated.

"Obviously, question him." She suggested, wondering why she had to think of everything.

"Based on what, Nancy? Suspicion of scamming old ladies out of their money? Making bad bets at the casino, and suspicion of murdering one of his clients to continue losing money at the casino?" he sounded angry again, "Do you have any proof that he is a scam artist, not merely a guy helping the older ladies of his community to be more financially stable as they age?"

Nancy didn't have an answer for that. She could tell Harry was exasperated by the whole conversation. He needed proof, she suggested, "I could help. Maybe ask his other clients about their encounters with him?"

"Are you out of your mind!" His voice rose to a new level, as well as sounding like a growl. "He has already threatened you. If you start poking around for evidence, you are setting yourself up as a target."

"I see what you mean, so what do you suggest I do to help you?" She asked.

"Help me by lying low, stay home, and don't stir up any more trouble for me to clean up. I'll give this guy a call in the morning and follow up on your assumptions, Nancy, but you need to quit this nonsense."

She heard the real concern in Harry's voice and realized that part of his anger was driven by his care for her safety. She agreed to stay out of his way, and he ended the call. Nancy sighed as she moved to the kitchen to make a cup of tea, saw the wine bottle from her daughter's previous visit, and reached for a wine glass instead of a teacup.

CHAPTER 27

The next morning, sitting in front of his computer, Harry had pulled up Enrik's data. The guy had an interesting life: a vintner in Croatia, a student at Oxford, and then Harvard Business School. He was now living in Carpio and teaching at UC Davis in Santa Barbara. Divorced twenty years ago, one son, and naturalized as a citizen ten years ago. No record or outstanding warrants. Nothing sinister there. He checked the address, added Enrik's cell number to his GPS, and headed to his car. He thought a home visit was less formal than asking him to the precinct for casual questioning regarding his relationship with Hilda.

Harry clicked on Enrik's number as he started the car, and his car audio beeped out the digits and the ring tones. Enrik picked up on the third ring, and Harry introduced himself, explaining that he would be in the neighborhood in twenty minutes and would like to stop by his villa with some questions if it would be convenient.

"To what do I owe this visit?" Enrik asked, sounding somewhat suspicious.

"We are investigating Hilda Hanover's death and talking to all her contacts. I'd like to stop by your home for a quick informal chat, that's all."

"I did not know Hilda well, but of course, stop by. I will be home most of the morning," he responded, sounding more comfortable.

"The conversation shouldn't take long. Thanks for agreeing to meet." Harry ended the call, thinking what a pain in the ass following up on Nancy's leads was. However, he did worry about her safety.

Harry arrived at Enrik's villa, taking note of the formal landscaping, detailed with few flowers but several different configurations of bushes and trees. Enrik opened the door before Harry rang the bell, obviously anxious about a visit from a detective.

He re-introduced himself and showed him his badge, "Thanks again for taking the time to meet." Harry began the conversation.

Enrik nodded, "Of course." and invited him into a well-appointed living area with a centerpiece stone fireplace surrounded by sleek and modern furnishings. Harry sat in a beige leather recliner while Enrik stood by a library table and reached for his coffee cup.

He asked, "How can I help you, Detective?"

"I understand Hilda was a client of yours?" Harry's comment was more of a question than a statement.

"I'm not sure you could call her a client; I did not have a formal arrangement with her."

"No contracts were signed. Is that what you mean?" Harry nodded in agreement.

"There was no need for signatures or a contract," Enrik responded.

"So she didn't move her investments to your firm?" Harry asked.

Again, Enrik, shaking his head, said, "I repeat that she was not a client. I have several clients within this community, but she was not one of them."

Harry pretended to be confused, "What was your business with her, then."

He scowled at Harry for a minute, then responded, "My business affairs are strictly confidential, and it is important that I do not share my conversations or client's information with others unless instructed to do so."

Harry sighed loudly, "Look, Enrik, I'm just trying to find out who would benefit from Hilda's death."

Enrik saw that Harry was sincere, "I think you should talk to Hilda's daughter; she has a power of attorney, and if I had any financial responsibility to Hilda, it would now be owed to her estate," he explained, attempting to be more cooperative.

"I didn't think you were being obstructive, Enrik. It seems that there is talk of you being the favorite of the women in the community and that the men aren't so keen on your investment strategy."

"That is particularly true, but I have spoken to several of those who previously questioned the validity of my recommendations but are now owners of that growth fund." Enrik shrugged.

"So you deny that you were scamming the vulnerable women of the community.?" Harry was blunt.

Laughing, Enrik asked, "That is a ridiculous accusation. I would give you a list of my clients, and they would tell you I am not cheating them. I can't share my contacts without their permission, and I wouldn't like to raise unscrupulous business suspicions related to a police investigation."

"I could always get a court order," Harry replied. Enrik stopped laughing and again scowled at Harry.

"What would you think if I shared that people have seen you paying large gambling debts at the casino?" Harry spoke again.

Still scowling, Enrik responded, his accent becoming more noticeable, "I would think you were very astute, but they were not my debts. I think it is foolish to bet on horses and teams or feed money into casino machines. I don't gamble. I did pay a large debt off at the polo field and casino for a client who didn't want his wife to know about the loss." He added, "It is a bad thing to deceive someone you love."

"Will the bookies at the polo field and sports bar or the casino cashiers confirm you are not a gambler?" brows raised; Harry looked at Enrik.

"First, you question my intent to meet with Hilda, accusing me of stealing money and planning her demise, then scamming vulnerable old women, as well as gambling with others' money. Now, you imply I am a liar. Where are these accusations coming from?" Wrinkled brow and scowl were evidence of his increasing frustration with Harry's questions. "I explained we are talking to all Hilda's contacts. I ask questions that I don't know the answers to and reinforce the answers to the questions we think we know. " Harry tried to reassure him. He did have to consider Nancy's accusation. "One last question: did you threaten Nancy Drouillard yesterday?"

Enrik scoffed, "Ahh, this is where all these questions are coming from. I did not threaten her. I warned her that she could be in danger. It was an attempt to dissuade her from setting up dates with other suspected murderers."

"She felt threatened, nonetheless," Harry responded.

"Well, she might have misinterpreted my words, as I was upset by her allegations. She had misrepresented herself. I felt set up and betrayed." Enrik shook his head, "I understand that she is seeking justice for her friend, but besmirching one's reputation is unacceptable. She is a difficult woman to understand." He shook his head at the detective.

Sighing loudly, "I will have another talk with Nancy. She has been informed numerous times to cease and desist. I regret that she involved you in her private investigation. She is persistent if nothing else."

Enrik smiled at that, "She had me fooled. It is not a bad thing that she wishes to find justice or her friend, tho'." He added.

Harry said, "She owes you an apology. I will speak to Hilda's daughter for the answers to my questions about your relation to Hilda's relationship status."

Harry got up from the chair to leave, and Enrik walked with him to the door, "Thanks for your time, Enrik,"

"I appreciated the opportunity to explain my involvement in your investigation," Enrik replied as Harry left.

Enrik closed the door, thinking about Nancy. She had that detective upset, but he had to admit that she had done her research related to his possible motive. Maybe I need to spend more time with her and find out why she is interfering with the police investigation. She is a power to be reckoned with, but one has to admire her spunk. Besides, she was an interesting companion and danced well. He kind of liked the feel of her in his arms. As he walked to the kitchen to grab an apple, he thought he needed a plan.

As he left Enrik's villa, Harry was furious with Nancy. He was still angry as he turned into the In and Out Burger Drive-Thru. Ordering a burger and fries, he thought hard about a shake, too. Surrendering to the urge, he added a chocolate one to his order. It was a good thing he was on duty; otherwise, he'd be heading to his usual dive bar.

Paying at the pickup window, Harry waited for his order. Rubbing the back of his neck, he was sure that his ex-mother-in-law was going to be the death of him, yet probably liver disease due to extreme alcohol consumption.

CHAPTER 28

The fact that Hilda was gone from her life weighed heavy on Nancy's heart as she hurried to the last meeting before the next day's memorial. Hilda was always a catalyst for fun and a magnet for gathering an interesting and entertaining group of residents. Sighing, Nancy was grateful to be included, especially after Ned died. At least she would be able to share her suspicions of who was responsible for taking her mother's money with Lisa. Harry didn't say anything about not letting Lisa know about Erik's scheme, so she felt comfortable letting Lisa know after the memorial meeting.

Nancy entered the Cup and Vine to see that Lisa was already there, sitting with the event planner from the clubhouse where the memorial was to take place.

As Nancy approached, she saw her pat Lisa's hand and heard her, "No worries, dear, it will be simple and lovely. Hilda would have been pleased."

Lisa nodded, thanked the woman as she left, and turned to Nancy, "I can't wait for this to be over. So many little details to finalize and so emotional."

"I know it is always so hard to focus on remembering the memorial details when one is experiencing grief." Nancy responded, "At least I have some positive news. I think I know who has Hilda's money."

Lisa looked surprised as Nancy continued, " I believe she invested it with Enrick Agani, a financial advisor."

Lisa smiled wryly, "She didn't exactly invest the $100,000. She gave it to Enrik, expecting him to make a transatlantic transfer to some scam artist she had been conversing with in Argentina!"

Shocked, Nancy asked, "She gave the money to Enrik to invest with a man in Argentina? Why involve Enrik?"

"According to Enrik, she heard him speak at one of the investment clubs she attended regularly." Lisa continued explaining, "Since he spoke with an accent and was a financial advisor, he said she knew he would know how to make a transatlantic transfer of that sum without the difficulty she would've had. She explained the investment opportunity to him and her plan to meet the man in question next month."

"So Enrik took the money?" Nancy asked. "Did he invest it?"

Lisa explained that Hilda had already withdrawn the money from her account and had a cashier's check ready for him when they met to discuss what Enrik thought was her portfolio. He worried about her keeping the check in her underwear drawer, so he took it to keep in his safe until they could discuss the purpose of the transfer.

"She agreed to give Enrik the cashier's check for $100,000, based upon hearing his financial advisor pitch?" Nancy asked, amazed.

"He told me he acted interested in the transaction and might want to get in on the deal if it was legit. Mother agreed to him keeping the check in his safe until he investigated the Argentinian's investment plan."

Nancy, still doubting Enrik's honesty, asked, "Was the plan legit?"

"Enrik got called to Croatia the next day due to a family member's death and explained that he would continue to look into her investment when he returned."

There were complications, and he was gone longer than planned, Lisa explained. "He hadn't been able to find any information regarding the Argentina man she was conversing with and, on his return, notified mother to end her relationship."

Rolling her eyes in exasperation, Lisa said, "Then she died before he could return the money!"

Nancy saw the other members of the memorial committee arriving and stopping to order at the counter, "One last question," she said, "When did he return the money to you?"

Waving to the others, Lisa responded, "The day after Mother died."

Nancy leaned back into her chair, thinking that Enrik wouldn't have returned the money if he had killed Hilda-who would've known? Closing her eyes, she envisioned the nasty scene in her garden when she accused him of scamming and killing Hilda and shuddered.

Bess sat beside her and, noticing the shudder, looked closely at Nancy and asked if she was cold. Shaking her head, Nancy denied being chilled. The other ladies explained the reason for their lateness. It seemed that the memorial flowers ordered for the table centerpieces were the wrong colors, and the vases would be too tall to talk over, so they had to decide on an entirely different arrangement that all three of them could agree upon.

The decisions were time-consuming, and they apologized for being late. Lisa gave Nancy a nod and smiled, explaining that the service was taken care of by the minister, and she had already finalized the seating arrangements and confirmed the menu selections that they had chosen. Bess shared a copy of the service program for final approval, and each member had a role in welcoming attendees and handing out the programs.

Lisa once again took care of the coffee bar tab, having tearfully thanked each of them for their concern and devotion to her mother. They all walked out together, and Bess noted that Nancy seemed distracted. "What's on your mind, Nancy?" She asked once the others left to walk to their villas.

"Well, it appears I made a terrible mistake and am not sure how to rectify it." Hand supporting her forehead, she sighed. "I need to call Harry before he talks to Enrik."

"Why? If Enrik threatened you, Harry needs to warn him off!" Bess said. Nancy asked her to walk to her villa while she recounted her conversation with Lisa. She finished an abbreviated version as they approached Nancy's driveway. "You have got to be kidding me, Nancy!" Shaking her head in disbelief, "What a mess. No wonder Enrik was so angry, and Harry is going to be livid if he met with Enrik."

"I know. Enrik will be even angrier if he's been questioned by Harry." Nancy hung her head, trying to think straight.

"I have a hair appointment in twenty minutes, but if you want me to stay and help you figure all this out, I can reschedule." Bess offered.

"No, no, please don't cancel!" Nancy answered, "I need to be alone to sort this mess out." They hugged and parted ways.

"It will all work out, Nancy; try not to stress," Bess shouted from the driveway across the street, waving a thumbs up at her.

Entering her house, Nancy wondered how to approach Enrik; knowing that she had been wrong to accuse him of cheating Hilda out of her money and implying he was responsible for causing her death was inexcusable. How was she to recover from that? She laughed humorlessly at the idea of calling him up to say she was sorry. She lured him into a situation that led to questioning his integrity. Entirely basing his guilt on conjecture on her part was irresponsible.

"No problem, Nancy. Most of us, at one time or another, have found ourselves accusing the wrong person of theft and murder. Happens to the best of us; all is forgiven." Nancy said in a gruff accented voice, talking to herself. As if that conversation would ever happen, she thought, shaking her head.

CHAPTER 29

Thinking about calling Enrik, Nancy looked for her phone, realizing she had left it in her purse. Retrieving it, she noted a missed call notation. There was a voicemail. Clicking on play, she heard, "Nancy, this is Harry. I would like to see you in my office at your earliest convenience. Please call the desk sergeant and set up an appointment."

Frowning, she thought his message was rather abrupt. Her hope was that he had found the real murderer and wanted to share with her rather than chastise her for implicating Enrik. Doubtful about the outcome, she knew the sooner they met, the better she would feel about her mistake. She called the precinct and set up an appointment to meet with Harry in an hour. She did a quick touch-up of her lipstick, brushed her hair, and headed for the garage and her car.

Arriving at Harry's downtown station, Nancy was escorted to a chair outside his office and assured he would be with her shortly. While waiting, she tried to think up a proper apology for involving him in her suspicions and threats from Enrik. She held out hope that Harry hadn't contacted Enrik yet. When he opened the door of his office and gestured for her to enter, that hope was dashed.

"Thank you for responding so quickly. I suppose you know why I asked you to meet at my office," Harry said.

"Um, I set up an appointment as soon as I heard your message. As to why I was summoned to your office, I am not certain, but I'm sure you will be sharing that with me," she responded pleasantly, smiling at him.

"Nancy, this is a serious matter. I have been to see Enrik, and although he was polite, he was annoyed at your suspicions and denied threatening you. He insists you set him up and then accused him of theft and murder."

He watched her expression, frowning at her effort to appear contrite. "Involving the police could result in you being sued for libel for false accusation. As I have consistently restated, interfering in a police investigation is a criminal offense, as you well know. I am not going to ask you again, Nancy; you need to stop playing amateur detective and let us do our job."

"I was just trying to help!" Defiantly raising her chin, she said, "I should have talked with Lisa before confronting Enrik. I didn't know that he had already met with her and given the money back."

Harry asked, "He gave the money back? Did she tell you why he had taken Hilda's money in the first place?"

Nancy repeated the conversation she had with Lisa before the memorial meeting, explaining Enrik's innocent involvement.

"That clears up a few things and completely exonerates Enrik. It also demonstrates why you need to stop interfering with this investigation. Also, I believe you owe Enrik an explanation and an apology." Harry said.

"Hilda was a dear friend. I didn't mean to cause problems. I just felt compelled to assist in finding her murderer, and it seemed like it was a task that needed to be done." Tears were forming as Nancy spoke.

"But it isn't your task to do; it's mine and the departments." Harry stated, still angry, "I understand that it is painful to lose a friend. I'm sorry you lost Hilda. If you want to do something useful, help with the memorial, support her daughter and her other friends within the community." He suggested in a kinder voice. She nodded in his direction. "No more interfering," he added in a much sterner tone.

Contrite, Nancy nodded again, "I get it; you want me to stay out of your way. I can do that," she agreed.

"No, I want you completely out of the picture." He stated, looking directly at her.

"Can you do that?"

Sighing, Nancy agreed. She stood up to leave, and Harry came around his desk, "I appreciate your cooperation in this," he said as he escorted her to the door.

As Nancy drove home, she replayed Harry's conversation about meeting with Enrik. The fact that Enrik shared being manipulated by her was a clue that his anger hadn't abated. She still hadn't any idea of how to mend that fence as she turned into her street and saw her daughter's car parked in front of her house.

"Damn! Harry, why did you have to get her involved again?" she said to herself as she pulled into the garage. Ann was sitting at the snack bar, with a glass of wine at her elbow, leafing through the latest AARP magazine in the kitchen.

"Wow, what a surprise," Nancy said ironically, slamming her purse on the snack bar. "I can only guess why you are here."

Ann turned to her, "Mother, I'm seriously concerned about you. First, you share that your life has been threatened, then Harry calls me to say he may have to kill you himself if you don't stop interfering with his investigation."

"Well, you can rest assured that he won't kill me as I have just returned unscathed after meeting him at his office."

Relieved but not reassured, Ann said, "This is not a mystery adventure. There is a murderer out there. You are not protected from being another victim if you poke the wrong person. Harry is really worried about your safety and has frightened me. "

Nancy got a wine glass from the cupboard, reached for the open bottle in front of Ann, and poured a generous portion, "Ann, I have reassured Harry that I understand his concerns and have listened to his threat of being arrested for messing in his investigation" she said, sipping from the glass she added, "Neither of you understands how useless it feels to be able to do nothing to find justice for Hilda."

"Harry's on it, Mother. This is not a Nancy Drew undertaking. This is real life, with a real murderer. Please do what Harry asks."

"I don't really have a choice, do I?" Nancy answered, trying to reassure Ann. She added, "I know that Harry has my best interest in mind; it's hard to feel old and incompetent instead of useful."

"Mother, you never seem incompetent, rather pushy and determined, but never feeble!" Ann smiled.

Nancy sat beside her daughter and took her hand, "I'm sorry for causing you to worry. I didn't mean to give Harry an excuse to nag you. I will listen to him and trust that he will be able to solve the mystery of Hilda's death." Nancy patted the hand she held, "You'll see, I'll be totally out of the picture. Harry will forget I even exist!"

Hugging her mother, "Glad to hear it, Mother." She said she had committed to attending a Girl Scout organizational meeting and needed to be on her way. She finished her wine and slipped her empty glass into the kitchen sink as she hugged Nancy again on her way out the door.

Nancy sat at the snack bar in front of the half-empty wine bottle. Looked at the bottle for a minute, then poured herself another glass. Saddened by the attitude of both her daughter and Harry, she felt dejected. The same way she had felt after her encounter with Todd, the son of her lawyer friend. Nancy realized that she didn't have the same youthful appearance, which was apparent every time she looked in the mirror, but she still had a flexible body, a good memory, and a functioning brain. Yet her own daughter sneered at her wannabe Nancy Drew's deductive reasoning and problem-solving skills.

Shaking her head at her maudlin thoughts, Nancy stood and wandered about the kitchen. She realized she hadn't eaten anything since breakfast, and after several glasses of wine, the evening wouldn't end well if she didn't find something to eat. She found some hummus and carrots to nibble on, still feeling sad and powerless.

Tomorrow was the memorial. She promised Lisa she would be there early. Nothing like a gathering of friends at a memorial to cheer one up. Shaking her head at the thought, she realized that she must've already had too much to drink.

CHAPTER 30

The next morning, Nancy awoke with a nagging headache, feeling like a block of wood exerting pressure on both eyes. A confirmation that she had indeed drank too much wine the night before. A shower would help, but coffee first, she thought. As the kettle steamed to a boil, she ground her coffee beans and prepared her pour-over. As the aroma of beans tickled her senses, she began to feel more awake and less of a headache. Cupping the hot coffee mug in her hands, she sat outside on the deck, breathing the early morning air and feeling the beginning morning warmth that would soon be bathing the deck.

Her thoughts slid easily to the day ahead, Hilda's morning memorial service at the community clubhouse followed by a move to the community supper club, the Bit and Brace, for a light brunch that Lisa and Hilda's good friends arranged. It wasn't going to be pleasant, as she still wondered who had wanted Hilda dead. She hadn't any further clues as to who it could be, either. She sniffed; at least Harry would be glad of that.

Lots of people had the opportunity. Hilda always had someone visiting at her condo, either a committee meeting, or social gatherings on her deck. Probably a third of the community residents have been to her condo for some reason or another. The issue was a lack of possible killers who had a motive; everyone liked Hilda. The other missing factor was who would have the means. Who among the people Hilda knew would she allow to enter her home, who would also know how to weaponize a mattress pad with a cigarette? The answer lies somewhere within those questions, but the quandary is which question would lead to the answer.

She could use the service and brunch to observe Hilda's close friends, looking for possibilities to answer those questions. She wasn't very hopeful, though, having exhausted most of her leads and ruling out most of the guests. As she made her way to the kitchen, frustrated at the lack of suspects, Nancy let her thoughts drift to what to wear. A simple shift and a pair of sandals seemed perfect. After all, it would be a simple service, and she felt understated would be the appropriate appearance. She peeled a banana and ate it on the way to the shower; her stomach was still somewhat queasy from the previous night.

While drying her hair, her cell rang. She saw that Bess was on the line and answered.

"Good morning, Nancy. I was wondering if you wanted to leave early and check in at the Bit and Brace before the service to ensure everything would be timely and that place settings were ready." Bess asked.

"That's a great idea. I planned on walking to the service, so I will meet you there." Nancy responded.

She hurried to find the sandals that coordinated with her dress and grabbed her shoulder bag and a sun hat since she was walking as the day was warming up. She left along the pathway to the clubhouse and supper club. Her thoughts turned to Hilda, how the community wouldn't be the same without her, and how much she would miss her. Hilda's vibrancy and enthusiasm for life added so much to any activity in which she was involved.

Her pre-dinner happy hours were always fun, and many friendships were formed there, as well as a few romances. Nancy sighed as she remembered the evenings she and Ned enjoyed her company. As his muscle weakness and fatigue increased, Hilda made sure he was comfortable and distanced from the more boisterous of the group without treating him as special. She was so kind; what could she have done to inspire someone to murder her?

Seeing Bess ahead of her, Nancy called out and waved. Bess returned the wave and walked toward her. They entered the supper club together and were greeted by the evening hostess.

"Hello Myrtle, up early for the brunch?" Bess asked, noting she usually didn't start work until opening at 4 p.m.

"We thought we'd stop by to see if there were any questions or problems with the brunch plans," Nancy said.

Myrtle nodded to both, "I'm glad you stopped. We are ready here. It should be a lovely memorial luncheon. Don't you ladies worry about a thing." She nodded at them.

"Thanks, we trust it will be fine. You are the pro, after all." Nancy assured her, "We appreciate your attention to detail."

They waved at the staff setting the buffet serving dishes out and left to cross the street to the clubhouse, where the other memorial planners were busy directing guests and handing out programs. Everything appeared to be under control, so Nancy and Bess joined the other guests mingling in the foyer, waiting for the service to start. Nancy noticed her palms were damp as she rubbed them together nervously. Closing her eyes for a minute, she took a deep breath, remembering why she had avoided all funerals and memorials since Ned's death. She felt an enormous sense of grief for the loss of her friend and a flood of sadness as her loss of Ned was momentarily rekindled.

"Nancy, are you all right?" Bess touched her arm, concern evident in her frown.

Opening her eyes, Nancy sadly smiled at Bess's anxious tone, "I'm fine, but the loss of Hilda hurts my heart."

Bess agreed as more community members gathered. Seeing Lisa enter the foyer, Bess nudged Nancy, and they started to head the guests into the clubhouse auditorium. Lisa moved to the front of the hall and spent several minutes shaking the hands of numerous friends of Hilda. As the lights fluttered, everyone took their seats, and a video of Hilda's earlier life with numerous pictures of her in various stages was shown on the screen across from Lisa, sitting in the first row with Ronald and Marcy.

Lisa appeared transfixed at the video and sighed heavily at its end. There was a murmur from the audience as she stood and began to speak. "Thank you all for your attendance here today. Mother would be pleased to have so many of you join us. She so loved this community and called many of you her dearest friends." She smiled at the crowd, her voice quivering and tears forming in her eyes.

"I would be remiss not to mention a special word of heartfelt thanks to the administrative staff here at the community, especially dear Ronald; Mother loved you dearly." She added, smiling at him tearfully. After a few more words of gratitude to several of the support staffers, housekeeping, facilities, and dining were included, Ronald also added to the memories, as did several guests. Bess elbowed Nancy, encouraging her to speak.

Others spoke of their memories, some moving, but most were humorous, and laughter filled the room, dismissing some of the sadness of knowing Hilda wasn't there to reminisce with them. Nancy shared a story of getting lost with Hilda in Santa Barbara, and Bess brought a roar of laughter when she spoke of Hilda's fear of spiders and her actions stumbling into a spider web. Lisa thanked all those who shared and invited all the guests to join her at the Bit and Brace for brunch.

As she walked across the street, Nancy caught sight of Enrik in conversation with SueLi Smith as they walked toward the restaurant. She hesitated momentarily as Bess, following her and busy talking to one of the male community members, bumped into her. They tripped, causing the man next to Bess to grab her to keep her from falling. Startled, Bess let out a screech, calling attention to the three of them. As the exiting crowd turned to see the cause of the disturbance, Nancy saw Enrik observing the confusion. Her chin raised defensively, and she managed to look away just as he nodded acknowledgment.

After the three disentangled themselves, Nancy held Bess back from the crowd. "Why aren't we going into the brunch, Nancy? They might run out of the cinnamon rolls before we get a chance to hit the buffet table."

"Bess, I just saw that Enrik is here," Nancy said, "I didn't realize he would show up for the memorial. I'm not sure what to do." She clasped her hands in front of her nervously.

"First of all, why wouldn't you have considered he'd be here? "Bess said, surprised by Nancy's lack of confidence. "After all, you once thought he murdered Hilda. Obviously, it stands to reason they had a relationship!" She shook her head at Nancy's lack of foresight. "Having recognized his reason for being present, your next step should be to apologize." She added.

Nancy thought about her suggestion, knowing that she would eventually have to apologize. She didn't think it was appropriate to broach that subject at the memorial of the woman one has been accused of killing. But then again, she reasoned a quiet, private conversation away from the crowd but near enough to be overheard might decrease her embarrassment and shorten any recriminations from Enrik. She turned to discuss the options with Bess, who was leading her determinately toward the entrance and the buffet.

"So, should I approach him here?" Nancy asked.

Beth joined the buffet line, so Nancy followed. "Why not? He probably wouldn't want to embarrass you in front of this crowd."

Nancy agreed and decided that she was hungry herself. After filling their plates, they sat with six other community members. They shared their sadness over their joint loss, eventually though the attention turned to the current community's planned activities. One of the gentlemen at the table asked Bess if she had signed up for the "Glamping Expedition."

She hadn't heard anything about it and questioned him about the difference between camping and Glamping. He explained that one was rugged, and the other was an exploration of the wilderness with all the comforts of home.

One of the ladies stated that she wouldn't think sleeping in a tent on the ground would be comfortable at all. Then, another woman spoke up and said that Marcy, the assistant director, oversaw the activity. She assured her that before she agreed to sign up, she had ordered mattress pads that fit the cots. "She said they would be part of the activity package, as well as a wide array of luxurious lodging solutions for those attending."

Bess asked about the food, remembering that at Girl Scout campouts, everything had a smoky flavor that she found distasteful. The gentleman who started the conversation added that Marcy hired a chef to prepare their meals, and he had a great menu planned. Turning toward Bess, he encouraged her to check if any spaces were open. He nudged her arm, "It would be a hoot to have you along, Bess." She admitted she didn't much like camping, but smiling at him, she said glamping might be more her style. Nancy was surprised at Bess's interest in glamping as she always avoided any strenuous outdoor activity.

Watching her talking with Glen, the glamper, Nancy smiled knowingly. Bess was probably more interested in him than an excursion into the wilderness. Her smile failed as she watched Bess and the gentleman flirting, reminding her of the evening she and Enrik enjoyed.

Her gaze searched the room in response, looking for him. At the same time, she found him in a group at the far corner of the room, and he met her gaze. She quickly looked away, embarrassed to be caught. Flustered, she excused herself from the table and walked to the nearest exit. She needed a quiet place to gather her thoughts on what to say to Enrik and overcome her embarrassment while finding the courage to speak to him.

CHAPTER 31

Nancy was unaware that he had watched her leave and followed her through the exit. She walked to the outdoor patio, around the seating area, and down a small path to the shade of a stand of coastal redwoods. Looking up at the majestic limbs, she relaxed as she recognized that, in the scheme of things, her problems in life were minuscule compared to the scope of space and time. Her life was merely a blip in the millennium of the past and the future, and being embarrassed, fearful, resentful, none of those emotions really mattered.

What mattered was the present. She needed to apologize to Enrik and move on. Sighing, Nancy turned to go back to the clubhouse when she saw Enrik watching her from a few feet away. "Oh, you startled me," she said, hand at her heart, "I was coming to look for you, hoping you hadn't left the clubhouse yet."

"I saw you leave and thought you were going home. I felt we needed to talk, so I followed you out here." He spoke.

"I'm glad you did, Enrik. I am so sorry for insulting you; it was unfair, and I am ashamed of my behavior." Nancy walked toward him. Hoping his reaction would be to forgive her.

"I have given my behavior some thought, and yet I don't see how I could have led you to believe that I would cheat and harm Hilda or threaten your welfare." Hands outstretched in a defeated posture, he looked hurt and confused.

Nancy reached for his hand and walked toward the park bench nestled in the trees. "Sit with me for a minute, and I will explain." She said, "It had so little to do with you and was so much my own personal issue."

She explained about her meeting with Todd, how she had been feeling useless and insignificant and thought she could do meaningful work for her old law firm, nothing major, an occasional ad litem case or two. The son of her friend operated the law firm, and he laughed at her idea.

She told Enrik, "His attitude had made me feel like a useless, foolish, old woman." She was embarrassed but felt compelled to share, "On my way home, I felt hurt, but the more I thought about his attitude, the angrier I became. It was at that point I determined that I would no longer merely exist; I would find a purpose."

Looking at Enrik, she raised her chin defiantly, "I promised myself that I would find somewhere my talents could be utilized. When I arrived home, I found that Hilda had died from smoke inhalation, having fallen asleep while smoking in bed. I knew it couldn't be true. The police wouldn't believe me or any of those who knew that Hilda wouldn't smoke in her condo, let alone her bed."

Turning away from Enrik, embarrassed, it was obviously difficult for her to continue, "My observations having been dismissed by the police, I took the opportunity to prove I wasn't just a foolish old woman." Enrik noticed a slight quiver in her voice, "I learned early in my life, while still in law school actually, first they ignore you, then they laugh at you; finally, they fight you, but eventually you win!"

Nancy took a deep breath, "So you see, Enrik, it wasn't about knowing you were guilty. I was determined to find her murderer. I was sure you had a motive, probably an opportunity, so I set you up. "

She looked at him sadly, "I would have accused anyone that even looked at Hilda suspiciously. I needed a fall guy, and it wasn't personal. It was my need to be taken seriously that drove me to accuse and insult you. I am truly sorry."

After a moment of looking at his hands, Enrik raised his eyes to her. Seeing her earnestness, he spoke quietly as he patted her hand, "Thank you for absolving me of guilt. You meant well, I believe." They sat in silence, shoulder to shoulder, for a few minutes when Enrik smiled and said, "So, who is the poor guy you will suspect next?"

Nancy scoffed as she bumped his arm, "You will be relieved to know I am off the case. Harry has promised to arrest me if I don't stop investigating, and my daughter and Bess are on his side. Besides, I haven't any other suspects who have the opportunity, motive, and means." She shrugged, trying to appear contrite.

"Surely there is some poor soul you can falsely accuse," he teased.

She looked at him and said, "Seriously, I am sorry about thinking you were a suspect," her voice caught in her throat. "But Hilda deserved justice, and it didn't seem like anyone was concerned about finding it for her."

She found a tissue in her pocket and dabbed her eyes. "I just wanted to help, to feel like I had something to offer. To be significant." She sniffed.

Looking at her, Enrik could see she was convinced she had failed Hilda. "So, do you feel the defeat of not finding justice for Hilda is a confirmation of your uselessness?" He asked, "I'm worried you will lose your spirit of adventure and passion for making a difference if the detective forces you to give up your quest for Hilda's justice."

She shook her head, "It appears that I am merely a foolish woman on a questionable quest, causing embarrassment and discomfort to others by my actions."

"Nancy, I will forgive you for the insult and aggravation, but only if you don't give up searching for Hilda's murderer and only if you allow me to help." Enrik took her hand in his, "Is that a deal?" He asked.

Nancy, dabbing her eyes, stopped to look at him to see if he was serious, "Are you teasing me, Enrik? I told you that Harry insisted that I quit interfering in his investigation and let him do his work." She shook her head, frowning, "He said he would arrest me, and I think he was serious."

Enrik could see she wasn't happy, "But you still want justice for Hilda. Harry doesn't need to know that we are continuing to look for the killer. When we find whoever did that to Hilda, then you can blame me for getting you back in the investigation," He smiled, eager to engage her in her pursuit of justice.

"I don't know, Enrik," he could see she was wavering, "I have run out of suspects. My daughter and Bess are against my involvement, too. Besides, why do you want to help me after how badly I treated you?"

"I see your earnestness, your need to make sure that Hilda's death is resolved. I admire your commitment and determination. My hope is that with my help and support, you will discover who could be responsible for this crime." He answered.

"It is tempting to take you up on your offer," forehead wrinkled in thought, "but Harry wouldn't like it at all, and my daughter would be mad at me for lying to her and breaking my promise."

Enrik smiled at her, trying to deny the urge to defy them and go after Hilda's murderer. "Maybe Harry would appreciate the help if we find the murderer," he further tempted her, "and your daughter will forgive you. Children usually allow their parents to act against their wishes and act up occasionally." He grinned, moving closer to encourage her.

"Besides, if Harry arrests you, I will post bail!"

Looking at him, lips tight, she responded, "The hell with it, Enrik, let's do it."

"That's what I wanted to hear. Where do we start?"

CHAPTER 32

Standing up from the park bench, Nancy said, "Well, we can't start investigating here, at the memorial." Enrik nodded, "Since I have run out of suspects, let's go back to my villa and review the progress I made so far." She suggested.

Enrik agreed, and they found themselves walking side by side back to the hall. Each is pleased with their own thoughts. Nancy felt her thoughts were finally validated by someone other than Bess and was hopeful that Hilda would have justice.

Enrik was glad to assist Nancy in her pursuit of justice. She had spunk, courage, a strong sense of loyalty, and commitment to those she cared about. He admired that in a person. He couldn't completely kid himself, though; he had hoped to share another dance with her. Distracted by their seeming to match each other's steps, it felt like she belonged in his arms.

As they approached the hall, they saw Lisa and Ronald talking to another couple from the community. Ronald had his arm around Lisa's shoulder, appearing to offer support as she dabbed at her eyes, and the woman reached out to pat her hand. As the other couple left, Ronald kissed her forehead, pulling her against him, and they hugged for a minute or two before he took his leave.

"It appears that Ronald and Lisa are no longer keeping their affection for each other a secret now that Hilda is gone," Nancy observed.

"I was not aware they were an item," Enrik said. "Why was it a secret?"

Expecting an answer, instead, he heard Nancy scream, "Lisa, Watch out!" Turning toward Nancy, she stepped back just as the community van jumped the curb and hit the pole that Lisa had been standing in front of seconds before. Hearing metal scraping metal and Nancy's warning, Ronald turned back, witnessing the van crumble onto the pole, and hurried to Lisa's side.

As Nancy and Enrik ran to the scene, they weren't surprised to see the driver slumped over the steering wheel and airbags activated. Ronald held Lisa, obviously shaken but unhurt. Enrik opened the driver's door to check on the still motionless driver while Nancy, her cell phone already in her hand, dialed 911 for an ambulance.

A group of onlookers poured from the hall, asking questions and crowding them. One of the men tried to keep the group away from the scene when one of the ladies announced that it was the community van against the pole, and the onlookers all moved forward to gawk just as the ambulance, accompanied by the police, arrived.

One of the officers asked for those who did not witness the accident to leave. The other spoke to Lisa and Ronald and eventually came to talk to Nancy and Enrik, who were watching the EMTs remove Marcy from the car and lay her on a stretcher. She was mumbling and complained of her neck and head hurting.

"She'll be bruised and battered tomorrow," one of the EMTs stated," Those airbags might save lives, but they do a number on headaches, especially when one hits an immovable object like a light pole." the second EMT added.

They completed an initial assessment before moving Marcy to the transport vehicle. She was becoming more conscious as they loaded her into the ambulance, and the officer excused herself from Nancy and Enrik to speak to her.

Ronald asked Nancy to stay with Lisa while he checked on Marcy's status. Arriving at the door of the van, Ronald spoke quietly to Marcy. She could be heard begging him not to leave her.

Moments later, Ronald returned to Lisa, telling the officer he would take her home. Nancy retrieved Marcy's purse, briefcase, and broken glasses from the now-deflated airbags and gave the purse and glasses to the EMTs.

A tow truck was arriving as the ambulance left, and the police returned to them with more questions. Enrik answered most of the questions, and Nancy nodded in agreement to his comments. The police said it was evident that somehow the driver lost control of the car. After the officer left, Enrik mentioned to Nancy she was abnormally quiet while being questioned.

"I needed time to process all of this," Nancy agreed she was hesitant to answer the officer's questions.

"I think a stiff drink is in order before we try to sort things out." He said.

Enrik thought she might be in shock, so he suggested they return to the Cup and Vine. She agreed and chose a table in the back corner of the room while Enrik went to the bar to order a couple of bourbons. Returning to Nancy with the drinks, he found her looking through Marcy's briefcase.

"Did you find anything interesting?" he asked, wondering what she was looking for.

"Not yet, just a set of keys, fancy cigarette case, and lighter buried in the zippered compartment," She answered, "She was certainly a busy woman," she noted as she reviewed Marcy's daily planner.

"Why did you keep her briefcase?" He asked.

Nancy stopped looking through the daily planner, sipping her bourbon, "Did you see Marcy's face just before she hit the pole?" She asked. "When I yelled at Lisa, Marcy looked our way."

"I don't recall seeing her at all," frowning, he responded, "I didn't know who the driver was until someone said it was Marcy."

Nancy looked at Enrik, hand on her forehead; she said, "When she turned toward us just before hitting the pole, her face was distorted with rage."

"Rage?" Enrik questioned, looking alarmed.

"I can't get that picture out of my mind," she said, "Her face contorted and framed by the door window." Closing her eyes, she shuddered.

"Are you saying that Marcy purposely attempted to run Lisa down?"

Opening her eyes, confused and sad, "It looked like it to me." she answered, "as frightening as that seems."

"But why?" he asked, still alarmed.

"I don't know why, but maybe I will find something in her briefcase to lead us to that answer."

A quick examination of the briefcase contents didn't reveal a motive for Marcy to want to hurt Lisa. Nancy invited Enrik to her villa to help review the contents more in-depth, and he accepted immediately. Since Nancy had walked, Enrik drove them to her place and parked in the drive.

After walking in the door, she headed to the kitchen to make coffee while he sorted through Marcy's briefcase on the dining table. He set the daily planner aside for Nancy to continue to view while he looked at the remaining contents. There were copies of several emails, invoices, receipts from various sites, and an assortment of ink pens, paper clips, and multi-colored Sharpie markers.

Nancy slipped off her shoes and turned on the light above Enrik's working space, "The coffee will be ready in a few minutes," she said as she left the dining area and headed toward her bedroom. Changing out of her dress and into jeans and a short-sleeved, lightweight sweater, she returned to the kitchen as the coffee finished brewing.

"If I remember correctly, you take a splash of cream in your coffee," Nancy said as she poured two cups.

"Yes, thank you," he agreed as she sat his coffee on the table in front of him. They smiled at each other, both looking forward to unraveling the mystery of Hilda's murder. "Did you find anything of importance that I might have missed?" Nancy asked, blowing on the hot coffee before sipping.

"Maybe," he said, " I believe this small spiral notebook has a list of vendor websites and passwords related to them." He went on to explain that they seemed to be the email sites of various accounts and figured they were all business-related. Nancy joined him at the dining table, starting to tidy up the papers Enrik left strewn about. She attempted to return the contents in the order they were in when they first reviewed them. Most of the invoices appeared to be current and involved the glamping excursion planned for next month. Food, tents, delivery trucks, transport buses, and even fuel expenditures were listed. The rental agreement for the cots and non-off-gassing mattress toppers caught Nancy's eye.

As she tucked that paper into the folder, she reflected on the fact that a non-off-gassing eco-friendly mattress topper would have saved Hilda's life. "Lisa should have spent more time researching the topper she bought her mother," Nancy said, sorting through the papers. "If I could look up the brand Lisa bought, I wonder if I could find a table listing flammable content."

His coffee cup midway to his lips, Enrik hesitated. "That is a great idea. As we don't have her mattress pad, we could check out those on Marcy's list and see what she knew about the danger of flames and toxic content."

Nancy looked skeptical, "Are you thinking she might have known that Hilda's pad was flammable and the materials used in manufacturing would be toxic if exposed to flames?"

"It's worth checking into." He nodded, excited by the task at hand. "Let me have that notebook, and I'll research the mattress pads she was purchasing. It will be my first investigator chore." Reaching eagerly across the table for the notebook.

Nancy grinned at Enrik, enjoying his enthusiasm and use of the word investigator as if they were detectives. "Then hurry home to your computer and find a clue that will give us a motive or means for Marcy as the murderer." She handed the notebook to him as he rose from the table. Walking out the door to leave, he saluted her as she closed the door behind him.

Smiling to herself, she was surprised at how gratifying it felt to have another person engaged fully in her need to find justice for Hilda. Thoughtfully, she frowned, uncertain at the cause of her pleasure at Enrik's enthusiasm. Was it that someone besides her best friend believed in her abilities? Maybe it was just a vindication of her belief in herself that others also believed in her. Shaking her head at the self-indulgent thoughts, she sighed, walking into the kitchen for another cup of coffee, she realized she was hungry.

Having left her half-eaten plate of food at the memorial luncheon table, she wanted something easy to fix. Nothing in the refrigerator appealed to her. Opening the pantry cupboard, she decided on a tuna melt. Adding two jalapeño garlic olives and a healthy dollop of mayonnaise to the tuna, she slit a pita in half. Spreading the tuna mixture on one side and topping it with a slice of cheddar cheese, she browned the pita so the cheese melted. Finding a bag of nacho chips, she sat at the snack bar and nibbled on the sandwich. Focusing on the culinary task helped to concentrate her thoughts.

They centered on Marcy's motive for wanting to injure Lisa. Where did that rage she saw in Marcy outlined in the car window come from? What had Lisa done to her? It was frustrating; there was no specific obvious motive for either action, Hilda's death, or Marcy's attempt to run over Lisa. Maybe the two incidents were connected, she thought. What if the motive for both was the same?

Nancy mulled that over in her mind. Thinking about the motives being connected brought a different level of thinking to the process. Why would the death of both Hilda and her daughter be necessary? What would the murderer gain? Finishing the tuna, she cleaned up the scraps and loaded her plate and utensils in the dishwasher, all the while mentally trying to solve that question.

Leaving the kitchen, Nancy headed to her office whiteboard and erased the grocery list and appointment reminders from last week. She made two headings-one half the board had Hilda, and opposite, she wrote Lisa. That was as far as she got. Stalled, she needed another set of eyes and a fresh set of ears to listen to her new theory. Enrik had just left, so Bess was the next best candidate. Finding her cell phone, she wasn't surprised when Bess answered on the first ring.

"Hi there, Nancy. I just got home and was thinking of calling you to catch up." She said, "I had left the memorial with Bert, the glamping guy, to see his favorite view from the tar pits and missed all the excitement of Marcy's accident.

"Bess, it was no accident."

CHAPTER 33

Nancy hit the speaker button on her phone as she sat at her desk. Staring at the whiteboard, she added, "I'm sure that it was an attempt on Lisa's life, and somehow it is connected to Hilda's death."

"But my neighbor said that Marcy lost control of the van and ran into a pole. She didn't say anything about Lisa. What are you talking about?" Bess asked, her voice rising.

Nancy thought it odd that Lisa's near miss at the light pole wasn't the highlight of the gossip shared with Bess. She remembered the crowd only formed after the loud crash; she and Enrik were the only witnesses to Lisa's dangerous position. Even Ronald had his back to the scene.

"I need to bring you up to speed," Nancy said, "Why don't you come over, and I'll pour us a glass of wine, and we can brainstorm on my whiteboard."

"I can't believe I only got part of the story; I'll be right over." She grabbed her golf cart keys as she hung up.

Nancy dialed the hospital and asked for a status report on Marcy. As she wasn't family, they couldn't share any information, not even if she had been admitted. She couldn't get her head around the fact that Marcy could be a murderer, rubbing her forehead as she stared at the whiteboard.

Walking to the wine rack, she smiled at the bottle of Posti, the Croatian white wine that had been delivered yesterday as a gift from Enrik. Looking for a light red wine, she chose a Zinfandel from the rack, thinking she should chill the Posti so it would be available the next time Enrik was over. She could offer it to him as a gift to make up for the inconvenience she had caused him by accusing him of Hilda's murder, but she decided to keep it and surprise Enrik by serving it at her home.

She was uncorking the wine when that thought caused her to pause. Staring blankly at the wall in front of her, Nancy wondered aloud, "How could a murderer be living among us, working with us, planning glamping trips with us, helping with the planning details for the memorial of the woman she had just murdered the week before?"

Hearing Bess opening the front door, she shook her head in disbelief, thinking it couldn't be Marcy; what motive did she have to murder Hilda and run over Lisa? Hoping Bess would have an answer, she poured two glasses of Zinfandel and greeted Bess. Not wasting time on small talk, Bess asked,

"What's this about Marcy running into a pole with the community van not being an accident?" As she took her glass from Nancy.

"Lisa was standing directly in front of the pole just before I screamed at her to watch out. I saw the van bearing down on her, and Marcy was driving."

"So, everyone agrees on that and also that she lost control." Bess tilted her head at Nancy, expecting a big reveal.

"Marcy's face was contorted in rage, I mean serious anger, her lips were drawn, squinting eyes," Nancy shuddered, "Her intent was clear; she was going to hit Lisa."

"Why would Marcy want to hurt Lisa?" Bess was obviously confused, leaving her wine untouched.

"That's the question both Enrik and I are asking ourselves," Nancy answered.

"Wait, what do you mean, you and Enrik? Did you kiss and make-up?"

"Not exactly," Flustered at her slip in including Enrik, she had to explain, "He followed me out to the garden at the hall and I apologized for getting him involved in the investigation."

"Ah." Intrigued, Bess sat at the bar stool and sipped from her glass, "Tell all."

Nancy explained that she had confessed to Enrik that she had damaged Harry's investigation with her involvement. She shared with him that she had promised both Harry and her daughter, Ann, that she wouldn't be involved in the investigation.

"He could see how hurt and discouraged I was by their demands." Shrugging, "I think he felt sorry for me and offered to help me solve Hilda's mystery in the hopes I wouldn't feel so disheartened and useless." Nancy smiled at the memory of his earnestness; catching herself, she frowned, "But I didn't invite you here to talk about Enrik. If we think Marcy is somehow involved in Hilda's death and Lisa's accident, we need to brainstorm some kind of motive."

Bess sighed, looking disappointed that Enrik and Nancy's Garden meeting discussion was on hold. Before she could object to the abbreviated version of their reconciliation, Nancy suggested they start with what they know about Marcy.

Nancy erased the names on the whiteboard and replaced them with Marcy's name. They realized that neither had much information related to her personal life. They didn't know where she lived or her interests outside of the community campus. Nancy did know she was single and added it to the board, noting that Marcy never spoke of any close relatives or hobbies. She did know her mother was dead.

"When I had lunch with her after Hilda's death, our discussion revolved around her relationship with her mother." Nancy drummed her fingers on the desk, "I believe it was pretty rocky." She added '*Mother issues*' to the short-list on the board.

Bess added, "I know she drinks scotch occasionally. In fact, I have seen Hilda share her private stock with Marcy whenever she joined happy hour on her deck before dinner at the club." She thought for a minute longer, "I saw her smoking on the deck with William, the gentleman who had lost his wife to cancer last year; you remember him?"

"Yes, I remember him. He was always on the deck smoking. I wondered about that since his wife died of lung cancer; she was a smoker, too." Nancy said. "I never saw Marcy smoking. Was she and William an item?"

"Not that I have heard. In fact, I think the few eligible men in the community were too old to spark an interest in her. But I heard her speak of a boyfriend." Nancy remembered that she did speak about a romantic interest at lunch, "She was pleased that he was older and appreciated a career woman like her, unlike the younger men in her life."

Bess remarked. "She seems pretty devoted to Ronald, though, and lots of assistants have crushes on their bosses."

"I've seen them together on many occasions. He didn't seem to be overly attracted to her. Now that you mention it, she seemed pretty dedicated to pleasing him." Nancy said, "Perhaps they were involved but needed to keep their relationship quiet because of their employment in the operation of the community."

Bess nodded as Nancy added 'relationship with boss' followed by a question mark to the slowly growing list, "It wouldn't appear to be proper to the community property owners, at any rate, although the community does love gossip and an office romance would certainly entertain ."

Nancy agreed, recalling the interest each new property owner receives from the members of the community. She eyed the whiteboard's list of bullet points, "I'm just not sure we are on the right track, suspecting Marcy of being involved with Hilda's death. I just don't see a motive."

Bess poured another measure of wine into her glass, "I don't see it either," she said, "I'll have to think about the two incidents being related. She stared at the whiteboard for a few minutes while sipping her wine, "the connection escapes me."

She finally sighed. Looking at her watch, she left her wine glass on Nancy's desk and said, "I gotta run. Bert, my glamping guy, is meeting me for pizza in an hour to try to talk me into glamping with him. I must go home and get glamorous! Ha, did you see what I did there?" She laughed as Nancy shook her head at the silliness.

"Seriously, though, when you meet, bring up the accident and see if he has any personal knowledge about Marcy," Nancy suggested as she saw her to the door and returned to the whiteboard.

Means, motive, and opportunity are all necessary aspects of criminal investigations, Nancy repeated to herself. Means required capabilities, who knew that flammable gel-foam materials would deplete oxygen from a room, leaving occupants unable to breathe. Lisa might have known; after all, she bought the mattress topper. Shaking her head, Nancy sighed; Lisa had an alibi. No other suspect came to mind.

Stymied, she moved on to motive. Again, she couldn't think of anyone who would want Hilda dead. There was still no motive if one looked at Marcy, even given the attack on Lisa that she witnessed at the accident scene. She felt there had to be a connection, but the harder she tried to find it, the more frustrated she became.

Moving on to the final categorical trinity, opportunity. Nancy felt that was the easy part. Anyone in the community who didn't have a witnessed alibi could be a suspect. She rubbed her hand over her eyes; that sure didn't narrow down the suspects.

Looking at the whiteboard again, she felt she was missing something.

Marcy had the means, and she had researched mattress toppers. The opportunity was always there for the staff of the community. What could be a motive? "It would help if I knew more about Marcy," once again, shaking her head at her self-talk. Leaving her office, she saw Marcy's briefcase lying on the floor by the table. Picking it up off the floor to hang on the back of the chair, a set of keys fell out of the outside pocket.

Picking them off the floor, she looked at them and wondered what they unlocked. Bouncing them in her hand, Nancy decided they might be useful. Maybe she could get into Marcy's office just to look around, see if there was anything to provide insight into why she would want Hilda or Lisa dead. It would be a long shot, but after all, Nancy Drew would take up that opportunity.

CHAPTER 34

Nancy grabbed a black windbreaker from the back closet, slipped her phone and the keys into the pocket, and headed for the garage. After pressing the door opener and sliding into the seat of the golf cart, she stepped on the gas pedal. She parked by the side entrance to the clubhouse in the golf cart spaces to remain inconspicuous as she walked to the administration building.

The entrance was locked. She tried the largest key on the keychain and was surprised when she was able to open the door. Surveying the parking lot, she didn't see anyone, so she entered the building feeling unobserved. Passing the receptionist's desk, she found Marcy's door locked as well. Trying a second and then a third key, she was finally able to enter the office.

Once inside, Nancy stood for a moment, getting her bearings. Marcy's office windows faced the administration building employee parking lot, which was empty at this time of night. She found the light switch and clicked on the overhead lights. Blinking as her eyes adjusted to the light, she glanced at Marcy's desk. She noticed that she had a glass desk-top protector with various phone numbers, contact lists, and pictures of cats.

Smiling at the silly cat pictures, she moved the computer to better view a cartoon and noticed a photo barely visible under the computer. Sliding the computer off the picture, she saw a very attractive Ronald smiling at her from what appeared to be a promo headshot. Brows raised in surprise, "Well, hello, Ronald," she addressed the picture, "What are you doing there." Returning the computer to its original spot, she thought it was an unusual spot for a photo of one's boss.

Glancing around the room, Nancy noticed a bookshelf with framed pictures, plaques, awards, and various mementos. Wandering around the office, she stopped at the bookcase. Various trinkets were scattered among the books: a potted cactus, a dried rose, and pictures of her receiving multiple awards. The photos drew her to them. In several pictures, Marcy was accompanied by Ronald, who stood proudly by her side. They all appeared to be given by the corporation that owned the Santa Jose Community property. They must have been a busy team to win so many trophies and awards. Ronald and Marcy stood close together, and as he looked at the camera, she was looking at him, shyly smiling. Looking at Marcy's face in the framed picture, Nancy wondered at their relationship. Marcy was looking admiringly at Ronald. Nodding at the picture, she wondered if there wasn't something between those two.

He was her boss, after all. Maybe she was merely in awe of his leadership skills, evidenced by the award they were receiving. Checking her watch, she thought it was still early enough to check on Lisa. It would give her an excuse to talk to Ronald. Maybe he could shed some light on their relationship, wondering if they were an item before Lisa came into the picture. Perhaps it was just a workplace fling for them both, she thought, as she cocked her head at the picture and then nodded. "Or it could be love," she whispered to herself.

CHAPTER 35

Leaving the administration building, Nancy decided the most judicious step would be to contact Ronald. Maybe he could shed some light on his relationship with Marcy. She'd like clarification of their level of intimacy before Lisa came into the picture. Checking her watch, she thought it was still early enough to call him, using the excuse of checking on Lisa's recovery from the shock of almost being hit by a car. She could hint that from her angle, it almost seemed that Marcy purposefully tried to run over Lisa. His response would help her decide the next step.

Slipping her shoes off as she entered her home, she found Ronald's emergency contact information. Ronald answered the call on the third ring. He reassured her that Lisa was not injured but was having trouble sleeping soundly. It seemed as she rested, Lisa had recurring dreams of the van accident.

"That is not surprising, as it seemed like the van was headed directly at Lisa," Nancy stated. " It must have been horrible for her to feel targeted like that."

Ronald answered that she was quite frightened and was trying to rest and recover from the shock. "I didn't see what happened as my back was turned until I heard your scream." He admitted, "As far as targeting, you can't think Marcy would purposefully want to hurt Lisa, especially on the day of her mother's memorial service, do you." He said.

"Can you think of any reason she would?" Nancy asked, having heard a slight hesitancy in his voice.

"I'm sure she must have lost control of the van. Marcy has been distracted since Hilda's death. She seemed genuinely fond of her, and I think it upset her to find out she had been murdered." He said. "The memorial might have added to her distress."

Thoughtfully, he added, "The glamping trip has been a real challenge too. For over two months, Marcy was extremely busy with all the issues involved with those residents who signed up, all their questions and demands, as well as contracting with suppliers. "

Nancy agreed that Marcy was always in the middle of something whenever she stopped by her office. She asked him about Marcy's condition.

"Have you gotten any updates? Did they admit Marcy to the hospital?" she asked.

"She was discharged from the emergency department after a few hours. They ruled out a concussion." He added,

"They gave her some muscle relaxants for her neck pain from the airbags and sent her home with directions to rest."

"She was very lucky not to have been hurt more seriously," Nancy said. She also informed him that she had retrieved Marcy's briefcase from the van before it was towed.

"I wasn't aware that Marcy smoked; at least I never saw her smoking," Nancy said, "When I grabbed the briefcase, a lighter dropped on the pavement. Putting it back, I noticed a fancy cigarette case." Nancy said.

"I never suspected she smoked," Ronald said, "It's against the corporation's policy to smoke on the community premises."

"She probably didn't smoke while on the community property," Nancy said that Marcy seemed to be a conscientious employee and would respect company policy. She added, "In fact, whenever I met with Marcy in her office, I was always impressed by all her corporate achievement awards displayed on the bookshelves behind her desk.."

"Yes, the corporation appreciates their employees and likes to recognize them when they go above and beyond expectations." She noted a sense of pride in his voice.

She continued, "Actually, I was particularly impressed by the picture of the two of you. It looked like you were presenting her with a framed award of some sort."

"That was special. She was the corporate '*Star on the Rise*' award winner that year."

"It seemed like an impressive award," Nancy said, "Both of you look very happy, a cute couple, too."

Ronald laughed, "I was able to nominate her for the company-wide award for the work she accomplished during our last expansion of villas and condos. She was amazing, staying up late and showing up early. Bringing coffee and baked goods to the contractors in the mornings and picking up sandwiches for lunch."

"She looked very proud. I couldn't help but notice, in that photo, she also seemed to adore you." Nancy said.

Ronald coughed, clearing his throat, "Well, yes, we had a few late-night dinners together, and I am afraid she thought them romantic while I considered them a demonstration of gratitude. She seemed to understand when I explained that it was against company policy for administrative staff to be romantically involved."

"Do you think she continued to have a crush on you, regardless of corporate policy?" Nancy asked. "She seemed pretty determined for you not to leave her when she was being loaded into the ambulance."

He was quiet for a moment, then responded slowly, "She had become more possessive related to my time. I really didn't give it much thought until you mentioned it, but our relationship had changed."

Ronald hesitated before admitting that Marcy would plan late afternoon meetings that kept just the two of them in the office after hours, working on trivial aspects of one of her outing plans. Again, with some hesitation, he admitted to finally brushing her off several times in the last month.

"I didn't want to be disinterested in her projects; they were always well thought out and popular with the residents." He said. "It was that she would wait until almost quitting time before bringing a problem to my attention. I didn't want to down-play the importance of her issues, but they were trivial and would occasionally complicate my evening plans."

"Those behaviors seem to attempt to control your time. Could she possibly be jealous of your evening plans?" Nancy asked. "Did she know of your relationship with Lisa?"

"We didn't discuss personal issues," He said, hesitating for a moment, "But on more than one occasion, she might have heard me call Lisa to explain that I was still at the office and would be late meeting her."

Nancy commented, "Obviously, you have been a great comfort to Lisa since her mother's death. She never mentioned your relationship to the women helping with the memorial, though, or shared how long you had been dating. It had been a while, hadn't it?"

There was a long pause, causing Nancy to wonder if he had hung up when he answered, "We had met several times before about some issues with her mother's condo maintenance requests." Suddenly suspicious, he said, "You seem inordinately interested in my personal life. I'm not sure why you are asking these questions. Lisa and I had nothing to hide, but my status in the community made it uncomfortable for Hilda. It might have appeared that she was receiving special treatment due to our relationship."

"I could see where others might see that as a conflict of interest." Nancy agreed.

He said, "If you must know, after Hilda's death, I found it impossible not to comfort Lisa, and my affectionate display made it obvious to the community that we were more than acquaintances."

"Yes, I remember our previous discussion about your relationship when Bess and I visited your office to discuss housing options. You were hesitant to talk about it then."

"At that time, I wasn't sure how Lisa would react to our relationship becoming part of the narrative surrounding her mother's death." He responded. "But it is obvious we are a couple now," Again, he added, "I repeat, we had nothing to hide."

"There was no mystery to our meeting," he added, "I was in the office with Marcy several months ago discussing the option of providing the residents a glamping experience when Lisa came by. She was upset, thinking her mother was being scammed by some overseas financial set-up."

Following another pause, "I told her there wasn't much we could do as all our members are independent and have the right to do business with anyone if it doesn't affect the community. Lisa left after I gave her the AARP fraud hotline information as a research resource."

Nancy moved the cell phone to her other ear, pressing the start button on the electric tea kettle. She dropped a chocolate mint tea bag in her cup, waiting for the water to boil.

Ronald continued, "I saw Lisa leaving her mother's condo a couple of days later, and I asked if she got her mother's issues straightened out. She seemed distressed, so I offered to buy her a drink and discuss her options." He laughed, "We hardly talked about Hilda. We found we had a lot in common and agreed to meet for a beach hike to the tar pits the next day."

Ronald explained how their relationship blossomed from that meeting, reconstructing the last two months of their relationship. He hinted at Marcy's possible knowledge of their increasing fondness. His tone was almost wistful as if recounting a past romance. She sensed a tone of regret in his remembrance and wondered at the source. After a short pause, taking a deep breath, he added, "I need to check on Lisa."

"Of course," concluding the conversation on a positive note, Nancy said, "I hope Lisa recovers quickly from her encounter and that Marcy will be back to work soon, too." Ending the call, she added, " I also hope that after the police finish their investigation of Hilda's death, you and Lisa will find happiness together. Tell her I'm thinking about her and will be in touch in the next few days."

Realizing she hadn't made her tea, she pressed the kettle's on button again and wandered to the window, not seeing the full moon or the star-studded night. Her thoughts engaged in the previous conversation tumbled over each other. Did Ronald think that Marcy's jealousy caused her to try to run over Lisa? Was his wistfulness due to his belief that she might be capable of murdering Hilda to distance Lisa from the community and him?

Pouring the steaming water into her cup, she decided, "I need to talk to Marcy." Nodding to herself, she thought, Nancy Drew has nothing on me when it comes to deductive reasoning. Looks like I found a motive; we need to confront her,

Nancy phoned Enrik while pacing around the kitchen and shared her thoughts relating Hilda's murder to Marcy's attempt on Lisa's life.

"If you believe that Hilda's murder and Lisa's accident are related, we need to find the connection," Enrik said.

Smiling at the phone, she responded, "I have a plan."

CHAPTER 36

"I know it is getting late," Nancy continued, "Let's do a quick review now, shall we?"

After Enrik agreed, she took a minute to compose her thoughts and started at the beginning of what they knew. She noted they now knew Marcy had the knowledge and the means to have caused Hilda's death. As a frequent visitor to Hilda's happy hour gatherings and a member of the team that helped remove the offensive gel-foam topper from her bed, she also had the opportunity.

"We still don't have a solid motive," Nancy said, "But after the pictures in Marcy's office and talking to Ronald, we might be closer to why Marcy might want Hilda dead and a plausible motive."

"I believe I've established that she was jealous of Lisa's relationship with Ronald. I remember while at lunch, she shared a description of her lover, an older gentleman. She didn't mention him by name, and Ronald didn't state that they were having an affair, as it is against corporate policy, but he hinted at the fact that they shared some intimate times together." Nancy added.

"Yes, but why kill Lisa's mother? Why not just kill Lisa?" Enrik asked.

With a tired, lopsided grin at the phone, "That is the question, isn't it." Nancy responded. "After the conversation with Ronald, I will think about the motives rolling around in my head before going to sleep tonight. Perhaps the answer will be waiting for me when I open my eyes in the morning," she said. "You should do the same. We can compare our nocturnal solutions over breakfast. I make a terrific cheese omelet."

"I will agree to that plan, but only if you come to my villa. I will make breakfast for you. Do you have any particular wants?" he said.

Surprised, smiling at the phone again, Nancy said, "I didn't know you could cook."

"You will be surprised what you don't know about me. Luckily, we will have plenty of time to investigate our knowledge of each other, eh?" He said.

She laughed, "As partners in crime solving, we might find the need for some personal investigation is necessary. Still smiling, she added, "I eat everything offered, so don't worry about my appetite."

"I will see you at my patio around 9 a.m. if that is acceptable for you." Enrik said as they ended the call, "I will look forward to breakfast with you."

As she prepared for bed, Nancy thought it would be helpful to have Harry's advice on how to proceed. That thought caused her to cringe at what his response would be should he learn that she was still investigating Hilda's death. Her thoughts turned to Marcy again. It would be interesting to see if Marcy had any criminal history or issues before being employed at this community. Harry could do that, but she would have to disclose activities she'd rather not. Finished brushing her teeth, she headed to bed, hoping to fall asleep quickly. Yawning, head on her pillow, she mumbled to herself, "Why would a jealous person kill the mother of a rival instead of just the rival?"

CHAPTER 37

The next morning, Nancy found herself refreshed and prepared to work through the murder dilemma with Enrik. The problem was that she still didn't have an answer to why Hilda would be Marcy's target. She showered and picked out a dusty rose cotton sleeveless shift and dark green sandals. Running a comb through her hair while appraising her choices, she smiled at herself. Checking her watch, she headed for the garage, grabbed her bag, still stuffed with her notes, and drove the golf cart out of the garage toward Enrik's.

Enrik had set up the umbrella table on his patio for breakfast. Walking through the kitchen, the scent of warming pancetta and scrambled eggs filled the air. A plate of berries, flaky croissants, plums, and tangerines, along with squares of goat cheese, was in the center of the table next to fresh-cut roses. A carafe of coffee sat next to a pair of stacked china cups.

"How delightful," Nancy said, sitting in the chair he held out for her, "You must have been up with the sun to set up this lovely scene."

"It has been a long time since I have entertained in my home," he responded, pouring the coffee and adding cream to his, "It is difficult to host colleagues from the university in one's home as we are scattered throughout the county. Traffic makes meeting casually difficult unless within walking distance of the campus. Driving to and from Santa Barbara could add an hour or more to one's travel."

She sipped from her cup, enjoying the aroma, "That's a shame, as this is a perfect spot to meet and enjoy one's guests."

Removing the cover from the hot plate of the pancetta scrambled eggs, shrugging, he said, "Hopefully, my culinary skills will impress you as well."

A forkful of the fluffy and slightly salted eggs erased any doubt regarding his skills in the breakfast department. "These are fabulous eggs, and the light croissants are perfect," Nancy said, lifting another forkful to her mouth.

Enrik humbly acknowledged he liked to putter in the kitchen, and they discussed the various breakfast selections they enjoy preparing. Once the eggs were eaten, the fruit and cheese nibbled, and the coffee refilled, Enrik cleared the dishes while Nancy created an area on the table to work. Opening her file, she waited for Enrik to return to the deck from the kitchen. Stretching in her chair, she thought how pleasant the morning had started out. Arranging her notes so Enrik would be able to view them too, she had the notion that if they could only find a motive for Hilda's murder, it would be a perfect day.

Enrik returned and sat next to Nancy to be able to share her notes. "So, where do we start?" He turned to her.

"If we believe Marcy killed Hilda, based on her knowledge of the means and the opportunity, we must start with the question of motive. Why would she do it?" Nancy responded, "Let's start over with what we know."

"Okay, we know that Marcy had a crush on her boss, Ronald. We knew that Ronald was having an affair with Lisa. We know that Lisa and her mother were not especially close. Do we know why they weren't?" Enrik began.

Nancy explained the issues related to Lisa being sent to boarding school after Hilda caught her male friend molesting her daughter. She also explained that Lisa had told her that her mother eventually married and subsequently divorced that man, but Lisa never forgave her.

"So I now see why you suspected her before you decided that I had a criminal mind!" He shook his head.

"That is unfair to bring up the past. I thought you forgave me." She frowned at him.

"It was a serious accusation, not easily forgiven. I believe you owe me a nice dinner free of subterfuge." Enrik teased her.

"We will see how this partnership works out before I make any promises." Squinting at him.

He agreed, grinning at her. "How about Ronald as the murderer at the request of his lover, Lisa? That would be a motive." He said on a more serious note.

"They were both seen together at the Chamber of Commerce fundraiser at the estimated time of death. Besides, I don't see Lisa really wanting revenge. After Harry became aware of the timeline and found she couldn't have killed her mother, I reviewed my notes more carefully."

Nancy further explained that, given some thought, she decided Lisa hadn't forgiven her mother's abandonment and wanted to punish her. Looking more closely at the notes she had taken then, she pointed out the section to Enrik. "But the solid alibi nailed their innocence.

"I am impressed by your thoroughness." Enrik said, taking a deep breath before adding, "But that eliminates two of our suspects!"

Nancy had previously eliminated them, so she had already experienced his disappointment.

"I feel we are missing something important." Rubbing her forehead with the tips of her fingers, "We really need Harry's help, but I'm not sure how to get him involved without upsetting him and involving my office visit."

Enrik stood up from the chair, causing Nancy's notes to fly off the table. "I know; ask him if he was aware of Marcy's incident running into the pole. Tell him it was no accident," he said.

Nancy thought about that angle for a few minutes, "That might work. I could suggest that he investigate Marcy's past and see if she has a record or any legal issues. I'll call his office."

"Then we should talk to Marcy and let her know that not only you and I but Lisa and Ronald all think that her collision with the pole was no accident," Enrik said as he began to pick up the scattered papers.

"But that's not true," Nancy said, "Lisa or Ronald didn't see her face."

"She doesn't know they didn't witness her rage," he turned to look at her.

Nancy, chin on her hand, appeared to be deep in thought. Finally, she said, "For any of this to work, we need a plan," Raising her hand in front of her, she started to tick off items, counting on her fingers.

"First, we need to know when Marcy is back in her office so we can talk to her. Second, we need to get Harry to believe us and check into Marcy's background in the hopes that there is something we don't know about. Third, we need to figure out a way to find out if she killed Hilda and why."

"That third thing could be a problem. Do you think she will just confess?" he asked, beginning to pace in front of where Nancy was sitting.

"She might," Nancy looked at Enrik, raised her chin in the air, and answered, "I plan on asking her both those questions."

Frowning at her, Enrik shook his head, "Do you think that is wise?" He stopped pacing and stood directly in front of her.,

"The tone of her response will give us a hint to the answer." She said. "At first, she will be surprised as expected, but what she says or does next will highlight her involvement."

Nancy explained to Enrik that witnesses on the stand often try to evade direct questions. "Their surprise is followed by several responses, confusion, misunderstanding, immediate denial, and an attempt to distract, or they will be insulted." She ticked off the suspect's avoidance techniques on her fingers, "If that doesn't work, they usually try to implicate or blame others, and often the last evasion is to show how hurt they are that you would question their involvement." emphasized by her eye roll.

"I've seen it all in the courts," She added, "It isn't pretty, but eventually, you can tell if they are lying or telling the truth. We will see which way Marcy responds."

"I'll have to trust you on that point." Enrik sat down in his chair and topped off their coffee.

"Since we have a plan, what's our first step?" he asked.

Nancy was dialing her cell as he spoke, "I'm calling Ronald to see how everyone is surviving and ask when Marcy plans on returning to work." she answered as Enrik sipped his coffee.

She spoke with Ronald again, "Just checking in for an update on Lisa and Marcy." She was happy to hear that Lisa had recovered, though still somewhat shaken. Ronald confirmed Marcy was recovering, too. "Her headache and stiff neck are slightly better. She wanted to be at work today, but I insisted she takes at least a couple of days off." He added.

Nancy thanked Ronald for his time and, reaching for her cup, shared Ronald's information with Enrik. "So when can we visit Marcy's at her office?"

"Tomorrow, if she's there, I can't imagine her taking more time off. I'll call the receptionist; she'll know when Marcy plans on being there." She answered, "Are you available?"

"I have a lecture to present at nine. Why don't I swing by and pick you up around 10:30, and we can check on Marcy at 11 once you find out if she is working?" he suggested.

She agreed. Looking at her watch, Nancy realized she needed to leave or be late for her yoga class with Bess. Walking to her golf cart with Enrik, she thanked him for breakfast and confirmed she would be ready to confront Marcy with him in the morning. She said she would call Harry and hopefully not have to talk with him and could leave a message.

Nancy took a deep breath; she wasn't looking forward to that conversation, "He isn't going to be happy; he might not do what we ask, and he might even follow through on his promise to arrest me for interfering in his investigation." she said, sliding behind the steering wheel of the golf cart.

"Don't worry. If he does arrest you, remember I promised to bail you out." Enrik reassured her, laughing.

She wasn't sure how she felt about her willingness to be beholden to him. Besides, thinking about calling Harry wasn't really a laughing matter.

CHAPTER 38

Arriving home, Nancy changed into yoga pants and a t-shirt and decided to call Harry while waiting for Bess, as it was her turn to drive to their yoga class. Calling his office, she was in luck. He didn't answer, so she was able to leave a message. "I don't want it to seem like I'm still investigating Hilda's death," She mentioned. "But you might want to investigate Marcy's accident. She is in love with her boss, Ronald. As he and Lisa are lovers, seeing them together, her jealousy could make the accident purposeful." She added in a hurried breath, "Maybe even connected to Hilda's death as she had researched mattresses for a glamping outing."

Nancy hesitated, took another deep breath, and casually asked, "Maybe a records check to see if Marcy had any priors or was involved in any legal issues would be helpful. Just a suggestion." she added, rushing through the request. Hanging up after thanking him, Bess honked her horn, announcing her arrival. Sliding her phone into her cross-over wallet and grabbing her mat, she joined Bess in her golf cart.

Bess spoke as she stepped on the gas, "Where have you been? I stopped by for coffee this morning. I thought I'd get caught up on your whiteboard, but you weren't home." She said, looking expectantly at Nancy.

"Enrik invited me to breakfast so we could get an early start on making a plan," Nancy said.

"Breakfast with Enrik? Seems like you are spending an inordinate amount of time with that man." Raising one eyebrow, Bess was intrigued.

Ignoring Bess's implication, she responded as they reached the Community Center, "I'll let you in on all the details after class."

"Lunch?" Bess inquired.

"Of course," Nancy laughed as they entered the studio and spread out their mats. Nancy usually found the 40-minute class relaxing. They were a big part of her heart healing after Ned died. Grief was not unexpected, but Nancy wasn't prepared for the intensity of losing not only her husband, but he was also one of her oldest and dearest friends. She hadn't been prepared to experience the pain of love and having no place to go.

Sharing so many special memories through their time as a couple, it was painful to realize she was the only one left to remember them; now they were just her memories not shared. The yoga stretches and breathing exercises left her feeling refreshed and more able to face the grief. Each class brought her comfort and reinforced the belief that she was going to be able to survive the pain.

Today was different. Today, Nancy felt anxious and on edge, distracted by her thoughts. She couldn't stop wondering about Marcy's motive for murdering Hilda. Hilda was such a friendly and generous person. Those at the memorial spoke of her kindness and her thoughtful nature. Marcy seemed to enjoy Hilda's company. She would show up occasionally at Hilda's happy hour gatherings, joining conversations and laughing at the silliness that often was part of happy hour at Hilda's. Nancy recalled that Marcy and Hilda would share a belt, the term Hilda would use for a shot glass of her special liquor stash.

Frustrated with her lack of focus on her yoga stretches, she focused on her breaths during the corpse pose, finally relaxing into the restful end of the session. Looking over at Bess, she saw that she was obviously asleep. Moving gracefully into an upright position, she stepped to Bess's side and touched her shoulder, waking her.

"Time to wake up," she spoke quietly at Bess, turning to roll up her mat while the rest of the class began to collect their mats and equipment, " I don't understand how you always manage to fall asleep during yoga class." She laughed.

"A clear conscience and late nights." Bess grinned.

They decided not to bother with changing clothes. They stopped at Nancy's villa to switch from Bess's golf cart to Nancy's car on their way to the Rincon Beach Bar for tapas. They ordered chicken flautas with queso fresco and salsa. Bess insisted on a side of guacamole and a Margherita grilled flatbread to share.

"I'm so torn," Bess started the conversation after ordering lunch and a Margarita. "I can't decide if I want to hear about breakfast with Enrik or more about your murder investigation." Holding her face in her hand, elbow on the table, she smiled innocently at Nancy across the table.

Sighing at Bess's innuendo, Nancy responded," How about both, since they are inclusive?"

Bess nodded agreement as she thanked the waiter who delivered her Margarita, Nancy's iced tea, and a basket of corn chips and salsa.

"If you remember, we decided that Marcy's car hitting the pole was no accident. That being the case, tying Hilda's death to an attempt on Lisa's life was maybe a stretch but definitely a possibility." Nancy dipped a chip in the salsa.

"But you had no motive for either." Bess sipped her Margherita.

Nancy recounted her visit to Marcy's office, finding the framed photo of Marcy looking adoringly at Ronald. She also reminded Bess of discovering the research on gel foam toppers in Marcy's notes in her briefcase.

"We think that Marcy saw Ronald comforting and kissing Lisa, realized they were a couple, and in a jealous rage, attempted to run over Lisa. When I yelled at Lisa to watch out, she must have turned toward us and missed being hit by inches." Nancy explained.

"I can maybe see that jealousy played a role in attempting to run over Lisa, but why would Marcy want to kill Hilda?" Bess asked.

"That's the question we can't answer." Nancy responded, "Both Enrik and I can't see a connection, so we are going to ask Marcy that very question."

"That's absurd!" Bess looked at Nancy like she had lost her mind. "You think she'll just confess and explain why she killed Hilda?"

Nancy shrugged, "We'll see how she responds and take it from there."

Doubting the judgment of her decision, Bess raised her drink in Nancy's direction as a mock toast, "I think that is a dumb idea, but good luck."

Just then, the waiter brought the flatbread loaded with mozzarella, topped with basil, tomatoes, and Rincon's famous balsamic glaze, and their full attention was directed to eating. Once each had a slice in front of them, Bess returned to the previous discussion.

"So we didn't get to the part about breakfast with Enrik," she mentioned, "How did that happen?"

Biting into the flatbread, Nancy chewed thoughtfully before swallowing, enjoying Bess's impatient glare, "After the visit to Marcy's office, we chatted, but it was getting late, so we decided to meet in the morning to devise a plan. He invited me to his house for breakfast to figure out the next move, that's all."

Bess looked skeptical, "Seriously? A man invites you to his home and actually prepares a meal for you, and you don't think he's trying to impress you for some reason?"

"I don't know why you keep trying to make some romantic connection between Enrik and me. He's intrigued by this mystery. It's like a puzzle, and he is interested in solving it with me, just like you are." She downplayed their relationship.

"Just like you and me, huh?" Bess asked.

"Exactly; come to think of it, though, you never made me breakfast." Nancy nodded.

As they left the restaurant, Nancy checked her phone, hoping for a message from Harry to confirm his interest in her new suspect. No messages from him also meant that he wasn't sending an officer out to arrest her for obstructing his investigation, either.

Dropping Bess off in the drive to retrieve her golf cart, she reminded Nancy to let her know how the meeting with Marcy went and left for her home as Nancy pulled into the garage. Retrieving the weekly community newsletter from her front stoop, she skimmed the headlines of the paper. Sitting on the couch, she wasn't surprised by the article criticizing the police department for not solving the murder of one of their residents. Frowning, she thought Harry wasn't going to be happy about the remarks the residents made in the press. Hilda's memorial was included on the second page, as well as her obituary.

An account of Marcy's accident was reported and listed her, Enrik, Lisa, and Ronald as onlookers to her hitting the pole. She thought if Marcy read this, it would confirm the story she and Enrik would tell her about witnessing her attempt to run over Lisa.

CHAPTER 39

Sitting at his desk, drinking his morning coffee, Harry listened to Nancy's recorded message on his cell. He felt himself becoming more irate by the second. That woman just couldn't understand the meaning of stop and desist. For a well-known lawyer and respected judge, that seemed hard to believe.

What the hell was she thinking, insisting an accident was an attempt on the murder victim's daughter, so she continued to interfere in the investigation by adding suspects. He was beginning to wonder about her sanity.

On second thought, a conversation about her mother's sanity might be a good excuse to invite Ann out to dinner. His anger decreased; he figured there was no reason why a guy couldn't show concern for an ex-wife's aging mother's mental health. Rubbing his chin thoughtfully, maybe he'd give Ann a call. He started to dial her on his cell when his desk landline phone rang. The command sergeant was on the line, directing him to see the captain at his earliest convenience.

Sighing, he swallowed his coffee and headed upstairs to the captain's office.

Harry was irritated. There was nothing he liked less than being requested to stop by the captain's office first thing in the morning. It was never a good thing; in fact, it usually ruined the rest of the day, if not the entire week. Scowling, he waited outside the office until the captain hung up the phone and gestured for him to enter.

"Morning, sir," Harry said, careful to leave out the 'good' in the greeting.

"Harry, what is the status of the San Jose Community case," the captain asked, not even bothering to ask him to sit down. Standing before the captain's desk, he swayed from one foot to the other.

"We're kinda at a standstill, sir." He responded, hand rubbing the back of his neck, hating to admit it, knowing the captain was not going to be happy with that answer.

"Listen, the local paper is calling and wants to follow up on an article posted in the San Jose Village Newsletter. According to the reporter, his view was less than complimentary related to the police investigation." the captain, in a deceptively calm voice, asked. "What seems to be the problem?"

Harry blew out a deep breath. He hated it when the captain acted calm; the storm usually followed. "There is a lack of leads, sir. The initial suspects all alibied out; it appears the fact that all the residents seemed to love the victim is complicating the investigation. Seems an outsider might be the perpetrator, but she rarely left the community, so outside contacts are difficult to find."

The captain looked skeptical, raising his voice to make sure everyone in the area heard him, "Difficult or not, find the person who murdered the victim; it was obviously premeditated, Harry. It shouldn't be that difficult to find someone with a grudge or long-standing motive to wish that woman dead."

He added, still loudly, "Find the murderer before that reporter starts interviewing all her friends and relatives. We don't need any more negative press."

Harry agreed that they didn't need any bad press, but he couldn't bring himself to give false hope to the captain. The thought of Nancy's message still angered him as he left the office. What was she thinking, he wondered, accusing the assistant director of trying to run down the victim's daughter? Why would she want to hurt a family member of the victim?

Having investigated Hilda's contacts and activity, he was at a loss; he just didn't have any suspects, and there was no evidence that anybody wished her any harm. On the contrary, as he told the captain, everybody seemed to love her.

Against his better judgment, he considered Nancy's request to check and see if Marcy had a police record. Without any other leads, he grudgingly thought, it wouldn't hurt to check out Nancy's theory. He had his records office email a request. He didn't have any high hopes of help from the inquiry, but in the absence of any other leads, it was another avenue to pursue.

Harry was surprised to get a phone call an hour later from a detective in New Orleans, Marcy's hometown. It appears that her mother was found dead at the bottom of the stairs leading to her apartment. Her blood alcohol level was four times the legal limit, causing the forensic pathologist to question how she was even able to leave her apartment.

Also, she had Belsomra, a prescription sleeping pill, in her system, too, but she didn't have any in her apartment or a prescription from her family doctor.

The officer stated, "The daughter was questioned several times related to her relationship with her mother and her whereabouts the night of the fall. Her alibi was flimsy. A guy she picked up at a bar gave a statement she was with him most of the evening. But he admitted that he might have fallen asleep and wasn't sure when she left his apartment."

Harry asked, "How long ago did her mother die?"

"About three years ago." He answered. "But I remember the case because the daughter said that she was estranged from her mother and hadn't seen her in over a year, made up recently, but it had been several weeks since she had been to her mother's apartment." He added, "An older lady who lived next door heard the victim and another woman arguing. She said she heard the door slam and saw a young woman that looked like the daughter's picture leaving."

"But she wasn't arrested?" Harry seemed confused.

The detective explained that the neighbor admitted she only saw her from the back, and she wore a black raincoat.

We couldn't find a black coat of any kind in the daughter's apartment, and the neighbor was older and nervous about getting involved.

"She wasn't going to be a good witness, and the DA declined to pursue the matter. It was deemed an accidental death. So they dropped the case, but I always felt the daughter somehow played a part in her mother's death." The detective responded.

"Why did you think the daughter was involved?" Harry asked.

"She didn't seem to care that her mother was dead; there should be some sort of emotion." He was silent for a moment, "She just seemed so smug. It was that she acted like she hadn't done anything wrong, you know, the type, right?" Again, he was silent, then added, "It was like she was daring us to try to implicate her."

Harry did know the type and was also haunted by the memories of those who were smug in their guilt but also in their ability to skirt the law. Those were the hard cases, the ones where justice wasn't served. The detective said Marcy's other legal issues were mostly related to a brawl with an off-duty cop acting as a bouncer.

He said his office would be sending that information and the various daughter's interview notes related to her mother's death within the hour. Harry caught him up on his reason for inquiry, and the other detective was sympathetic.

"Nail her if she's guilty," he said, "Getting away with murder once is tragic. Twice makes her a serial killer with no respect for the living or the law." Harry acknowledged the truth to that statement, thanked him, and agreed to let him know if they arrested her and hung up.

He sat staring at the computer, processing everything he had just heard. He was going to have to visit the San Jose Village again and talk to Marcy about her whereabouts on the night of the murder. Hand to the back of his neck, again, he just didn't see a motive.

He guessed Marcy might think Hilda's daughter might know something that would implicate her; maybe Lisa knew Marcy's motive. He decided to talk to Marcy first and then meet with Lisa. He hoped that Marcy had recovered from her accident and was at work, as he grabbed his cell and left his office.

CHAPTER 40

Nancy, pondering the same question as Harry, decided to call the administration office to see when Marcy was expected to return to work. The receptionist answered the phone and, once Nancy identified herself, stated that Marcy was already in the office.

"Would you like me to put you through to her," she asked Nancy.

"No, thank you. I'll just stop by later. I want to check on her after the accident."

"She'll probably appreciate that." The receptionist said.

Ending that call, Nancy clicked on Enrik's speed dial. He answered, yawning, "Good morning, Nancy," recognizing her number. He had just left the campus after his lecture and was heading home.

"Good morning to you; want to go catch a murderer?" She greeted him, "Marcy is at the office currently. I think our plan to visit her today will work."

"Give me a half hour, and I'll pick you up." He responded.

"Fine, I will be waiting." Nancy sipped coffee as she headed to her bedroom closet to choose a pair of shoes. She again looked at her phone to see if Harry had called or left a message. Thinking no news is good news, she shrugged.

Enrik was at her door exactly thirty minutes after their call ended, anxious to present their suspicions to Marcy. Nancy had slipped on a pair of open-toed flats when Enrik rang the doorbell. Sliding the notebook and pen into her bag, she swung it over her shoulder, gathered Marcy's briefcase, and headed for the door. Opening it, she stood speechless for a second. She couldn't help grinning at Enrik's black turtleneck tee shirt and black jeans.

"You look very sharp in your apprehending a murderer ensemble," she greeted him. Looking down at his attire, he appeared to see nothing wrong and looked hurt by her flip comment. Continuing to smile but not apologetic, she added, "You look dashing. Let's go solve this case."

Enrik held the car door open for Nancy, "As a lawyer and judge, you seem pretty sure that means and opportunity go a long way in convicting the right person." He nodded at her.

"A confession of guilt is the gold standard in a court case. But a jury can be swayed by presenting means and opportunity as reliable evidence for the conviction of a crime. The suggestion of a strong motive can often be the true deciding factor." Nancy explained.

"The secret will be in how she replies when we suggest that her fingerprints might be found on the cigarette that started the fire." Nancy reminded him, "As Nancy Drew always said, it was the reaction after one was accused that pointed to their guilt."

While they were talking, they approached the administration building, but before entering, Nancy put her hand on his arm, "Remember our plan, good cop/bad cop? Right?" She said, "Remember, I'm the good cop." He snorted as he opened the door for her.

Marcy was in her office when Enrik knocked on the door frame. She appeared distracted. A large bruise covered the lower part of her face, and Nancy noted a slightly bruised bump on her forehead. She attempted a weak smile as they walked into the office, but Nancy thought she looked tearful.

"We worried about you and thought we would stop in to see how you are recovering after your run-in with that pole." Nancy looked at Marcy, concerned, wrinkling her brow. "Also, I recovered your briefcase from the van after the ambulance left with you. I didn't think you would need it in the hospital."

"That was kind of you. I have to figure out how to retrieve the items belonging to the community that could be salvaged and hope to find any items still in the wreckage at the repair shop." Sniffing, she reached out to take it from Nancy, her hands shaking as she placed it on her desk. "The insurance company said the van is totaled." She added.

Concerned, Nancy asked, "Are you sure you should be working today? You might still be in shock and should be resting at home."

Marcy responded, "A stiff neck from the airbags and a slight headache that the doc says will be short-lived are the only residual issues, except for the village van being totaled weeks before it is needed for the glamping excursion!" She attempted a smile and lighthearted approach, although the words seemed forced, as if caught in her throat,

"We also had another reason for our visit," Enrik said, "Nancy has been trying to find out the truth about Hilda's death. She says that you have been most helpful in sharing information with her. But we've been thinking that you might have had an ulterior motive for all that sharing."

Her sad smile faded, "What are you implying?" She asked.

Nancy answered, "Enrik thinks you know more about Hilda's death than you shared. I told him that he was wrong."

Stunned, Marcy stumbled as she backed from her desk, looking first at Nancy and then fearfully at Enrik, "Why would you think I know anything more than you do about her death?"

Enrik shook his head at Marcy, "I want to know how much you knew about Hilda's suffocation. Nancy said that she remembers seeing a consumer warning label on Hilda's gel foam topper. She doesn't remember what it said, but having removed it from Hilda's bed several times, she wondered if it wasn't a factor in how Hilda died." Erik responded. "Did you remember seeing the warning label?"

"I don't know anything about the topper's warnings, " she said.

"I heard you say that you were facilitating the community glamping excursion this year. I read that along with tents and facilities being set up for the participants, all cots would have the option of inflatable or gel-foam mattresses. Seems to me you might know something about them." Enrik added.

"I don't set up tents, cots, or mattresses; maintenance does. Besides, they weren't sure what killed Hilda, were they? Why the focus on the mattress topper?" Marcy argued, leaning over her desk.

Nancy joined the conversation, "Well, it appears that among your papers contained in your briefcase, Enrik discovered you had invoices from off-gassing, gel foam mattress pads. You had been researching gel-foam mattress adverse events reported to the consumer protection board."

"That doesn't prove anything. One of the women questioned the contents of the mattress pads because she had allergies. I researched the cots and the mattresses to reassure her they were safe. That information had nothing to do with Hilda's mattress topper. I never even thought about what hers was made of."

"It is circumstantial at best, but it appears that the cigarette found on the mattress hadn't been smoked, with no trace of tar or nicotine in the filter. Also, her fingerprints weren't found on the cigarette at all. The forensic department is trying to identify whom they do belong to." Enrik responded.

"It's only a matter of time before the police arrive. They know that Hilda's death was not an accident and know of your involvement. You had the means and the opportunity, but I wondered, what was your motive? Why did Hilda have to die?" Nancy wanted to know.

"I had nothing to do with her death; I enjoyed her company. How dare you accuse me of wishing to harm her!" Tears ran down her cheeks, and she wiped them away with the back of her hand.

"The forensic lab will soon know if those are your prints on the remains of the cigarette. The police are already on their way, so you might as well admit to it."

Marcy looked at Nancy, then Enrik, panic and fear evident in her wide-eyed expression, "I'm not waiting around for them. If they want to talk to me, they'll have to find me." She pushed Nancy to the ground, grabbed her purse, and hurried out the door.

Taken by surprise, Enrik shouted, "Wait just a minute, young lady," to her back as she exited the office. He went to help Nancy up from the floor, only to have her push him away. "Go after her. I can manage."

He quickly looked at her, nodded, and followed Marcy through the office and out of the building. He saw she had a head start toward the employee parking lot. A club golf cart with the key in the ignition was parked next to the building; hopping in, he followed her.

"Stop, Marcy, you can't escape," he yelled, almost catching up to her.

"Leave me the hell alone," she shouted as he pulled up even to her.

Taking his foot off the gas pedal, he lunged for her, and both toppled to the ground. They wrestled on the ground, with Marcy fighting to escape and Enrik holding her down.

That was the sight that greeted Harry as he pulled into the parking lot.

"What the hell are you doing?" he asked as he rushed to help Marcy to her feet and glared at Enrik.

"Don't let her escape; keep her close," Enrik grunted as he picked himself off the ground. "She killed Hilda!"

CHAPTER 41

The detective looked first at the disheveled Marcy, then at Enrik, dirt clinging to his clothes. He was about to comment when Nancy arrived, slightly winded from her rush from the administration office.

Rolling his eyes at her arrival, he commented, "I expect you have an explanation for this, Nancy." His brow furrowed, and the tone of his voice left no doubt he was angry.

"I thought that Marcy had killed Hilda and tried to run over Lisa, but when we accused her of those actions, she denied them, questioning our proof."

With her hand rubbing her chin, she said, "Her delayed reaction to our accusations was inappropriate." Nancy cocked her head. She looked at Marcy next to Harry, "I'm beginning to think I might be wrong."

Enrik looked at Nancy and then Marcy, "If she didn't do it, why would she push you and run away?" His confusion was tinged with frustration.

"Enrik, she didn't run away until we told her the police were on the way. That was what made her bolt, not the fact that we accused her of Hilda's murder!"

Nancy turned to Marcy and asked, "Why did you run?"

Pulling her arm from Harry's grasp, Marcy raised her chin defiantly, "When my mother was high on drugs and alcohol, the police thought maybe her fall wasn't an accident. They were sure somebody pushed her down the steps," she said. "They thought I would be a likely candidate to have done the pushing since there was a witness who saw a person leaving the stairway landing that looked like me." She sneered at Harry,

"Even though I hadn't seen my mother in several weeks, the detective hounded me for months. I couldn't take that again." Her voice started to shake, "I didn't want to have to go through that kind of ordeal ever again."

Marcy looked at them. Tearful, she lowered her head, mumbling, "I don't know what to think. The head injury from the car wreck must have muddled my brain. Can we go back to my office? I don't want to cause a scene in the parking lot."

Back in her office, she moved to her desk and sat swiveling her chair to face them. With her elbow bent and hand holding her head, after a moment, she looked at Nancy standing next to Enrik.

"I'm sorry I pushed you, Nancy, but I can't understand what's happening. Since the memorial service, I haven't been able to make sense of things."

"With a head injury, I wouldn't think it would be uncommon," Nancy explained.

"The confusion started before the accident, though. During the service, the way Ronald was supporting Lisa, holding her hand, and hugging her during the video, it became evident that Lisa and Ronald were a couple, more connected than I had realized."

"I thought Ronald loved me. We would have dinner at the club here and take a bottle of wine to my place. He'd often spend the night with me, leaving early so we wouldn't arrive at the office together."

Nancy nodded. "Bess and I had noticed them meeting in the administration parking lot, embracing a week ago. Later, Ronald admitted that they had been seeing each other."

"I thought it was just a passing fancy with Ronald. Once Hilda died, Lisa wouldn't be around anymore." She sighed, "I wasn't worried about losing Ronald, even at the memorial service. I was sure that would be the end of his distraction with her."

"But when I spoke with SueLi a few days ago about the seasonal flower choices for the memorial committee, she mentioned that she didn't realize that Ronald and Lisa were a couple." Marcy continued that Sue said she felt sorry for Lisa, losing her mother, and said how nice it was that the two of them got to see Hilda the night before she died.

"SueLi remarked what an attractive couple they made, all dressed up for an evening out." Marcy looked at Harry, "I explained that they were probably on their way to the Chamber of Commerce Fundraiser." Marcy continued, appearing to think out loud. "But she said they were probably stopping by after the fundraiser. "

Again, Marcy stopped, rubbing her hand over her forehead. "SueLi was at Sally's monthly book club and noticed them leaving Hilda's condo. She was in a hurry to get home to watch the 10 o'clock weather report. She said she didn't get a chance to tell them how nice they looked in their fancy clothes." Enrik and Nancy looked at each other, surprised, while Harry pulled out his notebook and began to record Marcy's statement.

"I mentioned to Ronald that his and Lisa's relationship was no longer a secret as SueLi had seen them together visiting Hilda. I told him that she commented that Lisa was lucky to have him to comfort her during this awful time. He looked at me puzzled."

Looking off in the distance, almost as if she was talking to herself, "So I clarified that she said you made a cute couple all dressed up when she saw you at Hilda's. But he didn't respond, almost like he didn't hear me." As if remembering there were others present, she frowned at Nancy, "I just thought he was embarrassed to be found out, or maybe thought I was hurt and expected an explanation for our relationship change."

Rubbing her forehead, Marcy turned to Harry, "Before they walked into my office," she nodded at Enrik and Nancy, "I had been on the phone with the corporate maintenance crew. They told me that the insurance company notified them that the van's brake lines had been tampered with, and they were going to have to file a police report before they would be able to process the claim."

"That really upset me." Taking a deep breath, she continued, her voice shaking, "Ronald insisted that I drive the van to the memorial in case it was needed to transport anything. I did as he asked even though I couldn't imagine why it might be needed."

"Do you usually drive the corporate van?" Harry asked.

"No, not usually, sometimes for events or vendor pick-ups that don't deliver goods." Shaking her head, "But as Ronald and Lisa left the clubhouse after the memorial, he asked me to take the corporate van to get gas. It was an unusual request, as the maintenance crew usually took care of servicing the van along with the other corporate vehicles." Looking thoughtful, Marcy shook her head again, saying, "I didn't think anything of it until this morning when I spoke to the maintenance manager."

Marcy said she was looking up the insurance customer service contact number from the last paid invoice, "I wanted more information. I was still trying to process who would've tampered with the brakes." She got up from behind her desk and started to pace, "I knew the customer service contact person was listed on the insurance invoices, so I checked the transportation and travel account."

She stared at Harry for a minute, hand to her mouth, closed her eyes, and with a quiver in her voice, added, "That's when I found the Delta airline receipt. As I always arranged all the travel plans for the administrative staff, I wasn't aware of any community meetings or corporate travel plans. I found that a ticket purchased for a red-eye flight to Vietnam had been made for tonight."

"Vietnam? Why Vietnam?" Enrik asked.

Marcy choked up and had to stop for a minute. Taking a deep breath, she continued, "Ronald had been talking about his brother's old ex-pat army buddies who were trying to get him to visit Vietnam. They had plans to open a 55+ community like this for ex-pats in Nam."

Nancy thought for a minute, "I remember noticing an eagle sculpture on his side table in his office. It was carved in a beautiful, rare wood. Ronald said it was from his brother, who sent it to him from Vietnam."

Marcy started to sob, "After finding the airline receipt, I called Ronald, and I told him I talked to the maintenance crew, and they informed me that the insurance broker said that someone had tampered with the brake lines on the van and that they would be notifying the police." Wiping away tears with the back of her hand, she explained that he said the insurance people just didn't want to pay the claim and he would handle it when he came in later today.

She said she asked him when he planned on coming to the office. I told him I'd meet him there, and he told her not to come to the office today, saying he knew the doctor told him she needed a few more days to recover from her head injury.

"He said he had a few personal things to take care of but would check in with me about the insurance and van when he got to the office."

Nancy turned to Harry, "Does it seem suspicious that the day after she mentioned that he and Lisa had been seen at Hilda's the night of her death, the brakes of the van he insisted she drive were sabotaged."

Harry nodded while continuing to scribble in his notebook.

Marcy, with hands to her face and tears running down her cheeks, looked at Nancy, "Do you think he tampered with the brakes? Did he hope to injure me?" Nancy moved next to her, sliding her arm around the heartbroken woman's shoulders, and let her sob. Nancy squeezed her shoulder, thinking he probably wanted you dead.

CHAPTER 42

Marcy pulled herself together and said, "I'm sorry this has all been such a shock, but it's even more bizarre. Sniffing, she shared that she found some emails on Ronald's personal account on his corporate computer. He forgot to close his computer after his last use. I was looking for his online calendar to see if he had a meeting in Vietnam scheduled and forgot to tell me, but instead, I found some weird communication with Hilda.

Harry and Enrik approached Ronald's computer, "So what am I looking at?" Harry asked as Enrik scrolled through several months of almost daily emails addressed to Hilda.

'Why would Ronald be sending daily emails to Hilda?" Nancy asked.

Enrik was scrolling through them, "They seem to be online conversational lonely hearts missives to Hilda from an Argentina spoofed email address."

"Spoofed? You mean fake?" Harry asked.

"Exactly, it's a scammer's trick to hide the real source of the email." Enrik nodded. "It seems, if I'm reading these emails correctly, Ronald set up a fake email account to romance Hilda," Enrik said. "After several months of emails, he talks her into sending him $100,000 to invest in a money-making scheme. That's why she wanted the money and wanted me to wire that money to her online romantic business partner."

"Are you saying Ronald was attempting to steal from Hilda while having an affair with her daughter?" Harry asked, confused.

Enrik scrolled through the emails to show Harry that Ronald was attempting to engage in a romantic relationship to scam money from Hilda. "After he caught her interest, the fake Argentina gentleman gets more romantic and suggests they meet. She agrees, but the emails reveal financial issues and an opportunity to invest in a sure-thing deal. The hook seems to be a great return on her $100k, all tax-free since it is an international hotel conglomerate, he's attempting to get her to invest in. But he can't meet her until he has all his investors lined up and cash in hand."

Shaking his head, Enrik angrily said, "That Ronald is a bastard!"

Nancy went to stand by Marcy, touching her shoulder. Marcy looked at her tearfully and asked. "Do you think he tampered with the van's breaks?"

Harry rubbed the back of his neck, "So why kill Hilda if she was planning on sending the money?" He asked.

"As far as I could tell from his emails, Ronald was in big trouble with the local casino. If I had sent the cashier check when Hilda gave it to me, he would've been clear. Since I left the country for a month before mailing it, he missed his due date, and the casino threatened criminal charges as he had not responded as promised to their collection agency." Enrik added as he scrolled through Harold's personal email account.

Nancy continued where Enrik left off, "According to Lisa, she was the sole recipient of Hilda's estate. She could've possibly provided the collection agency a promissory note until the estate was settled.

Again, Harry questioned, "Then why leave the country? After all, Enrik gave Lisa the 100k he had received from Hilda. The debt could've been paid."

Looking at Enrik for confirmation, Nancy said, "Because Vietnam will not extradite another country's criminals. Since Marcy shared SueLi's recollection, there was a loose end, and he needed to leave the country before he was incriminated."

Marcy again looked at Nancy. "He planned on leaving the country for good!" she sobbed.

Enrik nodded in agreement. Harry called for backup and requested an unmarked police car to provide surveillance at the administration building on the lookout for Ronald.

It was then that Ronald and Lisa walked in the office door, stopping to survey the scene in front of them. They paused, and Harry invited them in.

"Don't let us get in your way. We're just trying to solve a mystery here." Harry smiled at them as he closed the door, securing them in the office.

"Marcy, what are you doing at the office? The doctor said you were to stay home for a few more days. I told you not to come in; you wouldn't be needed here today!" Ronald sounded harsh, raising his voice in surprise.

With the back of her hand to her mouth, tearfully, Marcy mumbled, "Why would you care? You tried to kill me!" Ronald looked shocked at the accusation, but before he could respond, Harry questioned him.

"What do you know about the tampered brake lines on the van you asked Marcy to drive?" Ronald looked at the detective and then at Marcy, but before he could answer, Harry asked a second question. "More to the point, perhaps you could explain your plans to visit Vietnam tonight."

His eyes searching the room, Ronald sputtered, "How. . . how do you know I planned on traveling to Vietnam?"

Lisa spoke up, moving to stand close to Ronald, "He's been promising to take me there to meet his brother and his brother's ex-pat army buddies. Since this ordeal with my mother, it seemed like a perfect getaway from the whole mess."

"More like the perfect get away with murder or escape from justice plan," Nancy commented.

Regaining his composure, Ronald snorted, "I've just about had it with your continued harassment, Nancy. What is it with you and your need to pin Hilda's murder on someone? You can't prove a thing. What evidence do you have that either of us caused Hilda's death?" Looking at Harry, he asked, "Detective, can't you do something about these endless accusations?"

"You are right, Ronald; all we used to have was circumstantial." Nancy agreed. "But Marcy found your emails luring Hilda into a romantic adventure involving the exchange of money. She found the threats related to your gambling debts. I believe there is a law against email fraud schemes." Nancy looked at Harry.

"The use of email in a scheme to commit fraud is considered wire fraud and can be prosecuted under either state or federal laws." Harry nodded at Nancy.

Lisa looked at Ronald, and losing her innocent, self-satisfied attitude, she turned to him, "You should have deleted that scheme from your computer! You fool! You said we would be able to live in Vietnam like royalty with my mother's inheritance and her life insurance payout once the development was up and running!"

Lisa stepped away from him, sneering, "You were foolish even to use your work computer, let alone not hide the conversations or delete them. How could you be so stupid!"

Nancy added to Lisa's agitation, "He only bought one ticket to Vietnam, Lisa. Were you planning on traveling separately?"

"What, there must be a mistake," looking at Ronald, "You only bought one ticket; how was I to get there? Or did you plan on taking the money and leaving me here?" She started to reach for Ronald. He stepped behind Harry, who raised his hand to stop Lisa from slapping him. "Calm down, Lisa. He'll get his day in court."

"Hopefully, they will lock him up and throw away the key!" She sneered at Ronald. Marcy appeared in a state of shock, and Enrik was spellbound as the action unfolded in front of them.

"Lisa, you, too, will get your day in court," Nancy explained, her chin raised defiantly and purposefully avoiding looking at Harry. "The forensic evidence report discovered fingerprints on the cigarette butt that ignited the mattress. They are in the process of being identified," surprised Harry looked at Nancy, wondering what she was up to, knowing that was not true, "and you were both seen at Hilda's around 10 o'clock on the night of the murder, making your alibis worthless." Nancy looked at Lisa, "A jury will have no mercy on a woman who murdered her mother for an early inheritance to save her lover from debtor prison."

"What are you saying? I didn't have anything to do with her death. I told you before!" Her voice rose an octave as she looked at Nancy. "I didn't touch that cigarette!"

"Shut up, Lisa!" Ronald shouted. "Don't say another word!"

Lisa pointed at Ronald, "It was his idea!" Attempting to deny her guilt. "I didn't even know the mattress was flammable until Ronald told me."

"Stop babbling, Lisa; shut your mouth!" he tried again.

"I won't!" She spit the words at him. "He told me he had heard Marcy on the phone discussing the safety of gel-foam versus fiber mattress toppers. I swear it was all Ronald's idea. He needed the money. Initially, it was just a scam on Mother and served her right!" She added, as if it made a difference, "It was my inheritance money, anyway."

"But the money was withdrawn and lost, wasn't it?" Nancy led her on.

Lisa exhaled angrily, "When the money that she withdrew didn't show up in Ronald's offshore account, he couldn't pay his debt, and his life was in danger from some gambling goons "

"Dammit, Lisa!" Ronald hissed at her, stepping from behind Harry. "Shut the hell up!"

She shook her head at him, "He panicked. He told me there was no further opportunity to negotiate more time to pay his debt. His bank's collection agency was threatening to have him arrested, and he said the gambling guys had threatened to beat him and break his arms if he didn't pay up."

Harry was still taking notes when Nancy took a step toward Ronald, "So rather than spend time in jail and fearing for your life, you thought the solution to your gambling problem was to murder Hilda?"

Enrik had been admiring Nancy's skill and patience in fooling Lisa into admitting to setting the topper on fire. He saw her movement toward Ronald, heard her voice shake, and gently restrained her arm as she approached Ronald, who stepped back to cower behind Harry.

"Now is not the time, Nancy," he spoke softly.

Hearing Enrik's gentle warning, Harry looked up from his notes to see Nancy trying to free herself from Enrik's hold to reach Ronald.

"Hey, hey, calm down, Nancy, listen to Enrik, leave Ronald to us. I've texted the officers outside to haul these two to the precinct." he said just as the officers arrived and handcuffed both Lisa, who was cursing him, and Ronald, who was glaring at her.

Marcy sniffed, staring at Ronald as he was taken away, "How could he have murdered Hilda?" Wringing her hands together, "I loved him. I thought he loved me, too." She held her head, her eyes tearing, startling both Nancy and Enrik, who had forgotten she was in the office.

Pulling herself together, she looked at the detective and said, "I guess I need to call corporate headquarters and report that the director has been arrested," she sighed, "What do I tell them?" Still with her hand to her head, Nancy thought she seemed dazed.

Harry handed her his business card and told her to have her corporate contacts call him for detailed information. He called for an additional officer to escort her home when finished with her report to corporate.

Nancy recommended that after she made the call, she should alert the front desk to defer all inquiries until tomorrow. "You suffered a terrible head injury, and this new stress can't be good for you. You need to go home and rest." Hugging her, "And I'm really sorry we increased your distress, Marcy." She said as she led Enrik toward the door.

"Wait up, you two. Could you spare me a few more minutes of your time?" Harry asked, attempting a polite smile but failing miserably. His polite request showed that he was controlling his temper and dampened Nancy's hope for a quick escape from his ire.

"Sure, detective, no problem," Enrik smiled agreeably at Harry, missing Nancy rolling her eyes at him.

"Nancy, I told you more than once to cease your investigation. You put yourself and others at risk, and you might have caused Ronald and Lisa to escape, never to be found!" Harry said, exasperated.

Shaking his head, he continued, "I'm not sure what more I could have said or done to make you understand amateur sleuthing is dangerous and can affect the ability of the police department to do their job. I can appreciate your desire to seek justice for Hilda, but putting yourself and others at risk is unacceptable."

He continued, his attention focused on Nancy, "Suggesting to Lisa that fingerprints were found on the cigarette butt was an interesting ploy, and maybe an effective Nancy Drew move, but it is not a usual police procedure," he added as he shook his finger at her. "Those tricks need to remain in the pages of mystery novels, not played out in the pursuit of criminals."

Nancy looked at Harry, trying to appear contrite, while Harry grudgingly looked at both and added, "I would be remiss if I didn't thank you for your deductive reasoning that led to the capture of those two. But don't let me catch you in the middle of a police investigation again!" He pointed his finger first at Nancy, then included Enrik, too.

Nodding to Enrik, he proceeded to speak to Marcy and directed the officer to escort her home with the recommendation for her to rest and recover from her accident. He reminded them all that he would need their statements the next day as he left.

Nancy and Enrik walked out of the building in time to watch Marcy being assisted into the back seat of the patrol car. Enrik slid his arm around Nancy's waist.

"So, justice has been achieved for our friend Hilda, and Marcy is safe. Quite the accomplishment for a retired lawyer-judge who dreamed of being a girl detective, huh?" Smiling tenderly at her, he asked, "How does that feel?"

"I feel vindicated and believe that justice has been served. In fact, it appears that the once hopeful girl detective still has some sleuthing chops." She smiled back at him, "Maybe I'll give up the idea of resuming my law practice and instead put my refreshed detective skills to work." She cocked her head and gave him a side-eye look. She said as they walked to his car. "It seems that women of a certain age appear invisible to the unsuspecting. Obviously, the bad guys won't see me coming."

Enrik grimaced. "Just don't tell your former son-in-law." As he dropped a kiss on the top of her head.

THE END

ACKNOWLEDGEMENTS

This book that you hold in your hand or view on your e-book is the result of a variety of folks who support and believe in the hopes and dreams of others. The beta readers who followed this book's path over the years and read and re-read numerous rewrites- are the first that I wish to thank for their time, effort, and belief in this project. They are my twin and staunch supporter- Kris Downey, hometown tech supporter, -Mary Pat McCarthy, Gina Pollack, editor, and Nancy Drew conventioneer and first-round reader/editor,

Ericka Waidley. My Partner in Crime, Ingrid Flanders, is an avid Nancy Drew fan and always had encouraging words to share..

Also, Jennifer Frisher's generous contribution to the Toledo, Ohio Library is priceless and honors Mildred Benson, the original author of the first Nancy Drew Mysteries and a 1930s local news reporter. Nancy Drew was an inspiration to so many young girls and is the role model for my Nancy 65-year-old grown-up girl detective.

The supporters of the early days of my writing career deserve credit too,- John Szozda, who read my college composition essays as writing samples, when I applied for a news reporter job(in my eyes, a Lois Lane position). He suggested I write a humor column instead, which I did (on and off) for 20 years. I need to thank my children, Matthew, and Chelsea, who are glad I no longer write about them. But I will be forever grateful to them for providing me with great copy for the humor columns.

A shout out to my sister, Sharon Piper, who, upon hearing I was going to be writing for the local newspaper, sent me a dictionary and thesaurus (aware of my lack of spelling skills), which came in handy before computers evolved. My most faithful fan, Rebecca Crabtree, deserves a loving thanks for taking the time to cut out and save over 20 years of those columns.

Then there is Raymond Crabtree, my husband, he has been the tech support, emotional support, and the person whose strength has been there when mine has failed. His love is obvious in his tolerance and support of all my undertakings; numerous returns to classes while pursuing progressive nursing degrees, starting a business, achieving my Doctorate in Nursing, or writing a mystery novel. His belief in me has allowed me to grow and achieve my dreams. I am eternally grateful that he is the constant in my life and hope he knows how much he is loved.